Mr. SEBASTIAN

⊱ and the ⊰

NEGRO MAGICIAN

Also by Daniel Wallace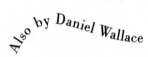

The Watermelon King

Ray in Reverse

Big Fish

Mr. SEBASTIAN

and the

NEGRO MAGICIAN

A Novel

Daniel Wallace

DOUBLEDAY

New York London Toronto Sydney Auckland

PUBLISHED BY DOUBLEDAY

Copyright © 2007 by Daniel Wallace

All Rights Reserved

Published in the United States by Doubleday, an imprint of The Doubleday
Broadway Publishing Group, a division of Random House, Inc., New York.
www.doubleday.com

DOUBLEDAY and the portrayal of an anchor with a dolphin are registered
trademarks of Random House, Inc.

Library of Congress Cataloging-in-Publication Data
Wallace, Daniel, 1959–
Mr. Sebastian and the negro magician / Daniel Wallace.—1st ed.
p. cm.
1. Magicians—Fiction. I. Title.
PS3573.A4256348M7 2007
813'.54—dc22
2006028103

ISBN: 978-0-385-52109-3

PRINTED IN THE UNITED STATES OF AMERICA

1 3 5 7 9 10 8 6 4 2

First Edition

To my kids:

Abby, Lillian, and Henry

Mr. SEBASTIAN

✦ and the ✦

NEGRO MAGICIAN

July 2, 1959

My dear,

I need to tell you a story.

After we buried your Henry and came home, I returned to Alabama. I had to. I was drawn back down there by the weight of everything I didn't know. Once there, I had an opportunity to speak to some of the people Henry worked with the last few years of his life—his final friends. You met them briefly. They seemed so odd at the time, didn't they? The way they looked at us as if we'd fallen into their world from the edges of some dark dream, and almost mute with grief. I knew they had something they could tell me, however, and I went back in the hopes that they would talk, and talk they did. They turned out to be quite friendly and forthcoming, not at all what you'd expect from people of their peculiar professions and unique dispositions. I think I told you I was off on a business trip to Savannah, a lie for which I ask your forgiveness now. But I wanted to know everything I could about Henry. I'd never stopped thinking of him. I've never been able to forget the look on his face on that final day. It follows me into sleep, as I know it will follow me into death. I did nothing wrong. But it's as if I were in the middle of a vast ocean, in a lifeboat with room for only two, and Henry was floating there, calling to me, reaching out—and I had to watch him sink.

This, what you have here, is all I know. We never expected to live the lives we have, and I'm sure Henry didn't expect or desire the life he was given. The difference is that we were lucky, whereas Henry was not. A part of me wishes Henry had remained a mystery forever, but in the end I think it's better to know what we can about people, to see beneath their skin, especially when it's about our own family—sometimes the most mysterious people we know. One day your son, my grandson, may read these papers. It's important, I think, that he know Henry's story and our roles in it. I did nothing wrong, but I hope you can forgive me just the same.

James

A Long Story

May 20th, 1954

Jeremiah Mosgrove—the proprietor of Jeremiah Mosgrove's Chinese Circus—hired Henry Walker four years ago, at the halfway point of the twentieth century, hired him almost as soon as he'd walked into Jeremiah's office: he needed a magician. He hadn't had a magician in the show for going on a year, not since Rupert Cavendish. Sir Rupert Cavendish was his full name, and he'd been a skilled prestidigitator—that is, until he lost most of his digits in a thresher. For a while they kept him on as a guesser of weight and age. But he always went high on both counts, and soon people began to avoid him. Last Jeremiah heard, he'd found work at a poultry farm, gutting chickens. Since then, nothing. And what is a circus without magic? You could hardly call it a circus at all.

Before he became proprietor, Jeremiah—a huge man, with hair covering most of his body—was the Human Bear: the tips of his fingers and the glow in his cheeks were the only evidence he had skin at all. But he'd always had dreams, and when the owner of the circus died (surprisingly, in this world of freaks and freak occurrences, of natural causes), Jeremiah used his intimidating size and verbal skills to ascend the throne, where he'd been ever since. Nothing changed during his tenure but the name: though there had never been a Chinese person associated with the circus, Jeremiah liked the sound of it. So *Chinese Circus* it was.

The day Henry came, Jeremiah's office was a slat of plywood balanced on two wooden horses, one chair, without walls or ceiling, carpeted in straw and horseshit, at the edge of the field where he'd chosen to set up the show. Henry had appeared from nowhere. Later, some would say they'd seen him wandering a long road alone, or crawling from a gully, or something like that, a story of a mysterious appearance to bookend the mysterious disappearance that, four years later, would follow.

"Show me what you can do," Jeremiah said to him, all business. But Henry—weak, thin, shaky—could do almost nothing. The pack of old cards he removed from his pocket fell like confetti from his nervous hands. Finally, he was able to force a card, produce a flower, change water into wine. But the truth was he had little more than his magnificent presence: he was tall, gaunt, doomed—and black. A black man with green eyes—a Negro—and this, in the end, is why Jeremiah hired him. A marketing tool of these dimensions was not something he could let pass by. For a magician was nothing, really, the same way a cow was nothing. But a Negro magician—or, say, a two-headed cow—now, *that* was something. Better even than a Chinese acrobat. Jeremiah felt that Henry's inability to do anything truly amazing (Henry thought of it as a kind of impotence, after so many potent years) might actually work in his favor, at least with the crowds of the small Southern towns where Jeremiah made his living. So he hired him, and his prediction came true. Watching a Negro fail was amusing. It was life-affirming. A white magician who performed as Henry did—fumbling his cards, accidentally smothering a bird in his jacket, and who, while sawing a woman in half, almost actually did (she was fine, after they bandaged her up)—would have been a sad and pathetic display of simple ineptitude. But *Henry, the Negro Magician*—the extremely unmagical Negro magician—well, it was comedy, and the crowds could not get enough of it. He played to a full tent every night.

The night Henry met the three young men was not the first night they'd come; it was their third. He had seen them enough—and overheard them speak to one another—that by now he'd been able to identify them. They were Tarp, Corliss, and Jake. All of them were at the tail end of their teens. Tarp: mean, merciless, lean and hard as rope. Corliss: a lard of mass and muscle, big as a horse but not as smart. And Jake. The quiet one. Tarp's little brother. Jake wouldn't hurt you, but he wouldn't help you much, either, cowed by his brother's will and Corliss's size. Each night they sat a bit closer to the front, and now they were in the very first row. Henry's tent wasn't that big—everybody, even the fat lady, had a bigger tent than he did—but full was full, and there was some small gratification in that, a minor delight at least. When Henry peeked through the curtain and poured a pail of water on the buckets of dry ice strategically placed out of sight around the stage, he had the illusion of success, which, in his current state, would have to do. Illusion had been his life.

The show began. A carpet of smoky fog set off by a trio of flashlights tied with rope to wooden planks preceded his predictable entrance.

His act, such as it was, was a parody of what everyone already imagined a magic show to be. He wore a fancy black suit with tails, a white shirt, a bow tie, the big top hat—everything. This alone sometimes got a snicker. But Jeremiah had insisted on all of it. "Look the part," he said. "Even if you can't play it."

Adding to the amusement was the expression on Henry's face.

It was deadly serious. He had no smiles for his audience as he took the stage. The smiles would come later. As handsome as any man you were likely to see, black or white, he held them all in his hands with his looks alone. He had a presence. Tall, wide-shouldered, legs like stilts. His face was thin, so thin you could see how it was put together: the high cheekbones, strong chin, and wide forehead. His long, sharp nose. It was his eyes, though, that were mesmerizing: they were shaped like almonds, but green, an emerald green. Every night Henry remained open to the possibility that this was the night his powers would return. Though nothing ever happened in the moments before he took the stage—no inward resurgence, no epiphany; in short, no magic—Henry—when it happened, if it happened—wanted to be ready for it. He wanted to be *appropriate*. And so he was, at least in the moments immediately before a show, wildly hopeful, even when there was absolutely no reason to be.

It was all a memory, but the strongest kind, the memory of the time when he was more powerful than anyone could ever possibly imagine. Those days were distant now, another life altogether. But this memory was in his eyes, in the fearlessness of his expression, his very stance. He was, simply, proud. And this, too, was amusing to the assembled crowd.

Amusing and—to Corliss and Tarp, especially—infuriating. Henry saw it in their expressions, in their postures, in their actions. The night before, as Henry walked out, Tarp spat into the sawdust floor. Corliss glowered. Jake, the third, brushed the hair out of his eyes—his long, thin brown bangs covered them like a veil—and tried to smile. Though they were all nearly men, newly grown, Jake's face allowed for the possibility of wonder, like the face of a little boy. He seemed to share with Henry, even on that third night, even after experiencing the two previous dismal failures, the expectation that something good would happen now, that they would all be treated to an evening of real magic. It was hard for Henry to watch Jake's growing disappointment, salt in the wound of the disappointment he had in himself.

As the last customers filed into the tent that night, Henry could hear JJ the Barker's daily refrain, which, though word-for-word identical every single time, he somehow managed to invest with the energy of a pulpit preacher coming upon the words for the very first time: . . . *and not just any magician, ladybugs and beetles. Do I look like someone who would ask you to spend your hard-earned money on a mere magician, on the tired spectacle of a poor man pulling a rabbit out of his hat, or sawing a beautiful woman in half, or making your wife disappear forever—though he will do that, sir, if you so desire (and I can see that you do). No! I wouldn't ask you to waste your time viewing such tired and pointless antics. For who and what awaits you beyond these increasingly ancient and semi-dilapidated tent walls is something much greater than all that. For this is a man who has met the devil himself—the devil himself!— and come away with Lucifer's darkest secrets, secrets that were he to tell would melt your very soul. But he will show, not tell. And that is where the magic lies.*

Henry and JJ were friends.

That night, Tarp and the rest had refused even to pay. Henry heard them arguing with JJ at the entrance. Tarp said, *We've already seen his show twice. It's shit—praise God.* And JJ said, *That puts me in mind of the woman complaining about an expensive meal: It not only tastes bad, she said, but the servings are small.* But JJ let them in, as anyone would have. Corliss, with one of his big arms, could have squeezed the life right out of him.

And so the show began. Seeming to glide through the knee-high fog, Henry stopped at the edge of the stage and regarded the crowd. Then he spoke, his deep voice tinged with the melancholy of a man who now knew he was about to fail as only he could: magnificently.

"Welcome, friends," he said. "I am Henry Walker, the Negro Magician. But the magic you'll witness tonight is not my own. The mind-shattering illusions—I could not tell you myself how they are done."

"Poorly," Tarp said, so everybody could hear. "Lord knows they are poorly done."

Henry glanced Tarp's way, but only briefly.

"The dark arts," Henry continued, "are dark for many reasons, are dark in many ways. Only the devil himself knows their source, for it is from the devil himself that they come."

"You got that right," Tarp said.

"*Keep an open mind,*" Henry continued. He felt more eyes in the audience on Tarp than there were on him. "And if you see the world as a place where magic can happen, you will see magic in your world tonight."

"Highly unlikely," Tarp said.

Tarp, of course, was right. From this beginning, the show proceeded in as dismal a fashion as it could have. Henry's hands were shaking as he produced the first deck of cards and dropped them; they landed facedown at his feet. He quickly knelt to gather them up, nimbly cutting and straightening them as he did. Already the audience gave off a nervous energy. *How bad could this possibly be?* they wondered. *How many conceivable ways are there to fail?* And in lieu of magic, is this what they'd actually come to view, what they'd come here to learn—that, no matter how low on the ladder of life they had been dragged down, no matter how miserable they were or would become, there would always be someone clinging to the rung below them, and his name would be Henry Walker?

Yet it was pretty snappy, the way he gathered up the cards. It was almost as if he had never dropped them. He smiled at the audience, a big smile, his teeth so white, so perfect, his eyes so hard and bright, his smile proved to them that his confidence was not remotely shattered. It wasn't even cracked. This could happen to anybody, and maybe—who knows?—it was a charming sort of forced ineptitude meant to endear: *For, though I will amaze you in a moment with magic that will melt your very mind, I am in fact no different from you. I make mistakes just like the next guy—not by a long shot am I perfect, just like you and you and you.*

But tonight there were other forces at work. Usually his audiences were composed of simple people who came to be entertained, and at this moment, at night in a small tent at a sideshow fair filled with freaks and weirdos and the concatenation of life's refuse, who didn't love the unmagical Negro? Most did. They loved him the way you love a three-legged dog, even though they were in northern Alabama now, not far from the spot where some genius got the idea for the Ku Klux Klan. People down here had a different way of looking at things. *No, he wouldn't be welcome in my home, and if he looks at my daughter I'm going to have to kill him. But, sure, he can show me a magic trick. I reckon that'll be all right.* Tonight, though, Henry felt the tent choking with real hatred and a malevolent kind of hunger that could not be quelled by anything except its own satisfaction.

Corliss cleared his throat as Henry neatly fanned the cards. Tarp laughed. Jake sadly shook his head. And when Henry cut his eyes at them, the life drained out of his face.

Tarp had one of his cards. "Looking for something?" he said.

Henry forced a smile. "Yes," he said, extending an empty hand. "Thank you."

He reached for the card, and just before he could grab it, Tarp pulled the card back.

"The card," Henry said. "Please."

"I'll give it back," he said.

"Thank you."

"First, though," Tarp said, pausing, lingering in Henry's embarrassment, "first, you tell me what it is. Shouldn't be hard for a man of your—" Tarp couldn't think of the word. He elbowed Jake.

"—prodigious," Jake said softly.

"Okay, right. For a man of your pro-digious talents."

"What it is?" Henry said. "You mean, which card? The card you hold against your chest?"

"That's right."

At this, a few people laughed. But they were all fixated on Henry and his plight, because no one thought, even for a moment, that this was a part of the show. They all knew exactly what was happening, and, good Lord, it was going from bad to worse really quick. Tarp pressed the card against his chest and stared at Henry, bright-eyed, daring him to hazard a guess or, failing that, actually attempt to take it from him. Which, as Henry walked toward him, seemed a real possibility.

But a few feet away, Henry stopped.

"I have a perfect memory," Henry said. "There is nothing I see that I don't remember. For instance, you, sir"—and he pointed to a farmer in the third row—"have a kernel of popcorn stuck to the bottom of your left shoe." The farmer looked, and darn if he didn't. Gasps all around. "And you, miss," he said, looking at a young girl just behind the farmer, "you should remove the tag from your dress. Five dollars is indeed a nice price for something so fine as that, but we don't all need to know it." The young lady blushed, more than a bit embarrassed. Then Henry looked at Tarp. "So of course I remember each of the fifty-two cards in this deck. In half a second I can look at the cards I am holding and tell you which I have and which I don't."

He gave Tarp a moment to take this in.

"But that would be too easy. Since you know what the card is, and in fact can think of nothing else at this moment but *what* it is, it will be an impressive but nonetheless simple exercise to read your mind."

Henry closed his eyes and took a deep preparatory breath. A

quizzical look appeared on his face. "I'm . . . I'm having trouble lo-
cating it. Your brain, I mean. Where do you keep it? Oh, there it is.
It was so small that for a moment I couldn't see it!"

He said this gently, playfully, and the audience loved it, they
laughed and laughed. Even Jake smiled. But not Tarp or Corliss.

Henry waved a hand magically in the air. "Oh, I see the card
now . . . Closer now, clearer, yes, I do see it, I see it as if it is emerg-
ing out of a fog and presenting itself to me . . ."

And suddenly Henry opened his eyes. "It's the three of hearts,"
he said.

Tarp stared at Henry, stunned, completely still. Then he forced
a hateful smile and threw the card at Henry with a nice hard spin
that sent it flying into his chest. Henry caught it before it hit the
ground, and showed it to the audience. They were delighted.

The three of hearts it was.

"Thank you," Henry said with a slight bow. "Thank you." He
waited for the applause to subside. "But this was not magic," he
told them. "Magic—real magic—is something much different from
this. This is a trick." And this is when he turned the deck around
and showed them: each and every card was the three of hearts. This
pleased them even more, of course, that one of their number had
been so totally fooled and in such a simple way. Only Tarp was
stung, and Jake had to hold him back from attacking Henry then
and there.

But if there had ever been any doubt as to their intentions,
Henry knew that they were at that moment sealed and certain.
There would be consequences, and soon.

The rest of the show was an amazing, colossal failure. The accidental success of his first trick yielded to five or six embarrassing
catastrophes that left the crowd murmuring in unsympathetic

disappointment. Someone threw a chunk of ice at him. Almost half walked out. Approaching the end, there was not a single friendly eye to rest his eyes upon. And Tarp and Corliss were in heaven. Henry always tried to put a good face on things by learning from disaster. Tonight, for instance, he made a vow that he would never juggle eggs again. Yet, night by night, his arsenal was shrinking, and since his assistant (who was really just a runaway urchin named Margie) was still recovering from wounds sustained when he had attempted to slice her in half, it was just him up there, sweating it out. How low he had fallen. The memory of all he had once been taunted him. Great men live in the glory of their achievements. It wasn't as if *he* had failed, but another man, one he scarcely knew. The simplest things—palming a coin, hiding a kerchief, vanishing a pack of matches, or producing a dove—even these things were beyond him. And, as he freely told the assembled crowd that night, this was not magic; these were *tricks*, and anybody could learn a trick, anybody . . . and, once, he had mastered them all. He still practiced constantly. Like an old retired athlete who stayed in shape in case one day he was called back to the majors, Henry worked day and night on the simplest maneuvers—forcing cards, cups and balls, sleeving coins—you name it. But he found them beyond his capabilities. Swallowing a sword was certain death. His false thumb tip was the wrong color. He was scared to start a fire out of fear for the entire circus, and a magician without fire is officially no magician at all. As Henry knew, the very first magician—a man with the same powers he had once possessed—was the man who discovered that.

The show over—the applause, such as it was, like a light, spattering rain—Henry ducked behind the curtain and walked through the tent's back flap to the edge of the midway. He stopped there to breathe in some of the night's dung-flavored sweetness and closed his eyes, another dismal performance at an end. Alone in the shadows, with the barkers at a distance calling out for business, not far from fathers trying to win stuffed animals for children and mothers comforting their exhausted babies, Henry stopped and simply waited for them to come. Blending in, of course, was impossible: Henry was the only Negro around here at night. Even the freaks— many of whom were mirrored gaffes anyway—stood a better chance of walking here than he did, beneath the whirling yellow and red and garish orange lights. The fair's unfortunate music—so jaunty and inviting, so cacophonous and exhausting—seemed at odds with its smells (the johns backed up by six every evening) and with the men and women who worked there, the sunken eyes on their thin and pallid faces always seeming to find you, to pick *you* out of the crowd drifting by their booth: *Give it a try, you can't go wrong, first toss is free.*

Tarp's hand fell on his shoulder, and Henry turned. Tarp brought a small wooden cross from his pocket, two sticks held together with a small brass nail.

"We're messengers of God, Mr. Walker," he said. "We're here to set things right."

"Is that so?"

"That's so."

"I'm surprised," he said. "God hasn't caught my show in a long time."

"Not a sparrow falls," Tarp said.

Henry looked around to see if anyone was watching this scene unfold. No one was. As always, he was on his own.

"I apologize if the show wasn't up to your standards," he said. "It wasn't up to mine, either. But, then, you get what you pay for."

"We didn't pay," Corliss said.

Tarp shot him a glance. "That's what he's saying, Corliss."

"Oh."

Jake lingered behind them, clothed in shadows, his eyes hidden once again beneath his bangs. With the toe of his shoe he drew in the dirt, looking up now and again to study Henry and the others, and then slinking back within himself, almost disappearing.

"So. God speaks to you?"

Tarp nodded. He looked at the little cross. "He speaks to everybody, Mr. Walker. It's who listens what makes the difference."

"And what does He say?"

Tarp blinked. The rest of him remained completely still. "Well, He says a lot of things. He's a talker for sure. But as it pertains to right now, He says that in His opinion a white magician would be better than a black one."

Henry considered this. "He said that? That surprises me. Because some white magicians are better, while some aren't. The color of your skin doesn't have a lot to do with it. I'm afraid a white magician might disappoint you as well."

"I'd sure like to find out," Tarp said.

Word by word, Corliss and Tarp moved closer to Henry, until now they were only a few inches away from him. Henry took a few deep, calming breaths and waited. He wouldn't fight them. He had nothing to fight them with.

"So—what now?" Henry asked.

"Now?" Tarp said. "Well, if it hadn't been for that card trick— the three-of-hearts thing you did—we'd probably just smack you around, say some ugly thing, and then be on our way. Now, though, we'd like you to take a little ride with us in the car."

Corliss took him by the arm, the sharpness of his grip stinging to the very bone. "The three of hearts," Corliss breathed into Henry's ear. "Why'd you do that to him?"

And then, just as Corliss was pulling him back into the darkness, something happened that could only happen on the midway of a small and seedy traveling sideshow: they were joined by Rudy, the Strongest Man in the Entire World. Rudy wasn't the strongest man in the entire world, he was not even the strongest man in the entire sideshow (Coot, the flatbed driver, claimed that distinction), but he made up for it by an insane fearlessness inspired by whiskey. It was the force of sheer drunken will that allowed Rudy to bend a shaft of steel as though it were a piece of taffy. His teeth were wrecked from crunching rocks; his cheeks and brow and enormous nose were covered in cuts and bruises that never healed from breaking pieces of wood with his face. His performance depended on items the audience brought for him to destroy, and he had never yet refused a challenge. One morning some months ago, Henry saw him completely sober for the first and only time in the four years. Rudy was crying in despair over the condition of his broken body, over the way he had chosen to spend his life, and over his relationship with Yolanda, the sluttish ticket-puncher. It was a painful moment, an unfortunate foray into reality. But it was nothing that a quart of bourbon couldn't fix. Sober, his life was a shambles. Drunk, he was the Strongest Man in the Entire World.

Rudy arrived and slapped Henry once on the back and brought him in close for a bear hug. Corliss relinquished his grip. Rudy was happy now. The smell of whiskey on his breath, all over his body really, was overpowering. And he might well have just left Yolanda's trailer, because he was never so cheerful as in the moments after that. Being with Yolanda—regardless of how many other men she'd had before him—was the high point of his day.

It had only taken him a moment to comprehend Henry's perilous situation; Rudy was far from dense. When he embraced Henry he was jolly, laughing with a big man's bellow, but almost instantly he froze up, became completely silent, and took it all in. Once he did, the expression on his face shifted. His eyes lit up. Especially when he saw Corliss, who he knew could inflict real damage on him if he wanted. But Rudy could endure anything: Corliss could hurt him bad, but Rudy would weather it, and then break Corliss in half.

"Well, hey, boys," he said, in a way that was both friendly and menacing. "What's shaking?"

Tarp shrugged. "Not much. Doing a little preaching here and there," he said. He showed Rudy his little cross. "Saw his show and thought he could use the Holy Spirit."

Rudy spat. It landed very close to Tarp's left shoe. Then he laughed. "Henry can't do a trick to save his life, can he?" he said. "But I find that quality endearing. That's one cute cross you got there." And he spat again.

Tarp slipped it back into his pocket. "God loves you," he said. "Hard as it might be for Him to, He loves you. He even loves Henry here. That's the Good News."

Rudy shook his head with a kind of sad despair. "Y'all look more like bad news to me," he said.

Tarp sighed. "Well, I guess it can't all be good," he said.

Rudy brought Henry even closer to him. He wouldn't let Henry go.

"Then all I can say is that it's a good thing you hooligans ran into him today," Rudy said. "A few years ago, he could have turned you into a pile of salt without even touching you. All he'd have to do is think it and—*voilà*—salt. Isn't that right, Henry?"

Henry looked away. His face seemed to draw the night shadows into it, making his face even darker, a shadow itself. "Doesn't matter," he said softly.

"It does, though," Rudy said. "What a man was may not be the same as what he's become, but we can't just forget about it. Just because George Washington lived two hundred years ago and is dust himself doesn't mean we don't want to think about him the way he was. As a hero. Our first president. There's books about him. Books! That's right, ain't it?" He was looking directly at Corliss.

"I reckon," Corliss said, shrugging.

"That's right," Rudy said. He looked down at Henry with affection. "I remember the dark and rainy night you came here, Henry, four years ago, asking Jeremiah Mosgrove for a place in the Chinese Circus."

"It wasn't raining," Henry said. "And it wasn't dark."

"It was dark that night," Rudy said. "Very dark. So dark you blended in with it. You were almost invisible. That's not a joke, either—it's a fact. We were in West Virginia then. That's where you found us. Before that you'd been . . . what?"

"Doing other things," Henry said.

"Doing other things," Rudy said. "That's right. Wandering through the wilderness, a lost child of God. You needed a place to rest your weary feet. You needed a family. And that's what we gave you, isn't it? Me, JJ, Jenny, and the rest."

Henry nodded. He stared at the ground, remembering.

Rudy gave Tarp a hard look. "This man's like my brother," he said. "It doesn't matter what color he is. He's my brother. Now, what do you think of that?"

"It makes me wonder about your sister," Tarp said.

At this Corliss laughed his idiot laugh, and Rudy shook his head. "I should kill you for that," Rudy said. "You and your friends, too. Instead, let me tell you a story."

"Great," Tarp said. "Just great."

Rudy, still with his arm around Henry's shoulder, led the others into Henry's empty tent. He motioned for them to sit down in three empty chairs. He and Henry stood.

"This is how it was, fellas," Rudy said. "Though I didn't know him then, by all accounts—or at least by his account—Henry Walker used to probably be the greatest magician in the world. Because he did *real* magic. It wasn't under the name Henry Walker, either, it was something different—a secret name he's never even told me. He wasn't like, you know, Houdini, or Kellar, or Carter, who only made things *seem* like magic. What they did is tricks;

Henry did it *real*. For instance: The others, they have strings tied to their levitating women. But Henry's women, they could really *float*. When he cut a woman in half—dear God, she was *sliced in two*. He didn't even use a box! He just sliced her in half and then, if there was a doctor in the audience, he had him come up onstage and examine her, not only to see if she was still living—which of course she was—but to study the organs which were now plainly on view. Then Henry put her back together."

Rudy knew how to tell a story. Tarp, Corliss, and Jake—they were entranced. Henry felt that he could just walk away now and no one would notice. But he stayed, and not just because Rudy's huge arm still draped his shoulder: Henry wanted to hear the story, too.

"It was nothing for him to make a card disappear and then to have it find its way into your back left pocket. Nothing to turn a rope into a snake. Nothing to fill the sky with pigeons. What amazed others was to him no more remarkable than a yawn. One might go so far as to say he had *infinite* powers, were he to allow himself to practice them. But he didn't. He couldn't. Because he had done that only once, and it led to a most tragic end."

"Not this story, Rudy," Henry said. "Please, not this one."

"But this is the *only* story," Rudy said. "There are no other stories besides this one. And you told it to me. It's my duty to tell these boys, and for them to tell others after that." Rudy leaned in toward Tarp and whispered, mock-conspiratorially: "Your duty."

"Rudy," Henry said, but Rudy squeezed him tight with his arm, and Henry found it impossible to speak again.

Rudy scratched his face, removing a scab the size of a quarter from his cheek. He examined it, and then let it drop to the ground. The open sore oozed.

"Henry was only ten years old when a very strange thing happened to him," Rudy began. "Before it, he was as normal as any child ever was, but after, he could not have been more different. His family—his father and precious younger sister, Hannah—had only just moved into a new home, a sprawling mansion which took up an entire city block. A grown man would have been awed by its immensity, but a mere child—which twenty-five odd years ago Henry was—would have felt as though he had discovered an entire world of rooms. Henry and Hannah—she was but one year his junior—explored it with the temerity of children who had yet to know fear. Floor after floor, each one yielding to the next, until it seemed there could be no more. And yet there were more floors, and on each floor, room after room after room. They could have slept in a different room every single night and not exhausted their availability for months. For, you see, it was no home at all they lived in now. His family had moved into a hotel."

Rudy knew this story because he was not the only drinker in this outfit; Henry joined him on occasion, huddled in the shadows between the trailers, in the backseat of someone's car, or at the picnic table behind Jeremiah's office. Together, they drank and told stories. This is how Henry heard about Rudy's experiences as a geek, long before Rudy even knew what a geek was. When he was a kid, Rudy ate the heads off of lizards to amuse his older brother's friends, to impress them, but it had won him no friends of his own. Henry heard about Rudy's growth spurt, too—an inch a week (either upward or outward) for half a year—and about his shyness, and how he played on the high-school football team well into his twenties, his plain immensity so scarifying that some teams refused to take the field. None of it was true, or perhaps all of it was. Henry wasn't sure anymore. His mind was full of so many things, crowded with the dead. The drunken storytelling—which became boisterous at times, like a show unto itself—was not bound by things as pointless and wearying as facts.

And yet it was possible that this was part of the dissimulation:

that the truth was being presented as fiction, and easier to tell because of that.

Rudy seemed to believe Henry, though. At least he wanted to. He listened: that was all Henry could be sure of. He was sure of it in the moment of telling, and he was sure of it now, as he heard Rudy repeat the story Henry had told him, verbatim and then some, with flourishes it would seem only the real teller of the tale could tell. For example, the "world of rooms" was Rudy's own invention, and Rudy's details made the story that much more believable; they drew Henry not only into the story, but back in time itself.

For it so happened that every word he had told Rudy was true— not factual, but true. Some parts he had skipped over, some chapters in their entirety, but those he shared were real. The hotel. His sister. The rooms. His family had been reduced to this. They had been prosperous once; then his father lost everything in the Crash. Like so many—almost no one was spared—but his family seemed especially cursed. Their mother was dying. Consumption, they said, TB, but Henry knew it was much more than that. Her life had been taken from her, a life of dresses and jewels and splendid parties and nice shoes and ribbons—of possibility—a picture-perfect life, gone now forever; no life was long enough to recoup what they had lost. They couldn't even afford to take her to a sanitarium, but the doctor said it would have been little use to her: the disease had progressed that far. She was dying in the home that would soon be taken from them.

The children weren't allowed to touch her. Henry and Hannah could only watch from the other side of her first-floor bedroom window. Hannah was so small Henry had to lift her up to see their mother. Standing between two fat shrubs, they waved at her, and their small, soft arms scratched against the branches, welting with thin lines of blood. Their mother waved until she couldn't anymore.

She turned into a ghost before their eyes. They could see the life draining from her, her breathing torturous, her lips edged with dried blood.

Then, one day, the doctor came and took Mr. Walker to another room to speak to him, and somehow Henry knew what the doctor was saying. He came inside with Hannah, left her in the hallway just outside his mother's door.

Stay here, he told her. He didn't want to run the risk of anything happening to her. *I'll only be a minute.*

She waited there, alone in the hallway, until she couldn't stand it anymore. As Henry had known she would, she opened the door and peered in. He shook his head to hold her there, and then he leaned over and gave his mother a kiss on the cheek. *And one for you,* he said to Hannah, and kissed his mother again.

She died that day. A week later, the bank foreclosed on their mortgage. And so Henry, Hannah and Mr. Walker left their beautiful home forever and began the next chapter in the story of their tragic lives.

"Henry's father was hired as the hotel janitor," Rudy continued. "A man who had worn bow ties and seersucker suits. Who had tried to get his kids to pronounce the word 'potato' *potahto.* A man whose hands were as soft as water—now a hotel janitor. Is there no end to it all? A point at which we can rest in our big comfy chair with our feet up, a drink on the table beside the chair, and say, *So this is what it was all about, getting to this place, this comfy chair?* No. There is no end. The family lived in the room between the kitchen and the laundry." Rudy had laughed so hard when he heard this—between the kitchen and the laundry!—as if it couldn't have been true, as if this detail had to have been added for effect, to give the story even more power. But it *was* true.

"Between the kitchen and the laundry," Rudy said softly, again, peering into Tarp's eyes as he said it, challenging him in a way to come up with something worse than that. *Sure*, Rudy seemed to be saying, *you may live in a shack with a busted septic tank and a mean dog growling beneath the porch, but at least you don't have to watch the high-and-mighty ones who have it better than you milling about in their fancy clothes, walking their fancy dog, people who—if they even think of you— hate you for being poor and for reminding them that there are people in the world with less, with near to nothing.*

"Dark times? You bet," Rudy said. "At the end of the day, their father had almost nothing left for his children. Nothing but the sense of his own perseverance, his unwillingness to give up, to lie down and die. Through his actions they could see he was heading toward the same star he always was, and that it had never had anything to do with money, or big houses, or nice chairs. It was about being alive, and staying that way until the last day came. Until he gave all that up as well. Every ounce of his strength was spent fixing things he didn't know how to fix. The lie he told to get the job: *Been working with tools since I was this big,* he told the mustachioed hotel-owner. *I'm a doctor of the mechanical world.* The truth was he didn't know which end of a hammer to use. But he had a roof, four walls. His children had food. He would have sold his body piece by piece to provide them with that.

"Even so, even with all of this, Henry and Hannah had a little fun, you know? Kids know how to do that. A kid can transform the world with a stick. Henry stole his father's keys, and the little scamps investigated the unoccupied rooms, jumping from bed to bed, listening to radios, and pretending to be people they weren't— the high rollers all around them. Hannah played the wife, Henry the husband. *We'll be late if you don't hurry, dear,* she'd call to him from the bathroom. *I can't find my cuff links!* he'd say. *Silly!* she'd say. *I have them right here. I believe we'll have an astonishingly good time at the Schneiders' this evening.* And Henry'd say, *Yes, I think so, too.*"

How Rudy remembered all this, when he had been drunk then and every day since then, made no sense to Henry. Because it was what Hannah had said exactly. *Astonish*—it was her favorite word of all time. *These potatoes are astonishingly good! Don't sneak up on me like that—you astonished me! I have an astonishing announcement: the couple in Room 311 have checked out—and they left some money on the dresser!* A fancy word for a nine-year-old. The only fancy word she would ever learn.

"And then there was the old standby, the perfect game to play in their new digs: hide-and-seek. It was on just such a day when they were playing this game that it happened—the moment I mentioned before, the one that changed Henry forever, the one that made him, if you will, the man you see before you today."

"Stop," Henry said. "No more."

"But I just got started, Henry," Rudy said. "I'm just getting to the good part. And I know you boys want to hear it, don't you?"

Jake looked at the others, but they were stone-faced. "I do," he said.

Rudy nodded, rubbing the back of Henry's head. "And if these boys want to hurt you, Henry, and I believe they just might"—Rudy glanced at Corliss, who affirmed that with a carnivorous smile—"they should know who it is they're hurting."

Rudy's objective was painfully obvious. He was hoping to turn Henry into something more than just a *nigger* in their eyes. He wanted them to see Henry for what he was. A man. A man with a story. They couldn't have known Rudy had no other weapon, that, as big as he was (a hairless ape, a human throwback, an anthropo-Gargantua), he couldn't fight to save his life. He withered at the prospect of causing pain to anyone other than himself. There is no way they could have done anything to him that he hadn't already done to himself, but in any case he would never have exacted a revenge. If he could have, he would have swallowed all the pain in the world.

"It was Room 702, if I remember correctly," Rudy said. He had, of course, remembered correctly. "Henry thought the room was empty. It was a great room to hide in, because it was the last room on the highest floor. Based on the occupancy sheets he'd glanced at in the office earlier, a couple from Wisconsin had checked out that morning. So, when he opened the door and slipped into the room, he was surprised to see someone, a man, sitting in a straight-backed wooden chair, staring right at him.

"Henry froze, apologized, and began to back out of the room. But it was as if the man had been expecting him. His deliberately placid expression didn't change. *Please*, the man said. *Come in.* Henry wasn't sure what to do. He and Hannah had always been so careful. This had never happened before. *Please*, the man said again, and Henry—only ten years old then, and without the will to object to an adult—let the door close behind him. *There's something I want to show you*, the man said. *I think you'll find it quite interesting. Come closer.* Henry did as he was told. He took a few slow steps closer to the man in the chair, who had never stopped smiling at him. The man was dressed in unusually fancy clothes, jet-black jacket and trousers, a white shirt, and a silver tie, which was fancy even for this hotel, especially since he didn't appear to be going anywhere and it was early yet to be dressed for dinner. He had thick, wavy black hair held in check with an overabundance of styling lotion, and a face so milky and pale that years later Henry would say that he was the first truly *white* person he ever saw. Because he was not tan or pink or a light shade of orange, like the rest of us are—but entirely white.

"*Closer*, the man said, and as Henry took another slow step, the man's eyes began to glow a bit, as if the pilot light inside of him had been lit, and those eyes, together with a knowing smile and his cold white skin, were *haunting*, positively *disturbing*, and even as I talk about it now, I feel the blood in my veins begin to slow and thicken into a red paste and harden." Rudy lowered his voice. In a husky

near-whisper he said, "For this was no man. This was no human being." Rudy paused, and slowly whispered, *"This was the devil himself!"*

Now even Tarp and Corliss were rapt, so deep into the story that
they had become a part of it, they were *in that room* with the young
Henry, standing inches away from a man who, it turned out, was no
man at all, but the devil himself. Corliss had been holding his
breath, and when he exhaled could be heard to say, *Holy Christ
Almighty.* His reason for being there was forgotten. Rudy had all
three men under his spell; only Henry remained above it. He tried
to remember if he'd told Rudy this. He was trying to remember
which version he'd told him—the one with just the facts in it, or the
slightly more elaborate one that was the truer. But it must have
been the truer version, because Rudy was getting it right. Every
word.

"The devil," Rudy continued, "has no name, so there was no introduction. Henry simply knew, as you would know, too, God forbid, were you ever to meet him yourself. He smiled at the boy, and
the boy simply stood there, unable to move at all. The devil possessed him. Enveloped him in his dark light. No breath came until
the devil allowed it to come. Henry could hear his own heart beat
as if the room itself had become his heart, as if he had been swallowed up and turned inside out. The devil's eyes glowed red, grew
large, like tunnels he could walk within. And then, as though com-
manded to, walk within them he did, the cold and glowing windy
tunnels that were the devil's eyes. Baptized by evil on that day. And
it was over.

"And just like that, the man was gone. Henry was alone when
Hannah opened the door and found him standing there facing the
empty chair. She touched him gently on the shoulder and said,
You're it. And he was. But he never told her exactly what *it* was he
had become. He didn't have the words."

Rudy paused, grimaced, and rubbed his jaw with one of his huge hands. He appeared to have a toothache. He opened his mouth and explored it with his fingers, finally discovering the culprit, and in front of all of them ripped the tooth from the gum, examined it, and tossed it off to one side. He swallowed his own blood.

"This is the day Henry became a magician. Not the kind we're used to seeing—the tricksters, the illusionists, the I'll-do-this-over-here-while-you're-looking-over-there kind of magician. Henry became a *real* one. Nothing he ever meant to be or wanted, but what he was now. Do we ever become who we want to become? How many of us can look at ourselves and say, *This is it, this is what I've always wanted, what I imagined I would do with the life I've been given*? A precious few. I'm one of the lucky ones, I guess. Henry—not so much.

"Until the day he met the devil, he'd seen himself in relation to one person: his sister. His mother dead, his father's spirit crumpled up and tossed away like a piece of carbon paper, Hannah was all there was in the world to keep, to save, the last good thing. Henry loved her more than we have ever loved anything and more than anything he has ever loved since. But now he was a part of a greater power. The accidental magician. For all he had to do was think a thing, and whatever he thought would come true. He could actually move things with his mind. At dinner, the salt shaker dashed across the table into his hand, his father too tired, and soon too intoxicated, to notice. A broken vase was restored. He could make cards disappear into thin air, and have them reappear beneath a table, or in your hair, or beneath the superficial layer of his own skin. Hannah loved it. She was only nine years old, remember, and didn't know such things were impossible, and that her brother was an agent of the devil. An agent of the devil though not evil himself. But an agent of evil, for he was possessed of powers no man should have, let alone a young boy.

"Which brings me to Henry's first magic show. It was Hannah's idea: something to distract their father from his dismal life. In the lost-and-found she procured an old top hat, and Henry turned a tablecloth into a cape that he tied around his neck in a clumsy knot. Hannah wore her most frilly dress. And she found a room in which to stage it, but since it was the weekend and the hotel almost full, there was only one room left unoccupied. The devil's room. Room 702. Henry said, *No. No. We'll find another room*, he said, *or wait until Monday, when the others clear out.* But Hannah insisted, and he could never say no to her for long. So Room 702 it was.

"Hannah and Henry each took a hand, dragging their dad upstairs. *What's all this about?* he wondered aloud. *Where in the world are you taking me?* But Hannah only placed a finger across her lips as they climbed the stairs, all the way from the basement to the very top floor, and then to the room at the far end of the hall, the very last room in the entire hotel. Hannah was about to open the door when Henry intervened. *I'll go in first*, he said. And a lifetime passed with his hand on the doorknob, his breath stopped in his chest. But then he turned the knob, he opened the door, and the room was empty. He breathed again. *What's this, now?* their father growled. *We could all get in trouble with this, you know that, don't you?* But Hannah was having none of it. She sat him on the edge of one of the twin beds. *Henry's going to do a magic show for you*, Hannah said, *and I'm going to help!* He said, *A magic show? Well, this should be fun.* And he settled in to watch.

"Henry began with simple moves from the well-known library of the trickster magicians. Only Henry had never practiced a one. He didn't have to. The tricks did themselves. He held out a deck of cards and knew before he chose it the card his father would draw. *Astonishing, isn't it?* Hannah said. She bowed, one arm across her waist, as if she'd done the trick herself. Henry made a spoon levitate, as his father peered in closer to find the strings; not seeing them, he was truly amazed. Hannah clapped. Henry produced a rabbit from his hat, a pigeon from his sleeve ... These things seemed to surprise Henry himself. *A rabbit,* he had thought, and so it happened. *A bird.* It was that easy and, yes, as Hannah would say, that astonishing. They watched as the furry white thing scampered beneath a bed, as the pigeon flew against the window. And their father smiled for the first time in years. Hannah and Henry exchanged a happy look—exactly the expression they had hoped to obtain. Seeing it emboldened Hannah. She stood up proud and straight. *And now,* she said, *for the most magical and wonderful and astonishing thing of all. For your viewing pleasure this evening, the Incredible Henry—my brother—will make me disappear!*

"Hannah's idea. They'd never done this before. Henry had never wanted to do it. He never wanted Hannah more than a few feet away from him, in his sight, day or night. This was the boy who waited just outside the door while she took a bath. She slept in a twin bed within an arm's reach of his. But he agreed, because she insisted. Surely nothing would be more fantastic than that—to disappear Hannah, and to reappear her, in the same spot, right in front of their father's eyes. A perfect colossal ending. *This should be something,* their father said, winking. And it surely was.

"Henry threw a sheet over the top of her head, and she stood there, perfectly still. She looked like a statue about to be unveiled. Then Henry waited for a moment, feeling the dark power within him beginning to surge, growing even bigger than he was himself, a bigness stretching at his very bones until he felt he might explode. Finally, he thought the word *Disappear!* and waved a hand above her head for effect. *Voilà!*—he actually said *Voilà!*—and Hannah was gone.

"The sheet, empty now, fell like a weightless body to the ground. Henry and his father both stared at it in a stunned sort of pleasurable horror. Neither could believe it had really happened. But it had. His father rose and lifted the sheet. She wasn't there. He looked at Henry. *How did you*—but he couldn't finish the sentence. *That was—I can't believe it. Is there a hole in the floor?* But there wasn't. *Then I don't—I can't for the life of me figure out how the two of you did that. My goodness me.* And he shook his head as he took his place again on the edge of the bed. *Now for the part where you bring her back*, he said. *Yes*, Henry said.

"And they waited. And Henry said *yes* again, now for that part, the part where she comes back. But as he prepared to think the necessary word, he felt oddly . . . normal. He felt empty, as though something had been taken from him. *Now for the part where I bring her back*, he said, but his voice sounded small. He thought the words that should do it, the words that had done it with cards and books and even once a small table—*Come back!* he thought—but this time nothing happened at all. The sheet on the floor remained still, lifeless. *I'm waiting*, his father said, an edge to his voice. Henry said it aloud this time, screamed it at the top of his lungs: *Come back!*" Rudy paused, his eyes sad and dark. "But she didn't. And she never did.

"For the real magician here was the devil himself, and this was *his* trick, *his* plan, same as it always was: to steal from man all that is lovely in the world, and to have it delivered to him via the hand of man himself. This is what Henry had done. In return for the gift of magic, his sister, the dearest thing in all his life, was lost."

Rudy looked at Henry's stricken face and continued in his soft, sad voice. "He has never seen her since. And yet a day hasn't passed that he hasn't looked for her." Then he looked at the three boys, seeming to take all of them into his eyes at once. "But one day he did find the devil, my young friends. He found the devil—and he killed him. Not with magic, no. He didn't need magic. Henry did it with the power of his immeasurable grief."

· · ·

Rudy stopped talking. He closed his eyes, took a deep breath, and began nodding—nodding as if he had been not the one telling the story but the one listening as, word by word, the dark secrets of Henry's past were told. But he knew he had lost. Whatever impression he'd hoped to make on these boys—and really it was just, *Deep down we're all the same, fellas, isn't that right?*—he hadn't done it. One losing battle after another: that's life for you. Winning doesn't even exist, really, not as something you can hold on to; it's just something that happens between losses. Whatever good Rudy did tonight would be undone tomorrow. He looked at Henry, at his bright, sad green eyes, and knew that there was nothing he could do to save him, and, knowing that, still knew he would never stop trying to, because they were friends, and that's what it's all about when you're friends: trying.

Tarp lit a cigarette. Jake wiped his nose with a swipe of his shirt-sleeve and appeared caught in the web of some big thought. Corliss spat, but it wasn't meant as commentary on what had just transpired, it was just something he had to do.

The midway was completely empty now. All the booths were dark and dead. They could all hear somebody laughing, but it was coming from far away, behind the trailers. Life was elsewhere now, in the private night. Rudy was already thinking about Yolanda.

"Well," Tarp said into the quiet. "That's the longest goddamn story I've ever heard."

"And he was only ten when it happened," Corliss said. "By the looks of him, we got about twenty years 'fore we catch up." He looked at Rudy. "How much more you got?"

Rudy sighed. "That's all I got," he said.

Tarp tried to tap down a yawn. He looked at Corliss, at Jake. "I don't know about the rest of you, but I'm beat. I say we head on back. Still got time to pray. Always have time to pray."

"I reckon," Corliss said.

Jake looked relieved. He took a penny from his pocket and began flipping it, grabbing it in midair with one hand, saying either *heads* or *tails*, and slapping it with a childlike delight on top of the other hand. Henry could easily read his face each time after he examined the result. Sometimes he got it right, and sometimes he didn't. "Come on." Tarp nudged him, and the three turned and walked slowly away.

Rudy finally let Henry go.

"That went all right," Rudy said, nodding, watching them go. "I wish I could have hurt them for you."

"That's all right, Rudy," Henry said. "Worked out pretty good. For tonight, anyway. But about that story, I should tell you."

"Yes?"

"That's not quite the way it goes."

At dusk the next afternoon, they returned. They ambushed Henry as he was leaving his trailer, tied him up with his own chains, and threw him into the back of an old Fleetline Tarp drove. Corliss sat with Henry, and broke one of Henry's ribs on the ride out. Jake was in the passenger seat, where he kept busy flipping his coin, the slap of one hand on the other, and the occasional, almost unconscious whisper—*Heads, tails, heads*—until they arrived in a spot in the middle of nowhere, a cow pasture, where Corliss and Tarp began to beat Henry with all the righteousness they could muster. They took turns, one after the other.

"God told you to do this?" Henry managed to ask them, already spitting blood.

"He's one mysterious son-of-a-bitch, ain't he?" Tarp said.

Then Corliss broke Henry's hand with his own. Tarp kicked him in the face with the side of one of his mud-covered shoes, bent down close, and smiled. Remarkably, Tarp had all of his teeth, maybe more than all. They looked crowded in his mouth, one over-lapping the next, like a busful of people.

"Where'd you get those green eyes?" he asked Henry. But he didn't wait for an answer. "Damn if they're not the same color as mine."

Tarp stood up. He was still wearing that Sunday-go-to-meeting outfit. There was blood on it now; spattered on the white shirt, it made some sort of design. Henry blinked, staring at it, trying to fig-ure out what it was.

"Corliss," Tarp said, "help me out here. How many total niggers have we killed?"

This caught Corliss off guard. "Total niggers?" he said.

"Total niggers," Tarp said.

Corliss touched the end of his fingers, counting, and sighed. He counted again. "I'm thinking seven at least." He looked at Tarp to see if that was a satisfactory number.

"I'd say eight," Tarp said. "Eight if you count that dog."

Corliss frowned. "Can a dog be a nigger?" he asked.

"If it's a nigger's dog it can," Tarp said.

Corliss didn't like the idea of a nigger dog. "That's something you can't always tell by looking," he said.

Jake looked up and shook his head. When he spoke, it was so muted and under his breath that the breath itself was louder, clearer, easier to understand than the words.

"We never killed anybody," he said.

"*Jake,*" Tarp said, disgusted. "Shut the hell up."

Henry knew, felt his body was almost finished. A cheekbone welt shut his left eye, and the right one was filled with blood. His entire face was swollen. His tux (which he had changed into just be-fore they arrived to kidnap him) was ruined, the tails torn off and used to cuff his hands until they'd discovered his box of chains. Tarp had circled the chains around Henry's body so tight that they cut his wrists and made it nearly impossible to breathe. Luckily, from years of practice, Henry knew how not to breathe, to live on almost no air at all; preparation for his low-rent Houdini water-immersion escapes had come in handy more than once. But never before had his left arm been broken, his ribs cracked, and his pants soaked in urine as his were now—not a fear-inspired leak, but simply because he had to go, and holding it, beneath the pressure of the chain, proved impossible. Letting it out was the single moment of relief he'd experienced since his ordeal began.

There was a time when Henry would have lived through this. Had it happened ten, fifteen, even twenty years ago, these punks would have earned the most malicious retribution. Think a pack of wild dogs. That's all he'd have to do. Think a pack of wild dogs, and a pack of wild dogs would appear from the depths of the dark pine forest behind them, howling, some of them red-eyed and some yellow but all glaring murderously, teeth bared like hacksaws, their black hair coarse as tree bark, wild dogs like monsters, ravenous and immortal, capable of tearing a man into the smallest pieces without bringing death, until death itself would be his best desire. And Henry Walker, the Negro Magician, would have walked away unharmed. But not now.

"We've never killed anybody," Jake said again.

Tarp shook his head. He was hating his brother now, Henry could tell. "I did run over a dog," he said.

"That was an accident."

"Well . . ." Tarp mumbled.

The day was quickly coming to an end, the shadows growing taller than the trees. Small patches of sun turned the grass yellow in places, and a rogue beam warmed the top of Henry's head. This is what he tried to absorb, to remember. Light touched every sense; Henry could almost smell it. He thought of Hannah as living through the sun, the goddess of light; the moon would have been too cold for her.

Jake walked over to Henry. He removed an oil-stained rag from his back pocket, knelt, and reached out to wipe some of the blood away from Henry's eye.

"Don't," Henry said. "Please. Don't."

But Jake did. He placed the rag along the edge of Henry's right eye and gently rubbed around it and blotted the little puddle of blood that had settled beneath Henry's lower eyelid. He wiped across it, and with a bit more pressure around the corners. Henry winced, and Jake pulled back, squinting, still just a few inches away from Henry's face. He looked at Henry's eye, and then he studied the area around it. It was as if he were seeing Henry for the first time, and, in fact, he was. Jake looked at the rag, red with blood, then swiped Henry's cheek again, this time even harder than before, and it stung. Jake sat back on his heels and considered Henry and his face, rapt in a moment he couldn't comprehend.

"Jake loves to make things better," Tarp said, and laughed. "You know that story, Corliss? About the bird? A bird flew into one of the porch fans last summer and he put it in a box, fixed it up till it could fly again. Fixed it up perfect. Then the cat got it."

Corliss laughed. "That's called something," he said. "There's a word for that."

"Sad," Jake said, standing up, moving away from Henry without taking his eyes off of him. "The word is *sad*." Then he turned to look at Tarp. "We should go," he said. "We've done enough."

But Tarp wasn't listening to Jake.

"Sounds good," Tarp said. "But I think I have a better idea."

Tarp slipped a pistol from his suit pocket. Henry saw the cross fall out at the same time, saw it disappear into the dark grass. Tarp didn't. He was interested in the gun now. He looked at it as if he hadn't known it was there.

From somewhere deep in the woods, they could all hear a dusk owl sing.

. . .

Now. Now would be about the time when Jeremiah and the rest would figure out that Henry was missing. The ship that was Jeremiah Mosgrove's Chinese Circus was not tightly run. A few minutes late rising from the only home you had—your moist and mildewed trailer with the fold-out bed, the hot plate, a picture of a woman you maybe used to know tacked on the wall beside you near the pillow where her head would be resting were she here—lingering was no surprise. Alone, without the rest of the world there to tell you what you were, you were the same as anybody; only outside did you become the other, the exception to the rule. Enjoy it while it lasted. Who'd choose this kind of life? Yeah, there was the camaraderie, that close warmth that came with knowing you're not alone in this aloneness. But these friends, these crazy misfits—who'd choose them if they didn't have to? Beyond even knowing that, beyond the disdain they felt for the rest of the world, there was this dream: a house in a neighborhood. Nothing particularly grand, just a nice little house with a yard and a lady next door who hangs her laundry out on a clothesline across her backyard. A lady who makes pies, and grows yellow flowers. Where everyone's house is white, and has a television antenna—half again as big as the house itself—wobbling precariously on the shingled roof. A couple of kids, too. Stuff that, when you add it all up, equals belonging. That's *normal*, and normal is good. When you're normal, people smile, they ask you for directions, they give you a job, you marry their daughter. So, if you spend a few minutes longer in your trailer, the only place where you can at least dream this sort of world, no one's going to stop you.

Eventually, though, they would discover he was gone. Rudy might put two and two together and figure it all out, but it didn't matter, not at this point. They would never find him here, because they wouldn't even look. Leaving the confines of the fenced-in park where they staged their performances rarely happened. The circus was like a little town all its own, an ecosystem where life forms evolved into the dark-night terrors of children's dreams. From time to time, someone would leave, disappear. Usually it was an old drunk who helped set up the tents and rides, disposed of the uneaten sugar bread and cotton candy. Very rarely it was one of the performers. Agnes the Alligator Lady left a while ago, moved back home to Florida to take care of her mother. Then, a month ago, they lost Buster, the fire-eater, to the army. Now Henry was nowhere to be seen. About to be slain, a prisoner in his own chains, bleeding in a cow pasture.

"Come on," Jake said as soon as he saw the silver barrel like a sixth finger jutting from the end of his brother's hand. "I mean—*damn*, Tarp." In Jake's voice Henry heard a small cry; the boy had only now figured out where all this was going.

"You come on."

"You don't want to use that gun, Tarp," he said. "I'm telling you."

Faster than Henry thought possible, Tarp's right hand—the one with the gun in it—slammed into the side of Jake's face, cracking it with the sound of glass. The blow forced Jake into the hood of the car, his lips pressed softly against the hood, as if in a kiss. He stayed that way for a minute.

Tarp stood over him, breathing hard. "You're like that bird," he said. "Careful that the cat don't get you."

Tarp, his hand shaking, held the gun high above his head and shot it. The sound was vaguely reassuring to Henry, who'd imagined it would be the last sound he'd hear on earth. His eyes swam in the last light of the sky that hung above them. Tentative, like Henry, barely there.

"We will *never* have this chance again," Tarp said. He turned to Henry and pointed the gun at him. But he was gripping the handle, not the trigger. "Never. Look at him. Look at *them*. They used to belong to us. Like a table or a chair." Tarp spat. "Now they can get on TV and say any goddamn thing. Be doctors, dentists—*magicians*. It's not going to stop. It's like a train. Run you over, the world will. Maybe I can't change that, but I'd like a vote. I'd like it on record how I feel."

Corliss dropped another card into the mud at his feet. He looked at his watch. "I'm with you, Tarp," he said. "Kill him."

"Don't do it," Jake said.

"Henry, the Negro Magician. Shit. He ain't no magician."

Jake wiped the blood from his face with the sleeve of his shirt. He looked at Henry. Henry shook his head. But Jake ignored him. "That may be," he said. "But he ain't a Negro, neither."

Tarp laughed once, and shook his head.

"You take the cake," Tarp said. "You really do. What does that even *mean*? Have you lost your stupid mind?"

Jake moved away from the car toward Henry. Tarp and Corliss followed. And Henry thought, *Hannah*. Just that one word, *Hannah*, and from the depths of the dark pine forest he saw her, glowing, the way little girls do, the way he had last seen her over twenty-three years ago, in her blue dress with the delicate ivory buttons down the front, her black shoes, white socks. She smiled and waved, and with the hairpin he kept hidden in the sleeve of his coat he unlocked his chains, and raised a hand to wave at her. Tarp cocked his gun and aimed. "Don't move another inch," he said. "Not one inch." Henry's hand froze mid-wave as Hannah watched the three approach him. He could see her eyes, and he could see she still loved him. But they were sad eyes all the same, because there was nothing she could do for him, not now, not ever. She was only what she always was: his, his beautiful little sister.

Jake knelt down and began wiping at Henry's face with the rag. What little light there was had turned the world a faded gray. But

Corliss and Tarp could see Henry's face: Jake seemed to erase all the color from it. His cheeks, his nose, his neck. Beneath the thin layer of black was another man, a white one. Jake was the magician now, turning one thing into another, doing the impossible, the unbelievable, the extraordinary.

"What?" Tarp said, not to anyone listening, or even to himself.

"An illusion," Henry said. "The only one I have left."

Hannah was gone.

Tarp ripped the rag from Jake's hand and began pawing at Henry's face, edging into his cuts and wounds, rubbing harder and harder until he, too, turned black to white.

Tarp dropped the rag and moved back, staring.

Corliss stared, too. "Can you do that to all of them?" he said.

They were all completely still.

Tarp dragged his fingers through his hair and closed his eyes. "This is not making *sense,*" he said. Another long and complete silence.

Then Corliss spoke. "Remember what his friend said? About the devil?" He took a step backward. "This looks like his work."

"Shut up, Corliss," Tarp said, but he wasn't looking at Corliss. He was staring at Henry, and Henry was staring back at him. "You ain't a nigger," he said. "And you ain't a magician. So . . . what the hell are you?"

There were lots of answers for a question like this. Lots of them. But none of them were easy, and Henry could only barely speak now. "That," he said, but so softly and slowly that Tarp had to lean in to hear him, "that could be a long story."

Tarp stood. *"A long story?"* he said, shaking his head, his anger rising in every word. Everybody looked at him, waiting for the commencement of his rage. He looked at his brother, slit-eyed, smoldering, then at Corliss. "Another long goddamn story," he said.

And then the very last thing anybody expected to happen, happened: Tarp laughed. He laughed like a crazy person. Then Corliss laughed, because Tarp was. And then Jake laughed, because he knew no one would be getting killed today for sure. But Henry, who discovered he wasn't going to die, didn't. He sat there staring at something far away, the night rising and falling above him like everything dark in the world.

The Secret Dog

as told by JJ the Barker

May 21, 1954

This is how it went.

Ladies and gentlemen! Boys and girls! The balding and the blue-haired! All of you strange dispossessed and clueless backwoods know-nothings, mouths gaping, desperate and lost in the new world that is just being born . . .

Welcome! You have come here for a show, for a few brief moments of respite, to be transported from this sad, plain reality to a place where birds appear from nowhere, where rabbits live in hats, where a man can tell you not only what you're thinking but what you're *going* to think, which card you will pick and why, and how many times you've cheated on your wife—in short, to be amazed—even flabbergasted—by a man with powers beyond your limited comprehensions.

But you will not see that show tonight.

For the showman is gone. Missing. A sadness grips my heart, as no doubt yours is gripped, too. It tears at me, at all of us, our insides are torn completely to shreds to know that this valuable member of our little troupe, this man through whom you had hoped to forget your cares and woes for a single night, only to have the reality of your sad and pathetic existence come slamming into your chest like a huge iron hammer sometime later—where was I?—oh yes—I am just plain depressed that he is not here to entertain and delight.

Henry the Negro Magician is gone. But why, and where?

If I knew the answer to that question, I would own this town and everything in it.

Theories abound, of course. He found love, he found Christ, he found himself, he found some money! Or is it, as some have suspected, an ambitious new trick gone awry? For there's a reason magicians use fat ladies and lifelong bachelors for their most dangerous illusions: if something bad happens to them, they are rarely missed . . . Don't judge me for that: even the fat lady near the back laughed at that one. But I digress and . . . in all honesty . . . I will continue to: digression, I'm afraid, is all I know, and all I need to know for my work, such as it is. But it's a purposeful digression—like a dog following a scent: it's how I get to where I'm going. The good news is I am almost there.

Ladybugs and gentleworms! Tonight you are going to witness something that has never before been attempted in this patchwork conglomeration of freaks and castoffs we call the Jeremiah Mosgrove Chinese Circus.

I'm going to tell the truth.

To begin with, there are a few very basic things I think you should know.

None of us are what we appear to be. The Strongest Man in the Entire World? A weakling. He cries himself to sleep at night. *Spiderella* is a trick done with mirrors. (There is no such thing as a spider with a woman's head, especially a head as fetching as that of Katrina's, who I've always had a little crush on.) And Agnes the Alligator Lady? No more than a very bad skin disease.

Which brings me to Henry.

Take the hand of the person next to you, however unattractive they may be, for what I am about to tell you might make the hardiest among you dizzy, and faint dead away. Those of you with a heart? Prepare it to be broken. And those of you without an imagination—why are you here?

Here is my news: Henry, the Negro Magician, is not a Negro at all.

He's white.

White! As white as you or me.

I'll give you a moment to take this in.

Not everybody knows this, even here at the Chinese Circus. I think you can understand why. Have you ever heard of anything quite so shocking in your entire miserable lives? And outside of vaudevillian circles of bygone years, the death of which mirrors the death of this, us, the freak show and all the freaks who compose it, I don't know of a single instance where this can be said to have happened. Think of it. Why would a man do this to himself? A white man turn himself black—in this day and age? It is as if a king chose to become a pauper. Cary Grant a leper. Marilyn Monroe a toothless, acne-ridden truck driver. A three-legged dog donating a leg to science. That is what it's like, isn't it?

Except worse. Except harder to believe. But, as with everything inexplicable, there's always an explanation, isn't there? And that is what I offer you tonight. We were friends. We were, perhaps, the best of friends. He shared a part of who he was with me, a part he shared with no one else, late nights camped before a bottle of red wine. I alone can tell the tale. But I can only tell it to you as he told it to me, using his very own words, and in this way I hope to make him real—re-create him, if you will—have him appear before us as he once truly did but even clearer now, more substantial—for now he will be illuminated by the truth.

.   .   .

A ten-year-old motherless boy growing up beneath the dark clouds of the Depression—that's where we begin. Where the once well-to-do are forced to beg for a solid meal, if that. Proud men forced to clean up after horses for a pair of shoes. And Mr. Walker, a prosperous accountant with his own firm, reduced to maintenance work at a grand hotel. Henry's little sister, Hannah, the only bright spot in his entire life—literally—for her golden hair shone even at night. What is missing from his life?

Well, almost everything. Almost everything there is in the world to miss. But most of all *wonder. Possibility.*

Magic. Is there anything else we need more? Each and every one of us? Me, for instance. Not a day goes by I'm not shilling for one freak or another. It's me telling you where the show is, and the show is always in there, beyond this weathered circus tent, behind the garish paintings of nature's mistakes. It's always the same, no different than working a nine-to-five really, if you don't count Yolanda, who will occasionally meet me near the sinkhole beyond that stand of pine. We talk. By her own admission she's been with every man within shouting distance—except me. We haven't, never will. She's a true vision—her Gypsy-dark beauty and all—and I have been tempted. It's peculiar, though: the fact that I alone haven't touched her in that way makes me feel more intimate with her than the rest of them. Like we're married, and no one but me can have her in this way. This is magic, isn't it? For me.

Now picture this. Summer, 1931. Though they were only recently released from school, school was already a distant memory. He and his sister were free to roam, explore, to do anything they wished. And at their disposal: the Hotel Fremont. Picture this lovely, sad ten-year-old boy, during a particularly ambitious multi-storied game of hide-and-go-seek, turning the knob on the door of a room he believed was vacant *but instead discovering a man there,*

sitting in a chair facing him directly, almost as though he were expecting him. The man was wearing a black suit and a bow tie and
the shiniest black-and-white shoes Henry had ever seen. The man
was smiling, but his skin was so white—sheet white, cloud white—
that his teeth yellowed a bit in comparison. His hair was moist. On
the lamp table beside him, a book and a pen, but the pages were
entirely blank. In his hand was a coin, which he casually turned
back and forth over and under his fingers.

"Henry," he said. "What a pleasant surprise."

"You . . . know my name?"

"Lucky guess," the man said, his smile frozen on his face as if it
had no other posture. "Names are funny. Mine, for instance,
changes from day to day."

"It does?"

"It does. Yesterday my name was Horatio. Today it's Mr. Sebastian. Tomorrow? Who knows. I'm considering 'Tobias.' "

Henry nodded as if he understood. But he was mesmerized. He
had fallen under the spell of this man in what must be record time.
Less than a minute.

"And where is Hannah?" Mr. Sebastian said, the coin moving
like a snake through his fingers. He knew everybody's name.

"Hiding," said Henry.

"I see," Mr. Sebastian said. "And you thought she might be
here, is that right?"

Henry nodded again, not taking his eyes off the coin. "How do
you do that?" he asked.

Mr. Sebastian's smile seemed to deepen, his eyes to glimmer.
"Oh, you know. The same way I do this."

And then, at that moment, on the very first day they met, Mr.
Sebastian did the impossible: he disappeared. Henry could have
sworn it. For a few seconds the chair was just a chair. He had not
taken his eyes off the man's hands, and the man's hands were gone,

too, along with the rest of him. Henry barely had time to look around the room for him before he returned, exactly as he had been, sitting with his legs crossed, smiling.

"What was that?" Henry said.

"That," Mr. Sebastian said, "was magic."

That night, in the darkness of their tiny room, the span of which their paper-thin mattress took up completely, neither Hannah nor Henry could sleep. Their clothes, hanging from a cord stretched across the length of the room, looked like ghosts. They could hear the water gurgling through the bare metal pipes decorating the walls as another guest flushed the toilet. Each of them knew the other was awake, knew the other was lying there in the darkness with eyes wide open: they were born barely a year apart, and it seemed as if a piece of Henry had stayed behind in their mother's womb and become a part of Hannah, the connection between them was so clear. Each could feel the other's eyes.

"Something happened today," Henry said.

Hannah gasped. "Me, too!" she said, almost squealing beneath her whisper. "Something happened to me, too." She slid closer, near the imaginary demarcation line separating his side from hers. "You go."

"No, you."

"Okay," she said. "I found a dog."

"What do you mean, you found a dog?"

"In the alley behind the hotel, there was a dog and I found him."

"What were you doing in the alley behind the hotel?"

"Reading magazines," she said.

"Magazines?"

She pulled something from beneath her mattress, and showed it to Henry. It was one glossy page torn from a magazine. *The*

Cunarder. It was a picture of a beautiful tropical island with a woman on the beach, next to a handsome man, gazing out across the infinite blue of the sea, a biplane high in the air above them. "There are lots of pictures like this, of different places. I'm going to go there someday."

"We," Henry said.

"What?"

"You mean 'we,' " he said. "We'll go there someday."

But Hannah didn't say anything then. She just stared at the picture.

"I was behind that big wall of trash cans," she said, "just looking at pictures like this. Been there for a while when I heard something. Turns out it was a dog."

"What kind?"

"Blue," she said. "Kind of. A blue dog."

"That's not a kind of dog."

"Well, I found him."

"Sounds like he found you."

"I went back after dinner and gave him some ham."

Henry stayed quiet for a little while, thinking about this. "Some of our ham?"

"Yes," she said.

"It's not like we have a lot of ham," he said.

"It was my part of the ham. Not yours. I didn't eat mine tonight, so I gave it to him."

"So that dog ate better than you today."

"I guess. But that's okay."

They were quiet for a little while, until she turned away. She knew how Henry would feel about this. She didn't have to be his late-arriving other half to figure this one out.

"It's my dog," she said, her back to him. "I'll feed it what I want."

And Henry knew better than to argue, because, as much as she was a part of him, she was just that much not. Let her feed the stupid dog. She could live in that alley and sleep behind the trash cans, for all he cared. This is what he told himself, anyway. She had rolled all the way over to the edge of the mattress now, farther away than she usually was, and Henry could feel the distance, and knew that if she could go farther she would. So it began. He fell asleep without saying anything about Mr. Sebastian or Horatio or Tobias, or whatever his name was that day, this secret the only comfort he had.

The next day, Henry returned to Room 702, again without Hannah, who had left almost as soon as she woke up, taking a piece of bread to the dog. Mr. Sebastian—he *looked* like a Mr. Sebastian to Henry, so this is what he called him in his mind—he was sitting in the same chair, wearing the same clothes, smiling the same smile. But instead of a coin he was holding a pack of blue-backed cards, and they moved from hand to hand as though they had little minds of their own, minds that had been trained to think what Mr. Sebastian wanted them to, slipping softly through the air one after another in perfect performance, magnetically connected but free as smoke.

Henry couldn't move or speak. It was as if he had just met his first true love.

"I can show you," Mr. Sebastian said. "If you like."

Henry slowly nodded. He would like.

I come from Oklahoma. My father was an oilman there. When I was a boy, we lived in a castle, a castle that rose up from the prairie like a crazy mirage. I have a picture of myself standing in front of it, a little boy wearing knickers. Knickers! My hair combed back wet, the way I wear it still. Then, when I was twelve, my father lost it all; he was a gambler, and a bad one, and that's an unfortunate combination. We left the castle, and my mother left us, and we lived in a walk-up in Norman. When I was fourteen, he got it all back—a tireless worker, my father, and brilliant, I even got a new mom—and when I was sixteen, he lost it all again, the same way.

I tired of this life. The uncertainty. Never knowing from one day to the next whether I'd be rich or poor, living in the castle or in a room above a meat market, motherless or mothered. So I left. I hopped a train out of Oklahoma City, and after a year of nothing much I ended up here, tearing down and setting up, until my predecessor lost his voice and the rest of his life in the fire of '49 and I was tapped to take his place, to flog for the freaks. I love them, of course, and they love me. And yet they're the stars. It's funny that way. They're the talent. I'm too normal to be somebody here, somebody important. All I can do is talk. What I'm getting at though is this, it's how Henry and I are alike: if it hadn't been for my father, I wouldn't have been here at all.

Over the course of the year they had been living in this hotel, Henry had watched his father's hands harden. Cut, bruised, and callused, they had refashioned themselves to become more like the tools they used. In the house where they used to live, his father sometimes held Henry's hand as his son fell asleep, and brushed the hair away from his forehead. But Henry didn't want his father to touch him anymore, because there was nothing comforting about it: it was like being caressed by an awl.

There was more to it, of course. His father's hands told the story of their sad lives. At dinner, Henry watched from the corner of his eye as his father grasped the fork and knife: it was as though he were strangling them. Then he attacked his food with a vicious need. Henry tried not to judge him, but the act of trying only served to harden his prejudice. Because it was *unseemly*, the way his father ate. He worked hard all day, he was hungry, and they didn't have a lot to eat or a lot of time to eat it. But as his mother had once said, *Just because you're in a foreign country doesn't mean you have to dress like the natives.* Henry remembered how his mother had shown him how to hold the fork and knife, how to sit up straight in a chair, how to ask for the butter to be passed, and he still did it that way, *her* way. He cut his food gently, and then impaled it on the silver tusks of his fork, and then he raised his food slowly up and into his mouth, where he chewed it, thoughtfully, always counting *one, two, three, four, five.* And so on. *Fletcherism,* his mother called it.

Hannah was somewhere in between the two of them. Knowing how her brother felt, she didn't want to disappoint him, but on the other hand she felt eating the way Henry did shamed their father, for somewhere inside of him he knew what he had become. So she sawed at the hard and dry leftover steak the hotel kitchen sent their way, but when she saw Henry watching her she reverted to the old, fine manners, and thus, in trying to please everyone, pleased no one at all. She was young, stuck between worlds, alliances, and affections. Henry knew this. He forgave her. She could eat however she wished.

Tonight's hotel leftovers included a vegetable medley, four crusty heels of bread, and a creamy fish dish the kitchen had made too many of, served on old tin plates.

"This is good," Henry's father said, his mouth full, little bits of cream edging out the corners of his mouth.

Henry and Hannah nodded, then Hannah sighed. "I'm full," she said.

Her food had barely been touched. Henry glared at her.

"You can't be full," he said.

"Well, I am," she said.

Their father smiled and rubbed the top of Hannah's head, and she flinched. "She's just a little one, Henry," he said. "Look at her:

a strong wind could carry her away! A couple of bites may be all she needs. We can split what's left," he said, already reaching toward her food.

"No!" she said. "No. I want to save the rest, for later. I expect I'll eat it then. Just not right yet."

"When?" Henry said.

"Later," she said.

"I can hear your stomach growling from here," Henry said. She looked at him, daring him, staring him down. "Growling like a dog."

She stood and left the table, plate in hand, casting a glance back at Henry to see if he was still watching her. He was. She left anyway.

"What was that all about?" his father said.

Henry considered telling his father the truth—that Hannah was taking her own food and feeding it to a stray dog she had found in the alley behind the hotel—but he couldn't betray her. Yet.

"I just worry that she doesn't eat enough," he said. "That she might get sick or something."

His father smiled and looked his son over, a dim light shining in his gray eyes. "You're a good brother," he said. "A good son, too. You I would worry about not getting enough to eat. You're growing like a weed! Pretty soon you'll be bigger than me. Pretty soon . . ." And he stopped and looked more closely at his son. "Henry, what's that?"

As his father conducted the inventory of his growing son, he had seen something bulging from one of his pockets, and his face lost all its spark.

"Are those *cigarettes*?" he said.

"No, of course not," Henry said.

"Because we don't have the money to buy cigarettes," he said. "I stopped with the cigars when things became what they are, and not because I wanted to but because I had to. And you are *not* going to be spending money—"

"They're not cigarettes," Henry said. "They're cards."

"Cards?" his father said.

Reluctantly, Henry slipped the pack from his pocket and placed it on the table in front of his father. Though he had spent a good half-hour before dinner staring at the pack, Henry still thought he had never seen anything more beautiful. Everything about it: the bright red of the cardboard box, the word *Bicycle*—so simple but so lovely—printed across the top, and the picture of Cupid riding a bicycle on the back: what a ridiculous idea! Cupid on a bike? What did this mean? Henry had no idea, but that hardly mattered. He loved it. The discreetly solid box in which so much was contained. Fifty-two cards. Already he was beginning to believe, though he did not know it yet, that there was more life in there than there was out here. More possibility. Magic.

Well," his father said, "I suppose I got upset for nothing. It's a pack of cards." Henry winced as his father reached for them.

"Don't—"

"What?"

"Don't hurt them," Henry said.

Henry's father recognized the tone in his son's voice: it was peremptory and patronizing. But he smiled. "How can I hurt a pack of cards?" he said. "They're made of paper, not fine crystal."

"Just, please, wipe your hands first?"

"Of course," he said. "Of course. Don't want to soil them, do we?" He rubbed his hands across his napkin before gingerly picking the pack up and examining it. "They look new," he said.

"They are."

"You purchased these?"

"They were a gift."

His father's glasses slipped precipitously to the end of his nose as he examined the pack. "A gift? From one of the guests?"

"Yes," Henry said. "That's right."

Henry's father shook his head. "They feel good about themselves when they give something to the less fortunate, even if it's a pack of cards." He laughed. "That's who we are now, you know, the less fortunate. And they are the more."

Henry fought back the urge to contradict his father. For, even though there was nothing wrong with what he and Mr. Sebastian were doing, it seemed to Henry that anything that had to be explained to his father would end up being called "a bad idea," and forbidden. He had not even told Hannah, because these cards were entirely his own. Not since they'd come here had he had anything entirely his own.

His father continued to examine them. "I used to play cards a bit," he said. "When I was . . . well, let's just say a long time ago. After work we'd clear off a table and play a few hands. The wager was a copper penny. The loser always blew a fuse." Mr. Walker smiled. "Cards have quite a history, you know. I'm not sure exactly what it is, but I believe the royalty on them means something."

Henry couldn't help himself. He blurted: "The king of hearts represents Charlemagne, the king of diamonds Julius Caesar, the king of clubs Alexander the Great, and the king of spades David, from the Bible."

His father peered at him over his glasses, somewhat amused. "Is that so?"

"Yes," Henry said.

"Do you even know who all those people are?"

"No," Henry said. "But I will."

"I'm sure you will, son."

His father turned the pack over in his hands and smiled. "I used to love to shuffle," he said. "Just the sound of it, especially with new cards like this. Want to hear it, how your dad used to shuffle?"

Henry went for the pack, but his father quickly moved them out of his reach, instinctively, like a dog guarding a meat bone. This is the kind of man he had become, the kind who would keep something from his son. Their bodies froze like that—Henry's hand out-stretched, his father's shoulder turning away—and they locked eyes. But whereas Henry's eyes were cold and hard, his father's had turned dark, and sad.

"You . . . don't want me to?" his father said.

He sounded as if he'd been shot and those were his last words. *You don't want me to?* And as much as Henry *didn't* want him to, he couldn't overcome this, the sound in his father's voice—how plaintive and wrecked it was, to think that his own son would deny him this, such a very small thing.

"No," Henry said. "Of course. I want to hear you shuffle. I was just going to open the pack for you."

His father smiled. "I know how to open a pack, son," he said. There was an iciness in his voice now. "I was playing cards before you were a glimmer in my eyes."

"What's that mean?"

"It just means that long before you were even born I was playing cards."

"But what's the *glimmer in my eyes* mean?"

"It means," he said, "that one night I looked at your mother, God rest her weary soul, and my eyes, they—you know—*sparkled,* and hers sparkled back, and we decided to make a baby, and that's who you turned out to be, the baby who was once just a glimmer in my eyes." Henry wondered what that would look like: his father's eyes glimmering.

"Did you and Mother play cards?"

"I don't think we did," his father said in his faraway voice. "We did a lot of things, but we never played cards. She—your mother spent a lot of time outside, in the garden. After you and Hannah, she loved her plants the most."

"Me and Hannah and you," Henry said.

"Yes, I think I made the list—right after the hydrangeas."

He laughed and Henry laughed and the spell was broken. Attention was turned to the cards. His father's thumb pressed against the box flap, and after two or three tries he opened it. Henry watched as though his father were performing an operation. His father's fingers looked gigantic and misshapen grasping the sleek perfection of the bright-red box. He shook it with one hand, and as the cards fell out he caught them in the other. Earlier that day, Henry himself had opened the box for the first time. *They're for you*, Mr. Sebastian said. It had been a long time since Henry had received something incidental, an accessory to life as opposed to a bare necessity. A toy. *Big things come in small boxes*, Mr. Sebastian had said. *And in this particular box, there are fifty-two things*. Henry couldn't speak but to say, *Thank you*, and even those words came out weak and didn't represent the feelings he had inside. *One day soon these cards will do whatever you ask them to*, Mr. Sebastian said. *I will show you how. We can't say what will happen in the rest of our lives, the good fortune or tragedies that might befall us, but over these cards you will have complete control.*

He had no control of them now. His father held them, fanned them out. He looked at his son as though something wonderful had just occurred. He shuffled them, and as he did he closed his eyes and listened to the sharp, smart sound. It *was* beautiful. It sounded like an audience clapping.

"I used to be able to shuffle them in the air," his father said, lifting the cards off the table.

"That's okay," Henry said. "I liked the way you shuffled them on the table."

"Let me give it a try," he said. "In the air."

"Father, really—"

But it was too late. His father held the cards before him and began to shuffle, but almost from the very first card it was out of his control, and instead of intersecting nicely and coming together as one, all fifty-two of the cards leapt into the air, as though escaping, and flew to as many different places as they could fly: the floor, the table, the stove. One landed on the edge of his father's plate; Henry could see a corner of the card soaking up gravy.

"*Father!*" Henry screamed, grabbing the card and wiping it on his shirt. He examined it; it appeared to be okay. Then he went after the others, enraged. He glared at his father. "You . . . Look at what you've done! *I'm* the only one who should touch these cards. It's my fault—I should never have let you do it. I should know by now that everything you touch—"

But here Henry stopped, knowing that the next thing he said would have been more hurtful than anything else he could possibly say.

"Henry," his father said. "They're only cards."

Which made things worse. "Only cards," Henry said. "*Only cards?*" He leaned over and picked up some more. Now he wasn't looking at his father. "Only cards," he said again, counting as he retrieved them from under a chair, the table, the refrigerator—they were all over the place, scattered across the cold and cracked linoleum like leaves in the wind. But he looked until he found them, and after cleaning his plate went to his room and counted them over and over and over again, until he was sure, until he was certain, that he had rescued them all.

Which reminds me of the day my father found me. I was standing on an apple crate, because the stand I'd been using had been crushed by a marauding elephant. It had rained the night before, so the ground was exceptionally wet and muddy, puddles everywhere, a very sad situation for the feet. I remember going into it—*Ladies and gentlemen! Boys and girls! The balding and the blue-haired!*—when I looked out into the crowd and saw him. He was standing toward the back, in a black suit and a bow tie—which was a muted orange,

I believe—and I thought (as my patter continued) maybe he had gotten it back. Maybe he was rich again. Good for him, I thought. He had his business, which he had hoped one day I might enter and take over from him—take the reins, so to speak—and now here I was standing on an apple crate crying out as though the world were on fire, *Spiderella! The head of a woman and the body of a man-eating tarantula!* And he just walked away. I watched the back of his head disappear into the crowd. Last time I saw my father, ever.

The dog, of course, was not blue at all. It was black from head to tail, and absolutely ferocious when Henry approached it for the first time. It was a real growler, the hair along its spine raised so high and strong it looked like the serrated edges of a knife. Henry froze. He was afraid to move any part of his body—his fingers, his eyes—because even when he breathed the dog's growl modulated upward as if to warn him against it. The stench was overpowering. Behind a row of scarred and dented trash cans lined up like tin soldiers along the alley wall, Henry and the dog stared at each other coldly as though only postponing the moment of inevitable combat. To prolong that moment, Henry stopped breathing.

This isn't how he had imagined things would go, of course, because this wasn't the dog he imagined would greet him. Hannah, he figured, had adopted a mangy, submissive, and pitiful creature who pulled at her little-girl heartstrings, whose life depended on the scraps she brought it, something he could scare off with a stick. But this dog was a monster, and he wondered if Hannah fed him out of fear for her very life. If that were the case, there was no reason for her to come back here at all. The Hotel Fremont was first-class all the way; the suggestion that life had imperfections was abandoned the moment a guest walked through its tall golden doors. Back here in the alley was the truth of it all. This was where it all went, the ref-

use of the pretense. Every form of human waste was here, the phys-
ical and the spiritual, too. The smell was terrific and ungodly, as if
something had died three or four times and then been left to
molder and crumble in the sweltering summer heat. It was a smell
so thick and pungent that he could actually see it, rising in clouds
and hovering around the cans.

It was impossible to imagine Hannah out here. He had never
seen her as anything less than perfect, the girl of girls, her hair so
blond and her skin so fair that dirt couldn't exist in a place where
she was. This alley was her opposite: dark and awful, evil almost,
what he imagined a corner in hell might be like.

It was the first time in his whole life he felt he didn't understand her.

After a minute had passed, he didn't think he could hold his
breath much longer. The black dog sensed this—was waiting for a
reason to attack. Its eyes looked red now, glaring murderously at
Henry, teeth bared like hacksaws; more and more it looked like a
monster. Henry felt the compulsion to die, on his own, before the
dog had a chance to kill him.

Then Hannah was there.

"Henry," she said. Unable to move, he didn't see her until she
was right beside him. She was wearing her faded pale-blue dress
with the ruffled sleeves, their mother's favorite tortoiseshell bar-
rette in her hair. She looked like an angel. She smiled at him. "I
could have told you this was a bad idea. If you'd asked."

Then she turned and called to the dog. "Joan Crawford!" she
said, in just the perfect way to call a dog, happy and forceful at the
same time. And Joan Crawford came, tail wagging, the sudden
transformation of character impossible for Henry to comprehend or
believe.

Hannah rubbed the sweet dog's head, and then down its back,
where the hair had bristled. Now it seemed as soft as down.

"You named the dog Joan Crawford?"

She nodded. He took a look beneath the dog's hind legs.

"It's a boy. Why don't you name him Blackie or something, like a real dog?"

"I like 'Joan Crawford.' "

Joan Crawford growled and edged a bit closer to Henry.

"Pet him," Hannah said.

"I don't think so." He couldn't let go of the fear that this was some sort of trick.

"That's how you make friends with animals," she said. "Being nice." She stopped and thought about that. "People are the same, I guess. If you're nice to them they'll be nice to you, too."

She looked at Henry and waited, and when he still didn't move she took his hand by the wrist and pulled it down. All the while, he was trying to pull it back, but she had surprising strength, and she brought his fingers to the dog's mouth. "Pet him," she said.

"Hannah," he said, waiting for the snap.

But Joan Crawford only gave a little sniff, and then tasted Henry's hand with his tongue. A little more of this, and he was done. And after that everything was fine.

Hannah took a piece of ham out of her pocket and held it out for the dog. The dog snapped it up, and in three quick bites it was gone.

"You can't keep doing that," Henry said.

"I can if I want," she said.

"We need that food."

"It's mine, not yours."

"You need it, Hannah."

"Joan Crawford does, too," she said. "I'm a good person to share with him, I think."

"Too good," he said.

"How can you be too good?"

"You are," he said. "You're too good."

She shook her head. "Don't worry about me, Henry."

"I have to look after you."

"No," she said. She smiled at him. "You don't have to do that, Henry. I'm fine. Besides, you came out here to scare him away. Didn't you?"

The dog was watching them now. He looked at Hannah, then at Henry, back and forth from face to face, as though he were having a little trouble following the conversation, but just a little. The sun broke over the edge of the grand hotel and like a spotlight hit them all, Henry and Hannah and the dog, baking the trash into its monumental smell. Henry stopped breathing again.

But not Hannah. She was fine. She rubbed Joan Crawford's head with her little hand, and the dog rubbed up against her leg.

"I taught him some tricks," she said. "Want to see?"

He said he did.

The next day, Henry went to Room 702 as he had the day before and the day before that. But that day, for the first time since Henry had known him—which hadn't been very long, but, still, it was the first time—Mr. Sebastian wasn't smiling. Henry knew what this meant: business. So Henry's face became all business, too.

"Sit down, Henry," he said.

Henry sat. Mr. Sebastian had been holding his ink pen, and he set it down gently beside the book, its pages still blank. Then he stared deeply into Henry's eyes. Henry had never felt this way before. He felt Mr. Sebastian inside of him.

"This is the beginning," he said. "The beginning of your life as a magician. But before we begin, you must take an oath. The magician's oath. For the things I am about to show you are secret from those who are *not* magicians, and if you were to tell them—"

He stopped, leaving the consequences to Henry's imagination. And Henry imagined things far worse than ever could have possibly happened: immediate and sudden death by fire, drowning, being buried in a hole, in a box, in a boat out to sea, in a world no one could see, invisible, dead, his tongue removed, mute forever.

"Agreed?"

"But I'm not a magician," Henry said.

Mr. Sebastian raised a brow, and lowered it. "Not a magician?" he said. *"Not a magician?* You are more a magician even than I. I mean that. Buried deep within you there's a special power, one so great you can't fathom it—yet. A power to conjure what in the hands of a lesser mortal would indeed be dangerous. And if you were to discover it before you learned how to control it—oh, woe to the unsuspecting world! A magician will eventually lose his powers. I am losing mine. But before they leave me entirely, I must give them to another. You see, for many years now, Henry, I have been looking for an apprentice, someone with the strength of character and potential to wear the mantle of that which is not of this world, that he might carry on after I'm gone. And I believe I have found him: in you."

"Me?"

Mr. Sebastian solemnly nodded. "And by taking the oath one is considered a magician and is allowed entrée into the magic world. Are you ready?"

Henry didn't even have to think about it, but he pretended to just in case. He nodded.

Then Mr. Sebastian removed a small knife from his breast pocket. "Give me your hand," he said.

Henry looked at the knife, then at his hand. Then at the knife again. Then—summoning that special power buried deep within him, the one Mr. Sebastian knew was there but he, as yet, did not—he held out his hand much as he had done with Joan Crawford the day before. Joan Crawford had licked him, but Mr. Sebastian quickly pierced the skin of Henry's index finger until a little stream of blood escaped and dripped to the floor. Mr. Sebastian stared at it for a moment, transfixed. Then he pierced his own finger, and as the blood seeped from his small wound he pressed his finger against Henry's and closed his eyes and spoke.

"As a magician," Mr. Sebastian said, "I swear never to reveal the secret of any illusion or even to *speak* of magic to one who is not learned in the dark arts, and who has not, as I have, taken the magician's oath. I swear *never* to reveal the source of my magic or speak the name of the magician who taught me, or to perform any illusion to a nonmagician without first practicing the effect until the illusion is perfect; otherwise I will lose all that I have gained. I swear not only to practice illusion, but to live within it, to *seem* but not to *be*, for only in this way can we fully partake in the magical world. As the blood of the magician and his apprentice are one, I swear these things now and forever."

"I swear," Henry said.

Sebastian opened his eyes. "Then we can begin."

It was all in the cards. That's what Mr. Sebastian said after Henry had taken the oath. *It's all in the cards.* Henry had frankly expected something more than that after the haunting oath, the blood, the severity of Mr. Sebastian's face. But it was all about the cards—"the building blocks of all that's to follow," he said. And so Henry practiced, constantly, until he was literally practicing in his sleep: he would wake up with the cards in his hands, going over some sleight he had been shown the day before. He practiced in the bathroom for the most part, because, as much as he wanted to, he could not show Hannah: Hannah wasn't a magician, she hadn't taken the oath, so he had to keep it secret even from her. During the day, there wasn't much of a problem, because Hannah was in the alley with Joan Crawford and his father was working, but when they'd come back, there was a lot of banging on the door, wondering what was going on inside there, and Henry, masking it as best he could, let out terrible groans and sighs as he flushed the toilet and left. "Do you need to see a doctor?" his father asked him. "You're always in there when I get home." Henry said no, he was fine, but his father looked at him suspiciously anyway, suspecting no good. The truth was, his father needed to be in there, too: behind the mop stand in the closet one day, Henry found an unmarked bottle of gin. He had never known his father to drink, but then, almost overnight, drinking began to be everything he ever did. This was where he did it, Henry understood, alone, in the bathroom. Like father, like son.

Mr. Sebastian had names for every single sleight he showed him. Montana Hideway. The Carpathian Struggle. Mountainous Mutiny. Houdini's Escape. There were dozens of them, and as though Henry were in school he had to memorize each and every one. But this wasn't hard. There was nothing hard about it, about any of them. The practice was grueling, and repetitive, but it seemed as if Henry had been caught at the perfect moment in his life, like learning a language, in which he was able to grasp the most complicated maneuvers in seconds and repeat them perfectly by the end of the day. Even Mr. Sebastian was astounded. *You will be great indeed*, he told Henry. *Special, even better than me. And the world will know without your telling them that it was from me you learned it all, for there will be no one else from whom you could have learned it. No one but Mr. Sebastian.*

Henry visited him every day. He waited until Hannah left to play with Joan Crawford, and then he would run as fast as he could up the six flights of stairs, past the bellhops and fancy guests staring. And every day Mr. Sebastian was there, waiting for him, in the same chair, wearing the same clothes, the same smile on his death-white face. Henry had wanted to ask him about his skin, because his hands were that way, too—wanted to ask if he had ever been out in the sun at all, because that's what it looked like, what *he* looked like, a man who had somehow never left a room, this room, had been born there and had all of his needs met by room service and the maids. But it seemed like the wrong thing to do, because maybe it was a disease. If Mr. Sebastian wanted to talk about it he would, but Henry knew he wouldn't. All they talked about was magic, and that was enough for them both.

It was all about the tricks at first. Get the tricks down and the magic would follow. *You're making a home for the magic,* he told Henry, *a place for it to come when it trusts you, when it feels at home.* Craft becomes art, and once it's art then it's no longer simply yours: you have to share it, you're compelled to share it. You have to find an audience who think they understand what's happening, that the effects in the performance are accomplished through some sleight of hand or legerdemain, misdirection, deception, or possible collusion with a member of the audience, secret mechanisms, mirrors. You will seek to present an effect so clever and skillful that the audience won't believe their eyes, and can't think of the explanation, but feel in their hearts there is one. But there won't be; even you won't be able to explain it. The sense of universal bafflement is part of the entertainment. It's a lie made true. Think of it: you will be master of one of the only situations in life in which people willingly allow themselves to be lied to—*pay* for themselves to be lied to. And only then, after they think they know the rules, only then will they realize that this was the biggest lie of all, and that what they have witnessed is beyond anything their meager minds could imagine. *Magic,* he said, again and again and again. *Magic!*

Henry was the perfect apprentice: he believed everything he was told.

. . .

Summer brought wave after wave of beautiful people to the Fremont, elegant, lovely, happy people. They did not even seem to sweat. To Henry, they all looked brand-new, as if they had just now walked off the human production line fully grown and infinitely rich and allowed to skip whatever process it was that scarred the rest of us, made us old before our time. The men looked so fine in their pressed white suits, and the women with their empire-waisted gowns and, at night, fox furs. So many animals gave up their lives for these people, but Henry thought they must have been happy to do so. Hannah was like them. She glowed like them.

The hotel was booked to capacity in July, which meant Mr. Walker had very little time with his children; he had very little time for anything other than work. The only opportunity the three of them had to be together was at dinner, and then it was only for a little while. It wore on Mr. Walker. This job—this life—was killing him, and there were ways he had begun to look dead already: the sallow pallor of his skin, the blank stare, the way the flesh on his face appeared to be sinking into his skull. Ever since discovering his father's secret bottle, Henry checked it every morning and lightly marked its level with a pencil. But that proved not to be necessary: his father drained the entire thing in two days, and then a new bottle took its place. His work, which at its best was shoddy, suffered; gin clouded his brain. Blotto. He forgot things: how to fix a toilet, make a key, plug a leak. He lost his tools. Henry overheard the hotel manager—Mr. Croton, "the big cheese," Mr. Walker called him, and the fattest man Henry had ever seen—scold his father about his appearance. "You look like a *bum*," he hissed, and made it none too clear that his job was on thin ice. "I have over a hundred applications for your position on file. I only hired you as a favor to a friend. I hope you know that. But friendship only extends so far. Guests have complained, Mr. Walker." At dinner, his father was quiet—everybody was—and they listened to *Flash Gordon* on the radio to fill up the room with human sounds. It was as though he weren't there at all.

So Henry and Hannah were on their own, now more than ever. While Henry learned tricks, Hannah taught them—to Joan Crawford. By mid-July, he could sit, stay, and beg. Henry could make the queen of hearts appear in the wallet you had been sitting on for the last half-hour. And their father could make a bottle of gin disappear in a day. Henry was dying to show Hannah the things he could do, but there was that oath—never to *perform any illusion to a nonmagician without first practicing the effect until the illusion is perfect*—and Mr. Sebastian hadn't said it was perfect yet. This was between just the two of them. So he continued spending his long hours in the bathroom, flushing every so often to give the illusion that he was doing something else.

Hannah's little hand always knocked three soft times.

"Henry," she said, "get a wiggle on. I need to use the bathroom."

"Use the one in the lobby."

"I need to go *now*." She turned the knob, but it was locked.

Henry made a groaning sound. "You don't want to come in here," he said. "The smell will kill you. I've got a problem, Hannah. A big one. What's coming out of me now is not good."

"That's bull."

"Is not."

"I know what you're doing in there, Henry," she said.

"I hope so," he said. "I do it same as everybody."

"No," she said through the door, "I *know* what you're doing. You're in there playing with cards."

Henry opened the door. She was standing there as if this were the spot she had stood all her life, the place she would always stand. Right in front of him, natural and beautiful and impossible to budge. They looked at each other now the way they used to, when

everything one knew the other did, too. There were no secrets between them anymore.

"He told me," she said.

"He told you," Henry said. There was some part of this he
couldn't understand. "He *told* you?"

"He said it was okay I knew," she said. She smiled. "Because
I'm your sister. And because he said I would make a good assistant
one day."

"An assistant," he said.

"A *magician's* assistant." She was excited at the prospect.

Henry nodded and said something he could not even hear himself say. This was too confusing. His mind couldn't rest on one thing
long enough to understand it. Mr. Sebastian had said not to tell anyone, and he hadn't, and now Mr. Sebastian had. It wasn't the way
things were supposed to go.

"You know Mr. Sebastian?" Henry said.

She nodded. "But that's not his name," she said.

"Yes it is," he said.

"It was. Now it's James the Magnificent."

"That's what he told you?"

She said it was.

"Maybe it's somebody different," he said. "A different man."

She shook her head. "The really white man," she said. "There's
only one of him."

She looked down at the cards Henry clutched in his hand. "So
show me something," she said.

"I can't."

"He told me you were good."

"I can't until he says okay."

"He told me—"

"How is it you know him?" Henry asked her, finally arranging
things in his mind long enough to understand what it was he
needed to know.

"He helped me with Joan Crawford," she said, "one day."

"Helped you?"

"Feed him. Joan Crawford needed more food than I had. I didn't want him to leave, to look for more of what he needed somewhere else. Then, one day, James the Magnificent appeared out of nowhere with a big pail of leftovers, and *voilà.*"

"*Voilà?*"

"It was like magic," she said, her blue eyes wide.

"Maybe it was magic," Henry said.

"It probably was. You've never seen a happier dog. Or a happier girl." She smiled, then lost a little of it. "We've been friends since then, James the Magnificent and me."

"Mr. Sebastian."

"Okay," she said, "you can call him that if you want." She looked at the cards again. "So you're not going to show me anything?"

But Henry wasn't listening to anything except his own thoughts now. "I wonder why he didn't tell me," he said. "About you."

She looked at Henry, shrugged her shoulders. She brushed her brother's dark hair away from his eyes. "What's to tell?" she said. "Don't look so grumpy. One day we met, and he became my friend. The end."

Out of nowhere, a hand caught Henry's shoulder as he raced through the lobby on his way to 702. It was his father, looming above him.

"You shouldn't be running," he said. His father looked around them nervously. "You could run into somebody, and then where'd we be?" Henry could smell the gin on his breath. He was half under.

"I'll stop," he said.

His father had an odd look in his eyes. "I need to talk to you," he said.

"Not now," Henry said.

"Now."

His father panned the lobby again: no one was looking at them. "In here," he said.

They went into the hotel conference room. In it there was a long brown table made of the finest mahogany, and green banker's lamps at every chair. There were portraits of important men hanging on the wall, men who looked like they thought they were God, men with faces of serene and powerful confidence. Important things happened here. It was a place where great decisions were made.

His father closed the door behind him, took his hat off, and placed it on the table. He rubbed his face with his hardened hand and closed his eyes and sighed.

"Henry," he said, "I know where you've been going for the last few weeks." He looked at his son for affirmation but didn't get it. Henry betrayed nothing. Everybody knew things they weren't supposed to know. This wasn't how it was supposed to be. "You've been seeing the man in Room 702. Mr.—whatever his name is. He has a number of names, I understand. He's become your friend."

His father paused and turned away. He looked at one of the men on the wall, a man who, not inconceivably, could have been him once, if everything that had happened hadn't.

"Unfortunately, it's not good news, what I have to tell you. He is going away. The manager here, others, people who make the decisions, have determined that his presence here is no longer good for the hotel. So he will be going."

"When?"

"Soon," his father said. "Very soon. Until then, I think it's best if you no longer see him. To get used to the idea of him not being there. And because I'm not convinced that it's in your best interest to see him."

"You don't want me to see him?"

His father couldn't look at Henry, but found it easier to commune with the eyes of the portraits on the walls. He went from one to another; it was as if he were speaking to them.

"It's best if you don't," he said.

"So I *can't* see him?" Henry said. "Is that what you're telling me?"

"That is what I'm telling you," his father said, and he looked at Henry briefly: one harsh passing glance. There was a hollowness in his eyes; Henry could see all the way to the bottom of his soul, and there was nothing there. Nothing. "I forbid it."

"Then I won't," Henry said, and he left his father in the room with all the great men and quickly made his way to Room 702.

Magic is hard. This is what Mr. Sebastian said every time Henry made an unforgivable mistake—lost a card, failed to misdirect with his direction, wasn't smart with his patter. Sometimes it was all he said throughout the entire session. *Magic is hard.* Or *Practice makes perfect.* Demonstrations followed. The cards like water, like air, like smoke in his hands, maneuvers Henry clumsily aped with varying degrees of success but never with the same ease, the same understanding. What Mr. Sebastian did *was* magic. Even if Henry knew exactly how what he did was done, he felt he couldn't do it. It was like language: no matter how fluent Henry became, a real magician would always be able to tell he came from another country.

But not since he'd learned how to shuffle had there been a day worse than this one. Mr. Sebastian seemed distant from the first, and even a little bit angry. The book on the table was closed. Henry didn't mention the conversation he'd just had with his father, and Mr. Sebastian didn't mention any talk he'd had with Mr. Croton. It was like just another lesson.

"Force the five of hearts," Mr. Sebastian said. But Henry forced instead the nine of diamonds.

"Palm the ace," he said. But the card was clearly visible in a chink between his fingers.

"Cut the deck." He spat out the words like a backfiring car. But now Henry's hand was shaking, and as he picked them up, the entire pack slipped from his fingers, and he dropped them, the way his father had that first night. The cards went everywhere. Henry quickly knelt to retrieve them, looking back over his shoulder at Mr. Sebastian as he did so, waiting for him to say something, anything. But he remained silent. He leaned back into his chair and quietly glared until Henry thought each and every one of the cards had been accounted for.

"I've shown you so much," Mr. Sebastian said. "And you've learned so little."

"I've learned a lot. You said I was doing well."

"You haven't even gathered all the cards."

"I have, though. I have them all."

"The three of hearts is beneath the dresser," Mr. Sebastian said.

"No it's not." There was no way Mr. Sebastian could have known that. From where he was sitting he couldn't see beneath the dresser.

"I've got them all," Henry said. "I counted."

Mr. Sebastian sighed and closed his eyes, and when he opened them again and saw that Henry was still standing there, he stared him down until Henry felt as if he were being forced through the power of Mr. Sebastian's singular will to look, and now he knew it was there, knew it had to be, that this wouldn't be happening if it weren't. Henry got on his knees and, seeing nothing, flattened himself against the floor. When he still couldn't see anything, he fished across the dust until his fingers stopped, feeling something that very well could have been a card, was almost certainly a card, was in fact—it had to be—the three of hearts. But his hand came out empty, or so it appeared. Failing on all other counts, he could still palm a card.

He stood and looked Mr. Sebastian in the eye. "Nothing's there," he said.

Henry was lying and Mr. Sebastian knew he was lying, and though this seemed, at the time, to mark the beginning of everything that was to follow, the lifelong rivalry, the Biblical antagonism, the single-minded hatred, Henry would have to become much older to realize that it had started long before that, lifetimes before, that it was out of their control, completely. There was nothing that either of them could have done.

"Why didn't you tell me?" Henry asked.

"About?"

"Hannah," he said.

"What's to tell?" he said, echoing Hannah. It was as though they'd worked out a code.

"Nothing," Henry said. "Only that you didn't."

Mr. Sebastian smiled. "But it has nothing to do with us. With this. With the work we're doing. You don't tell me about all the other things happening in your life, do you?"

But there was nothing else happening in his life to talk about. Henry had dedicated his every waking moment to this, to what was happening in this room.

"She's my sister," Henry said.

"She is also *not* your sister," Mr. Sebastian said. "In the same way that I'm your teacher, your mentor, but I am also not. I am Mr. Sebastian, but I am also someone else. For instance, we've never even talked about my lifelong interest in butterflies."

"Butterflies?"

Mr. Sebastian opened his right hand, and a beautiful butterfly, blue and brown and green, fluttered out of it and then around the room, as if it were looking for something in the air, something only it could see, finally alighting on a lampshade, where its wings opened and closed, open and closed. Out of his left hand came another. He opened a box on the table beside him, and three more butterflies escaped, then half a dozen more, until the small room was full of them.

"She's my sister," Henry said again.

"Yes. I understand that. But it's different now, between you and Hannah. Isn't it? Different than it used to be. She's said as much. I think Joan Crawford has changed things."

"Joan Crawford's a dog."

"At this point in her young life, Hannah cares more for that dog than she does about anything."

"You should have told me," Henry said.

"Anything, Henry," he said. "Even you."

"You should have told me."

"And yet the difference between what we do and what we should do is often vast, Henry," he said. "This is something we learn early on. Must I also teach you that?"

"No," Henry said. "I knew that. I knew that already."

Mr. Sebastian produced his pocket watch and studied it for a moment. "Then I think that's everything," he said.

"*Everything?*" He had not expected this. He had hoped for it, and feared it, but he had not expected it now. "What does that mean?"

"I think we're done here, Henry. Today was not your day, far from it, but you're a real magician now. Where it counts: on the inside. I have nothing left to show you."

"No," Henry said, "this can't be everything."

"It's not. But the rest you'll have to discover on your own."

Henry hated him. He wanted to hit him. He wanted to ball his hand into a fist and hurl it into his face. But something Mr. Sebastian was doing, some strange power, had sealed his feet to the floor. All Henry could do was stand there and breathe.

"One more," Henry said. "Show me one thing more."

Mr. Sebastian threw his hands up in the air and laughed. "But I have nothing!" he said. "You have soaked me dry! I have absolutely nothing left to show you."

"What about that first trick?" Henry said.

"The first trick?" Mr. Sebastian looked confused. He really had to think about it. "The first trick . . ."

"The one when you disappeared," Henry said. "The thing you did the first day. You never showed me that."

Mr. Sebastian smiled and looked Henry square in the eye. Compassion, love, pity, pride—it was all there, in that one look. Mr. Sebastian should have been his father, Henry thought. If Mr. Sebastian were his father, he would never leave and he would look at Henry like this forever.

"Ah," Mr. Sebastian said. "That one." He sighed. "I'd forgotten that one. I'd planned to show you that. But not today."

"When, then?"

"Tomorrow."

"Tomorrow," Henry said. "You sure?"

"Sure, I'm sure," he said. "Tomorrow. I'll show you tomorrow."

But tomorrow, of course, he was gone.

And so was Hannah, and so was the dog.

He took them, you see. He stole them. Like magic, they all disappeared.

Which brings me, ladies and germs, to the end of one story and the beginning of another. What is it, you may have asked yourself when I started my tale, what is it that could ever compel a man to change the very color of his skin, especially when the skin he had was so much better than the skin he got? Well, that question has been answered. I've told you all you need to know: a white man— the whitest of men, a ghostly-pure-white man—stole his little sister. How could he be linked with that color ever again? That's my take on it, folks. His life would become an antidote to that evil, and Henry would become whatever it was that his mentor was not.

A life takes its twists and turns, doesn't it? One thing leads to another, and then another after that. But how it all begins—that's the mystery. I know I'm here because of my father, and Henry the same. But there's more to it . . . There has to be. We can never go back far enough to understand who we are right now, because pretty soon it's all darkness, everyone is dead, and the little ones are getting hungry. I know you're tired of standing on your feet. Thank you for your patience and understanding. Those who still want their money back, please see Yolanda in the booth behind you. She'll be happy to help.

This is what I told them.

May 28, 1954

The Book of Lost Freaks

Hester Lester, the Chicken Lady. **Left us on the night of August 9, 1944. Her story begins as a sad one: Born with floppy skin. All over her body, the flesh just fell off of her. A little lady in a big skin suit. She became the Chicken Lady because of the skin, especially that around her neck: it hung off her chin the same way the stuff on a chicken does. Her eyebrows fell into her eyes, making them seem very small, like the eyes of a chicken, and she had a large rump, an arched back, and a mound of breasts. So her shape was appropriate to the job as well. Very popular. When the rubes came around, she'd twitch her head and squawk. In many ways the perfect freak: ostracized by the rest of the world, she found a home here and was well loved. Especially by Mr. Bob Simmons, our Fat Man. His skin, of course, drooped in a similar way, but in all honesty he was not fat enough to be a legitimate fat man. A disappointment and an embar-**

rassment when the crowd boasted a man even fatter. They left my employ together that same night, after a small party to wish them well. Love fills the human spirit with hope. Their hope: a normal life. Perhaps they found it, but I imagine they did not. Hester's optimism in the face of all she had endured was a great model to us all, and she will be missed. Bob, not so much.

Shelby Cates, the Human Pincushion. Not sure, but word was he died on a cold December night near Lexington, Kentucky. Born without the ability to feel, Shelby allowed himself to be stuck, cut, hammered into, sawed on, picked at, and whatever else the dark minds of the populace could configure. One rule only: all the body parts he had at the beginning of the show he had to have at the end. Otherwise it was a trade: eye for eye, toe for toe. Shel was an odd one. Bled without knowing he was bleeding, broke without feeling broken. We always kept a lady nearby, sexy as we could find, dolled up in a tarty nurse's outfit three sizes too small. She appeared to attend to him. Backstage we had a real doctor (inasmuch as anything here is real), Dr. Nathan P. Jones. A man who could be said to have attended a great deal of medical school. Could plug a wound with a piece of gum and sometimes did. Saved Shel's life eighteen times.

Shel's problem was twofold. He couldn't feel anything, inside or out. When he drank, he got drunk, but he didn't feel drunk. When he fell in love, he didn't feel in love, but he was. This created a schism that tore him up. He loved his fake nurse. She loved him, too, but he couldn't show her how he felt, because he didn't know. So he got drunk, but still did not know it. An insensate, brokenhearted drunk, he wandered off into the woods one cold night, never to be seen again . . .

. . .

Mark Markson, the Hairy Ape Man. Went bald. Took his own life. March 1947.

Whit the Stickman, the Thinnest Man Ever Born. X-rays not necessary, with the Stickman you can see every bone! For an extra quarter you can count his ribs! Feel his stomach and guess what he had for dinner! Has to stand in the same place THREE TIMES to cast a shadow. Whit tired of the nomadic life, settled in a hamlet near Baton Rouge, and opened a diner.

Bambi Dextrous. She could fold herself up into a ball small enough to fit inside a shoebox. We had a little thing. Her arms and legs twisting around each other, as nimble as a vine. Lured away one night in Montgomery, Alabama, by a man so intrigued with her talents he offered her a large sum of money to perform in the privacy of his boudoir. Probably a very rich woman today.

Henry Walker, the Negro Magician. Neither a Negro nor a magician, Henry was a lie from top to bottom and one of my all-time favorites, an American of the highest order: a self-made freak. Simply vanished. He, more than any of them, was lost, lost before he came here, and lost forever after he left. I cannot stop thinking of him, and wondering what really happened. Something of a mystery, a divergence of opinion, which can be divided into three camps.

I. Sucked into the vortex of the magic world he pretended to (and some say was a part of a long time before we knew him). It was said he was punished for dragging his art so low, gutter-low, removed from the world in order to make room for someone real. According to this theory, he is presumably floating through infinite dark space, or being chased by wolves over an infinite dark plain, or something equally painful and infinite . . . No real proof here, of course. Told by those who never knew him late at night in the quiet we are never accustomed to and thus fill up with our own nightmares. The fear of being sucked into another world even darker than this one is common among us. Maybe there is a word for this. If not I should make one up. Put that on the to-do list.

2. Abducted by a trio of hooligans for perceived crimes against their perceived humanity. Evidence exists to support this view. Eyewitness account from our own Rudy and others describing a confrontation in the midway and, prior to that, a nightly heckling. Investigation of Henry's trailer indicates a sign of struggle. Chains: missing. So was his photograph of Lana Turner. Theory maintains that, having been thwarted by Rudy's presence on first attempt, they returned the next day, fired up by failure and hatred, took him somewhere distant, and killed him for being a nigger. Which he wasn't. But dead because he would never tell them so. He was not so fond of life that he would save his own by turning his back on his own people.

3. Suddenly fond of life, he removed the shoe-black, he threw away his pigmentation pills, he returned to the world into which he was born, as a barber, or a vacuum salesman, or a housepainter, or a teacher, and he is happy, happier than we can imagine, a man who, passing others on the street where he lives, will engender a single thought, which is *There goes a happy man.* Jenny (our eternally hopeful Ossified Girl) is the single proponent of Theory No. 3, and she does not even believe it herself. The saddest of them all,

No. 3, because of poor Jenny, who loved him, and misses him, and yet only hopes for the best.

My heart breaks every day, and not just for Jenny but for them all (and for me, too, the King of the Misfits), and for the world itself, that a place like this can exist within it, that it's necessary, because without it we would all be

[Journal page torn.]

but No. 3 sounds right to me. There is the proof, of course, which is always nice, but also, even better, the hand of God for a moment briefly seen, the lid of a box snapping shut on a life, the beginning and the ending one and the same. Life is a sad thing, but authentic tragedy touches only a few and haunts the rest of us all of our lives. Like the same song playing over and over in our head forever. In my head. Henry. If that is his real name. We spent some time together, Henry and I, some serious time. A quiet man, but he spoke to me, told me things he told no one else. Before he found a home with us he was without one, a wanderer, in and out of jail for playing the three-card monte—and other things, no doubt. Not a man very fond of authority; the authorities were never very fond of him. I was a friend to a man who had none, perhaps the best he had in his entire life. And what a tale he had to tell. You can't forget such a story, especially when it's told in that voice, those green eyes, that weathered face, holding you to the edge of your seat. Impossible to render it again in any voice other than his own. His sister . . . abducted . . . stolen by a nameless man, or one who had too many names, a man who pricked his finger and shared his blood. Who made him vow a vow. His sister, who

[Journal pages missing here, followed by unrelated references to Mosgrove's loneliness, his desire for a true friend. Also mentions a woman named Jessie, a woman whom he loved but who could not love him in return. It was not him so much as it was his hair, she said, something she could not overlook.]

but she wasn't in the alley and neither was the dog, and when the day passed and then the night and still she wasn't there, Henry took his father to the room. They went there and knocked: nothing. No one. Mr. Walker opened the door with his master key (from the huge ring hanging from his pants; he jingled like a jailer everywhere he went), and the room was empty, pristine, the only sign the room had ever been occupied at all a playing card resting in full view on top of the dresser.

(Henry took the card and palmed it into his pocket; from that day forward, it never left his possession. Were he ever to turn up again, dead or alive, I would personally guarantee that card would still be with him. I would bet the farm.)

Henry couldn't speak at all after what happened to his sister, though he was surrounded by people waiting for him to say something, anything. Hotel security, local police, detectives, reporters from as far away as New York, a lot of men in wide-brimmed hats and cheap dark suits. There was nothing. Not a fingerprint. But Henry knew. He had at the very least a clue, something to go on. You could tell by his face. It was as if he'd seen a ghost—and he had. Mr. Sebastian was a ghost, and he had turned his sister into one as well. Those ghosts would haunt him for the rest of his life.

The heat cleared out of there sooner than one would think they might. Henry would have liked a more thorough going-through of things. But they were there, and then they were gone, and the investigation appeared to be over, and his sister was still not there. Henry couldn't help, not being able to speak a word. But there should have been more to it, he thought. When he finally opened his mouth to speak, he whispered. His father put his ear half an inch away from his son's mouth to hear what he had to say. "The king of hearts," Henry said, "the king of hearts means Charlemagne, the king of diamonds Julius Caesar, the king of clubs Alexander the Great, and the king of spades David, from the Bible." This he said over and over and over. His father must have thought he had lost him forever.

Henry could not venture far past one thought, as if monsters lay beyond it: *I let him take my sister.*

When the rest of words came, Henry told his father everything (within the parameters of the vow he took so seriously). But he had little to add to what was already known. No clues. How, after spending so much time with Mr. Sebastian, he could offer next to nothing surprised even him. When he described the face of this man to his father—the deathly-white skin, red lips, constant smile, thin black hair—the result was something from a dark fairy tale, the face of a human wraith.

His father cried and drank and gave his son a pat on the back, told him he was being very brave and they would have to carry on, they would find her, they would never stop looking, et cetera. But Henry knew this was a lie. Even he, a child, knew this. Life, such as it is, goes on. You could only look for so long and then you had to bury her. And they would bury her.

As for the father, the loss of his daughter was the final and greatest loss at the end of a long list of them; there was no room for another. He knew nothing about anything anymore. This loss pushed him over, greased the wheels of his descent. Prohibition couldn't stop him—he became a *drunk*, and so sad that it didn't matter, that nothing did: his daughter's disappearance sealed his fate. He would be drunk as a rat for the rest of his life.

Not long after the newsmen and policemen left, Mr. Croton had a talk with Mr. Walker, and in short order he was no longer an employee of the glorious Hotel Fremont, and he and his son spent the next weeks in a hotel that, in almost every detail, was *not* the Hotel Fremont, was even worse than the place between the kitchen and the laundry, lice-infested boxlike rooms with beds no thicker than a slice of bread, wallpaper stained by water dripping from the room upstairs, a bath they shared with strangers—the other hard-luck boarders—a toilet where wild things grew, the walls of the room itself a paper-thin protection from the cacophonous outside world, where other down-on-their-luck Americans scraped and begged for the hope a full stomach will give you. Henry saw the trajectory of things now. The truth. They had been treading water all this time, and now they were drowning. *We now commingle with refuse*, his gin-soaked father said, *because that is what we have become*.

A sad story. I'd cry if there weren't a million others just like it. Young boy. Scab-faced father. Drooping eyelids over bloodshot eyes, hopeless and poor and, frankly, boring. Henry practiced his card tricks, and as long as he did he could have been anywhere, because at these times the world around him disappeared, and he was freely floating in that no-man's-land of the imagination, somewhere between this life and whatever is on the other side. When his father was sober, he watched his son, absorbed and bewildered and transported himself. He studied his son. He had a thought buzzing around his head like a bee. He slipped on his tattered beret and grabbed his son by the wrist, pulling him along. *Bring the cards*, he said.

And this is how the cards saved Henry's life. And how they almost saved his father's.

It was like this. His father took him to downtown Albany, to a street corner where a crowd had gathered around a man who had set a table down there. A dozen men stood entranced, men from all walks of life. Some wore zoot suits, others the old plus-fours and slouch hats. A man without legs was there, too, rolling around a pallet with wheels. Mr. Walker and his son joined them. The man at the table had three cards, and he was moving them back and forth and around with hands that looked as though the flesh had fallen off of them, as though they were now only bone. His face was sharp, cheeks sunken, skin pockmarked, cratered; he wore a large-brimmed hat (everybody wore hats then) pushed back to reveal a huge forehead. He spoke in a wild but engaging patter. No one could move as they all listened to him speak, watched his lightning-fast hands.

Keep your eye on the red card, that's the money card; I'll show you where it is now—see?—to make it easier for you to follow when I turn it over. Slowly this first time, so you can be sure, and you are sure, aren't you, sir? I can tell. You're a sharp one. I should never have tried this with you. I was going to take a bet, but not with you—no, sir—but of course if you insist, a fiver, I'll risk it; we all have families we need to feed, and I'll feed yours or you'll feed mine. Now point. Show me. In the middle here, is it? Let's see . . . Ah! I'm sorry, sir! That's the one everybody points to, I'm afraid. Thank you, and, yes, I'll take your money, and my baby thanks you.

Mr. Walker looked at his son, and he saw something new in him now. *Can you do that?* he asked him. Henry studied it for another few seconds and shrugged. *Sure I can.*

And he did. Through the winter and into the spring, three-card monte—or Follow the Queen, or Find the Lady—fed them and clothed them and gave them a bed. It was a beautiful thing to watch, this young boy taking money from men twice, three times his age, ten times his weight. It was a dangerous and

[Journal text smeared with coffee, wine, ashes, tears—illegible.]

"Had no idea it was illegal," Mr. Walker told them.

[Journal page torn.]

whom he met in jail. He slipped it to Mr. Walker as though it were magic itself. The card read

---

TOM HAILEY'S MAGIC TOWN

MANAGEMENT AND REPRESENTATION OF

YOUNG PRESTIDIGITATORS WORLDWIDE

(if Albany is your world)

321 Malcolm Ave.

Albany, N.Y.

I know the card because I saw it myself: Henry kept it with him all those years. Tattered and worn, the edges crumbled in his hands, just like his three of hearts. Sentimental, Henry, if that was his real name. I'd have kept the card, too. Because Tom Hailey was important. He changed Henry's life.

Tom Hailey was the man who turned him into a Negro.

Tom Hailey! What a great man he must have been! Not like Rockefeller and Roosevelt are great men, but more like P. T. Barnum, had P. T. Barnum been born like him on the cobblestone streets of Albany, rooted there by a mother who never died, and whom, as her only child, he felt obliged to take care of until she did, at which point it was too late to leave. Think of the stillborn dreams Tom Hailey must have had! Think of Alexander the Great stuck in the backwater of Macedonia his whole life, and you'll get the picture. A tall man, preternaturally happy, his eyes all a-glimmer with possibility—the possibility that there was something you could do for him, something he could take from you that might make both of you richer for the theft. Attracted money like a vending machine, this one. But mostly small change. Everything about him was big. He had big hands and big teeth and big ears and a big nose and was powered as if by the energy of the sun and moon themselves. Tall and mostly thin, but with a nice little potbelly he was quite proud of. It looked good between his suspenders. He never met a man he didn't like or one who didn't like him. This was Tom Hailey.

[A long passage in which Mosgrove recounts the death of his parents— Mother: fire, Father: tractor—both of whom he desperately loved. "How strange," he writes, "that after forty years that love has not diminished one bit. That they are still alive in my heart."]

Tom Hailey's office was on the second floor of a four-story building at the edge of the warehouse district, not far from the paper mill. Soot stained every window, and the smell was terrible, poisonous, nostril-burning. A horde of bums and 'bos huddled beside an unhitched abandoned boxcar across the street, their haven from the wind and the freezing rain and things that go bump in the night. The streetcar's last stop was six blocks away, so Mr. Walker and his magical kid had to walk the rest, goddamn it. Henry's father hobbled, not because of a bad leg but because moving his legs, their entire extremity one after the other, was more than his pickled brain could suavely manage—there was just too much to it. He was lucky to be upright at all.

"Had no idea it was illegal," he muttered for the thousandth time. "Did you?"

"I had a good idea it was," Henry said, "the way that guy took off every time the policeman came."

Mr. Walker rubbed his son's head until the scalp burned. "You're a sharp one, you are. You take after me."

Which Henry knew wasn't true. He was, in fact, keeping a mental tally, a list of ways he was *not* like his father and would never be, a regular Ragged Dick with a poet's soul. Much more like his mother, he thought. Having never really known her, though, he had to invent her, and in doing so gave her the virtues he sought for himself—single-mindedness, passion, fairness, perseverance, and the ability to grieve. This last he had already perfected.

"So we broke the law," Mr. Walker said, shrugging. "What's the law done for us? What's the law done for those poor bastards over there? It can only get worse, too. They have their eye out for us now. That's why we need to go straight, you and me. That's why we need to talk to this Tom Hailey person. You know, things happen for a reason. Had we not gone to jail, we never would've gotten his card. I'm glad we spent a few nights there, you and me! Good things are about to happen, Henry. I feel it."

A feeling apparently shared by a dozen or so other fathers and sons, mothers and daughters, uncles and their nephews: Tom Hailey's tiny waiting room was nut to butt.

"Mother of Christ," Mr. Walker said. He looked around, overwhelmed by the competition. "What do we do now?"

"You wait like the rest of us," a large man with a killer stare said to him, gruffly, as if he could read their thoughts and objected to the one they had about breaking in line. "There's a sign-up sheet up front."

They signed up, and waited for three hours. Ahead of them was a boy holding a beat-up leather briefcase with golden snap locks on it ("Inside this case are more wonders than you could ever believe!" he said, but Henry could tell he was lying: Henry had seen wonders and doubted he had even a single one in there); a guy with a dummy on his lap ("Looks like a couple of dummies there," Mr. Walker said, much too loudly); a girl in a tutu who longed to be a magician's apprentice; and six or seven other young boys who could have been

Henry, Henry thought, kids who knew how to force a card, to lift a wallet, to mesmerize and tantalize and all the rest.

Henry didn't have a chance.

"Everybody's so dressed up," Henry said to his father.

"Maybe because they can be," Mr. Walker said, bitterly.

Because, even though Henry knew no one would be here if they didn't want a job, he and his father were the only ones who looked like they needed it.

By the time it was their turn, Mr. Walker had fallen asleep and was snoring like a submachine gun. Henry had been passing the time with his cards, the way he passed his whole life now—he and his *fifty-two best friends*, he called them—shuffling with one hand, with two, practicing the weave, the false cut, the Hindu, the Jordan, the multiple shift, all these beautiful things the legacy of the man who had stolen his sister. He looked up whenever the door opened, hoping his name would be called. Billowing clouds of smoke rolled out the door every time, as if something in there were on fire.

Finally, he heard his name.

"Henry?"

Tom Hailey's secretary caught his eye and smiled at him, and as he nudged his father awake and stood, she winked, the kind of wink that made you think that she'd never winked at anybody else ever before, that this wink she was saving for you. Henry liked her. She was pretty. Her hair was short and blond, cupping her big cheeks like a shawl. Her lipstick was fire-engine red. Her eyes were friendly and blue. Pretty. Henry was beginning to think like that. Her name was Lauren.

"Come on in," Lauren said.

There were a couple of old metal chairs covered in a torn and battered green vinyl; Henry and his father sat on them. It was dark in there. Wooden blinds were shut against the window. On the wall a framed diploma from a mail-order university. Before them a cluttered desk with a large black Bakelite telephone that had a built-in address book at the bottom. An unfiltered cigarette was burning unattended in an ashtray filled with others just like it, the nubby ends pressed flat and still a little wet. The phone started ringing as soon as they sat down, and Lauren picked it up.

"Magic Town," she said, and listened for a moment. "We don't take appointments, I'm afraid. First come, first served. No. Best not to bring a rabbit. Um-hm. Bye, now."

She hung up.

"Mr. Hailey will be with you in a moment," she said.

And he was. A toilet flushed, a small corner door opened, and Tom Hailey, all six and a half feet of him, suddenly appeared before them.

"Thank you, Lauren," he said, leering with the very tenor of his voice; anyone could tell they were an item. Lauren was a little heavy, but, as Tom Hailey would later tell Henry, *Sure, she's a little heavy, but heavy in all the right places*. And though Tom Hailey had a rule— *No fishing off the company pier*—he had never been able to follow it, and broke it for Lauren as often as he possibly could. He couldn't help himself. Tom Hailey couldn't help himself with any woman, though—a man happy to be enslaved by this particular desire.

Lauren left the room. Tom Hailey didn't take his eyes off of her until she was gone, and when she was, he looked like he missed her. Or the view, at least.

Now he looked at the fellows before him. He took a moment to gaze at them, at what was left of the Walker family. He tried to size them up, and he did, Henry could see him do it just that quickly. But he kept what he learned to himself. He looked at the puny cigarette burning away in the ashtray, picked it up, and with it lit another.

"Welcome to Magic Town, my friends, where the motto is *Magic is money and money is magic*. People like to forget. That's the service we provide here, forgetfulness. A sip from the river Lethe. I have a theory—unproven, of course, which is why I call it a theory—that God is actually a magician. He's simply the best one around. That's what we strive for here in Magic Town, anyway: to be God-like." He had said this exact spiel maybe one thousand times. He smiled at Henry. "I understand you do tricks with cards."

"Yes sir," Henry said.

"Not really as ambitious as creating the world in seven days, is it?"

Tom Hailey smiled wider, his fingers interlocked before his long three o'clock–shadowed face, looking at Henry, completely ignoring the father he'd brought in with him. He'd already dispensed with him.

"You're staring at my ears," Tom Hailey said.

Henry blushed. "Yes sir," he said.

"They're pretty big, aren't they?"

"Yes sir."

"They may be the biggest there are in the world," he said. "Far as I know. I've written Mr. Guinness to come measure them, but so far no response." Tom Hailey opened a drawer and removed a lady's hand mirror from it. He studied himself. "But I wouldn't say they're freakish. In their own way—and I am a harsh critic, Henry Walker, especially of myself—in their own way I'd say they're not unattractive. Lauren has compared them to the wings of a giant butterfly, one wing on either side of my face. But I don't pay her seventy-five cents an hour for nothing." He winked at Henry. This was Henry's second wink of the day. "They have their practical uses as well. I can hear *everything*. I can hear a roach sneeze from a mile away."

"Roaches sneeze?" Henry said.

Tom Hailey nodded. "I can hear your heart beating," he said, and he closed his eyes and with a pencil began tapping on the edge of his desk to the beat inside Henry's chest.

"And you know what they say about men with big ears," Mr. Walker said, and laughed.

"Yes," Tom Hailey said dryly. "They wear big hats."

And, turning his attention back to Henry, again forgetting the father, erasing him from the scene: "Let's see what you can do."

[One page apparently burned.]

everything, from simple to complex, following the evolution of his own education. Sometimes Tom Hailey told him what to do—the Four Friendly Kings, for instance, Seb's Bottom, the Three-Card Match—calling out names rapid-fire while Henry's father watched, dizzy and bewildered. Tom Hailey didn't betray a single emotion, though; sometimes he allowed himself a nod, which Henry would learn was the height of his approbation. But nothing else. Not even a smile.

Mr. Walker looked back and forth from his son to Tom Hailey. He rubbed his hands together, as if warming them—a nervous habit he'd recently developed, because his hands were always freezing. He breathed through his nose like a dog sniffing for a treat. He was overeager: even Henry, as he paused between tricks, could tell that. This was their first last chance, and Mr. Walker's presence was hurting whatever chances they had. He would interrupt the routine with a *That's good, son,* or *I didn't know you could do that!* Each time the comment came at exactly the wrong moment, until Tom Hailey had to tell him to quiet down.

"Okay," Mr. Walker said. "Okay. Sure. But—"

"But what?" Tom Hailey said, nailing him with a stare.

"But he's best at three-card monte," he said. "If you really want to see something, ask him to do that. It's how we've been eating for the last two months."

Henry stopped what he was doing, the cards appearing to freeze in midair. Not the right thing to say. Even a kid knew that. Tom Hailey sighed and rubbed his eyes. The silence was interminable, painful, and during the course of it Henry was forced to admit something about his father he hadn't been able to before: his father was wrong. Not wrong about one specific thing, but wrong in general. Something about his very existence was wrong. On the one hand, it was sad how he had degenerated into the pointless thing he was, like a piece of stale bread no one had bothered to throw away. But, on the other, Henry was angry. Henry couldn't help his father, and his father clearly couldn't help him. He was a drag, dead weight, holding Henry back from the rest of his life, and Henry knew with a terrible clarity that he had to cut himself free.

"Mr. Walker," Tom Hailey said after clearing his throat, "three-card monte is the magic of a street urchin. Three-card monte is the hole into which magicians crawl to die. That this extremely talented boy was forced to sully his art to make up for the failures of his father—and it pains me to say this, my heart breaks, it truly does—but it's like sending your own daughter into prostitution."

And at this, the mention of a daughter, Henry's father stood and threw his body across Tom Hailey's desk, falling headfirst into his chest, clawing at him with his fingers, ripping at his vest and suspenders, and choking him with his own tie. He made a sound like a wounded animal as he did this, wailing and sobbing, until Tom Hailey pushed him off, and then off the desk, and then to the floor, where he curled up into a shivering fetal wreck. Tom Hailey watched him for a moment, then looked at Henry, who hadn't moved.

"You have a sister?" Tom Hailey said to him.

"Had," Henry said.

Tom Hailey nodded. He looked down at the crumpled man on the floor, then helped him to his feet. "I'm so sorry, Mr. Walker," he said. "I shouldn't have said that. I didn't know."

"I would never do anything to hurt her," Mr. Walker said. He looked at Henry. "You know that, don't you, Henry? Never."

"Hurt her?" Henry said. "But you didn't—she was—"

Tom Hailey looked more and more alarmed by the second. "I'm very sorry," he said, "if I said something hurtful. I didn't know—I don't—" He looked away. He looked at his desk—all of his contracts, his girlie magazines, his fancy stationery, a total wreck. "Lauren!" he called out, and less than a moment passed before she opened the door and stuck her head in. "Next," he said.

"Next?" Mr. Walker said. He looked as though he had just awoken, and was unaware of the scene that had preceded this one. "Next? That's a lot of hooey! No one can do what my son can do. No one!"

"That's true," Tom Hailey said. "I've never seen anything like him. He's truly remarkable. But, as talented as your son is, I'm afraid there's nothing I can do for you."

"But . . . why?" Mr. Walker said.

Tom Hailey stood and walked to his office door, flinging it open. "Because of this, Mr. Walker."

They all looked. The waiting room was still completely full. It was as if in the world there were an infinite supply of boys with cards, and girls who wanted to assist them. When one left, another came.

"It's like this every single day," he said. "There are more magicians than there are people to see them. I have no idea how this happened. It didn't use to be this way. Something in the water now. In the air. They're everywhere. Henry is immensely talented. But so are they. The world just doesn't need another young white magician."

"So why did you even see us?" Mr. Walker said. "I was very hopeful."

Tom Hailey shrugged and studied him. "Then it wasn't a total waste. How long has it been since you felt that way?"

The audition was over. Tom Hailey opened the door a bit wider, waiting for them to go. Henry stuck the cards into his pocket and reluctantly stood; his father placed his hands on his son's shoulders, not to reassure his son, but to help himself stay upright. As they passed, Tom Hailey caught Henry's father by the elbow and pulled him close. He whispered something in his ear. Henry wouldn't find out what he said until later, but it went something like this: "Now," he said, "while the young *white* magician may be a dime a dozen, a young *Negro* magician is a rare thing indeed. A valuable thing. I have calls every day from people who want an authentic Negro magician. But I can't seem to find one anywhere. You could say I'm desperate for a young Negro magician."

Tom Hailey and Henry's father understood each other perfectly. No more needed to be said. Tom Hailey scribbled something on the back of a card and handed it to his father.

"We're going to be fine," his father whispered into Henry's ear as they were leaving. "We're going to be fine."

Tom Hailey's apartment was no palace, but it was clean and warm and, for the time being at least, it was free. "I'll deduct the rent and food from our future earnings," he said. "Which are sure to be substantial. A small percentage. Not to worry."

Henry and his father shared a room not much bigger than a closet, a naked bulb hanging by a wire from the ceiling. There was an old wooden crucifix on a wall, one small mattress stuck in the corner, a pile of blankets on the floor. Mr. Walker tested the mattress out first thing.

"Not bad," he said, his head falling hard into a cloudy stack of pillows. The pillows were top-drawer. "A little creaky. But better than a stick in the eye, I'll tell you what!"

Henry had begun turning the blankets into a pallet when Tom Hailey stuck his head in the room. "The bed's for the talent," he said to Mr. Walker, winking at Henry at the same time. "He needs his sleep. Tomorrow's a big day."

Mr. Walker climbed off the bed. Neither of them took off their clothes. A few minutes later, they turned out the lights, and all was quiet. Completely. How long had it been since they'd gone to sleep without the frantic sounds of the city burrowing into their ears? The streetcars, the fights, the lovers' screams and cries? Occasionally they'd hear Tom Hailey open and close something, turn the water on, flush the toilet. But these were the sounds of a home.

"A big day?" Henry said.

Henry looked now to his father, whose eyes were fluttering low.

"*Dad*," he whispered, "why's tomorrow a big day? I thought he said he didn't even want us, and then he did. What happened? What did he say to you? Dad?"

But his father was asleep.

Early the next morning, the smell of bacon frying seem to lift Henry and his father from their sleep and carry them as if on a magic carpet, still half dreaming, into the kitchen. Three places were set at the red Formica table with the rusty metal legs. Two strips of overcooked bacon, like thoughtless sunbathers, were stretched parallel across each plate, and as they sat down, huge mounds of eggs were dumped onto their plates. As hungry as he was, Henry took only small bites; his father shoveled the food into his own mouth as if he thought any moment someone might take it from him. Tom Hailey smiled, watching him. Tom Hailey pitied his father—Henry could see it in his eyes. Henry knew the look because Henry pitied him, too.

They ate in silence. As Henry followed his last bite with the last of his orange juice, Tom Hailey placed two small white pills beside his plate.

"Always take these on a full stomach," he said. "With water. Lots of water."

Henry looked at them. He had never taken medicine in his entire life. "What are they?"

"Magic pills," Tom Hailey said. He winked again, and Henry could tell now it was a nervous tic, the punctuation to almost every-thing he said. "A doctor would call them psoralen."

"You got them from a doctor?" Mr. Walker said.

"Sort of," Tom Hailey said. "An almost-doctor. As close as you can be to a doctor without getting the M.D."

"And these are what make it happen?"

"These are what make it happen," Tom Hailey said.

"Make what happen?" Henry said.

Mr. Walker took a deep breath. "Turn you into a Negro," he said.

"A *what?*" This was the first he'd heard about it.

"Not a Negro," Tom Hailey said. He gave Henry a reassuring pat on the back. "No one can become a Negro who wasn't *born* a Negro. That's simple biology. It's merely color that changes. White becomes black. Someone who didn't know better, and no one will know bet-ter, won't be able to tell. You'll still be you—Henry Walker from Nowhere, U.S.A. But they'll swear you came from darkest Africa."

Henry looked at his father. "Were you going to tell me about this?" he said.

"I just did," he said, running his finger along the edge of his plate.

[Long passages scratched out, unreadable.]

the car ride back to the office—he drove a brand-new Studebaker, and it was the first time Henry or his father had ever been inside one—Tom Hailey described the entire procedure, what would hap-pen. He had these pills, very safe, very wonderful, and every day Henry would take them and then spend an hour or so beneath a spe-cial lamp. Soon his skin would become quite dark. Then they would shave his head—Henry's hair, mercifully, was already thick and black—and—"Keep your fingers crossed!" Tom Hailey said—Henry would look as much like a Negro as a Negro did. The effect was completely temporary, he said. In just a day or two—without the pills and the lamp—Henry would begin to return to his natural color.

"But I don't know if I want to be a Negro," Henry said.

"And I completely understand," Tom Hailey said. He turned around to look at Henry, who was alone in the backseat. "But if you're not a Negro—and I explained this to your father—we've got a big fat nothing. Nothing. As I said, there's a glut of Caucasian prestidigitation right now. The market is flooded. Nothing I can do about that. But you possess remarkable skills, Henry. I'd hate for those to go wasted. And—on the practical side of things—you have black hair and features which, I mean, it looks to me like it could work. This doesn't work on the blondies. My point is, together I think we could do something special."

"But it's lying," Henry said. "Isn't it?"

Tom Hailey laughed. Then he looked hurt. "Lying? Hardly. Do you think I could be in business for as long as I have if I were a liar? Absolutely not. It's an *illusion*, Henry. It's part of the act. If people want to see a Negro magician, we will give them a Negro magician. Simple as that."

"But I'm not one," he said.

"Yet," he said. "Eventually you will be, and no one will know the difference. It'll make 'em happy. It'll make 'em forget. See, we'll tell them a story. The folks love a good story. An outrageous, phenomenal story impossible to believe—a boat, darkest Africa, I can already see it in my mind—and they'll buy it. They will! We'll be doing the work of the angels, Henry, you and me, fulfilling their desires. Do you know how important it is that we do that? And you can, simply by becoming a Negro. They will die a little happier because of you. Not a lot happier, but a little. And every little bit counts."

Tom Hailey pointed down a side street. "There's a soup kitchen right down there. A good one. And The Pilgrim House will give you a place to stay. For a night or two. If you're dead-set against this, I'll drop you off down there."

Henry watched the weak and hungry men in their rotting coats, as slump-shouldered as his father had become, making their way toward nowhere.

Henry stayed where he was. He nodded, once.

Tom Hailey smiled. He'd had them pegged from the jump.

Your name will be Bakari. It's Swahili and means One Who Will Succeed. You see, I've done my homework. It's the little details, you know, that make these things believable. Not that anyone will know the difference, but it means a lot to me. So from the darkest Congo you come. Hidden in a basket at the bottom of a freighter, you were smuggled into this country by a group of sailors who hoped to sell you on the black market—no pun intended. Okay, maybe a little pun. But they didn't realize the extent of your magic powers! As soon as you arrived in America, you turned one of them into a donkey, another into a pig, and a third you reduced to a plume of smoke. But, please, do not expect to see such powers in evidence today, I'll tell the crowds who come to see you. You are safe! Bakari has sworn off them. They are too dangerous. They also include calling on one of his many gods to help, and the gods don't like to be called on except in case of dire emergencies. But what you will see will astonish you. Abjuration, Alteration, Channeling, Conjuration, Divination, and Evocation will all be evidenced here today. You will become mesmerized, and when you leave here the name Bakari will reside in your mind forever. Bakari speaks not a word of English, but neither does he need to. His magic will speak for itself.

The lamp was no regular lamp. It was a light in a box, and brighter than other lamps, and hot. Sitting before it was like warming his face in the summer sun. For an hour every day he sat at the red Formica table with the lamp shining on his face (and later on his hands, and later on his entire body). He remembered lying on the ground in the little park beside the hotel with Hannah one day feeling like this. They'd been looking for four-leaf clovers. They couldn't find any, and after a while fell back into soft green clover and watched the clouds. There was one mountainous, billowing cloud almost right above them, and it partially blocked the sun. Rays shot out from the top of it, and the cloud itself seemed to glow, as if something were behind it, just shining. *That's where God lives*, Hannah said.

"I got the idea from my uncle," Tom Hailey said over dinner one night. He'd shovel a spoonful of mashed potatoes and a piece of meat into his mouth at the same time, chew for a second, wash the rest down with beer, and smoke his cigarette. He always kept a cig-arette lit and ready to smoke, from the moment he woke in the morning until he fell asleep at night. "He was taking these pills for a skin condition, and one day he's outside, the sun beating down on him like a whip, and his skin starts to turn this dark brown color. Called him Mandingo after that. Still do. But you know how the mind works. I had clients on the horn all day begging me for a black magician like the Armstrongs or William Carl. Where am I go-ing to get one in Albany, New York? The human mind is a miracle of science, is it not? Ideas like a pinball—seen those? pinball ma-chines? *binga-da-banga-da-bing*—I think to myself, Why not? Why not do what the two of us—"

"Three," Henry's father said. "The three of us." Surprising everybody that he was even there, much less listening.

"—what the three of us are doing here, now, in this little apart-ment at the corner of Blake and Austin? Just waiting on the right kid, you know, the perfect kid to pull this off. And I found him. In you."

Or, as he would later put it: *Someone desperate enough to give up his natural skin color just to live in the world. Someone with absolutely nothing to lose.*

"Do me a favor, kid," he said to Henry. "Give it a couple of days before you look in the mirror again. Better yet—"

He stood up, pushed away from the table, found a roll of yellowed masking tape in a kitchen drawer, and covered every mirror and mirrored surface with newspaper. Even the toaster.

"So it'll be a surprise," he said, winking. "At least, to you."

Meanwhile, they were captive in Tom Hailey's apartment, listening to swing music on the radio.

> *[Mosgrove writes the words* I wish *here,*
> *but doesn't complete the thought.]*

Lauren brought them lunch, Mr. Walker more bootleg gin. She had a trio of revolving hats: a cloche, then a pillbox, then a beret. Henry liked the beret best. It made her look like a friendly, beautiful spy. She sat down beside Henry at the tiny kitchen table, flush together, elbows touching, and their legs so close he could feel the pleats of her skirt against his thigh. She'd wipe the corners of his mouth with a napkin she'd moistened with her lips, and he'd let her, gazing at her skin and eyes as if she were an unknown specimen of something from an unknown land. He fell in love with her, not like a man, but like a boy with a claim to something precious. His father had a different angle on it—a man's angle—and for a couple of days he shaved for her and tucked in his shirt, until it was clear it made no difference. She hardly recognized his existence, so he quickly went back to his natural scruffy I-got-nothing-to-live-for look. Henry knew she came over at night sometimes as well to see Tom Hailey—he heard them through the walls—but she was always gone before morning.

"I think what you're doing is so brave," she told Henry. "Crazy, a little, but brave. And I haven't seen Tom so happy since he won a saw-buck at a dog race. Thanks for that, Henry." And she planted a kiss on his forehead. "Never kissed a Negro before," she said, winking.

"I'm not a Negro," Henry said.

"No," she said, "you're not. But you're as close to one as any of us will ever get."

When Tom Hailey left for the office in the morning, Henry and his father were on their own. His father slept late, but even when he woke, usually around noon, he still seemed to be asleep, or to have carried sleep with him into his waking life. Tom Hailey kept him well supplied with his favorite gin, and he drank a little with his orange juice first thing. So he was at least a little drunk every minute of his life. He listened to the radio and read the comics. *Plainclothes Tracy* was his favorite, though it wasn't that funny. "I like this Tracy," he said almost every single day, as if it were the first time he'd said it. "He's got what it takes." He said it as though he recognized a last little bit of himself in Tracy.

After an hour or so in front of the lamp, Henry practiced his routine. He had never had a routine before—a series of tricks presented in a logical order, one building on the next, ending in a big finale, like fireworks. In addition to the illusions he knew already—fantastic illusions Tom Hailey had never seen, or even heard of before—Tom Hailey showed him some things with ropes and disappearing water and even snakes, which he thought would work well within the theme of the show they were presenting. Because his fingers were nimble, and his powers of misdirection substantial, even without the traditional patter—since he could not speak a word of English—he could perform the illusions successfully. At least for his father, who was his only audience now. But he wasn't sure if his father was really looking at him when he did his tricks, and if so whether he could understand any of it. He seemed a step removed from the world.

Not Tom Hailey, though. Every day, Tom Hailey would return with raw energy and a new idea. One day he brought back a turban. "I know this is an Indian thing, but the joints we're playing aren't going to know the difference. And if anyone does know and calls us on it, the steamer docked in Bombay for a month, and you soaked up a bit of that lovely culture. Is Bombay a port? Maybe I should look that up. But it doesn't matter. I can tell them you're from the moon, and by the time I was through with them you would be. Believe me."

Henry wasn't worried. He had suspended that emotion for now, and put all of his trust in his manager. Tom Hailey told Henry stories impossible to believe, and Henry believed them all, at least for a little while, as long as was necessary for the average audience, for example, the length of time equal to that of the routine they were working plus the time it took to get out of town. *I can see you and Harry Houdini onstage together, Henry—you'd open for him, sure, but on the same stage. And you'll be just as famous. I can see it. And no, you're not the only Negro magician out there, and, I don't know, maybe not the only white Negro magician out there, but I'll say this much—they are few and far between, and none that I've seen have your innate skills. You're the cat's pajamas, HW. Where did you learn these things? From another magician, sure. But who? Tell me. Maybe I know him.* But Henry couldn't bring himself to speak the name yet. He wasn't even sure if he knew it. Sebastian. Horatio. Tobias. James. He'd probably made all of them up. From the beginning, Henry figured, Mr. Sebastian had been there to take his sister, and so nothing he had told him was true. It was why he would prove so hard to find.

In a matter of days, it was done. Tom Hailey came back from the office—*Anybody home?* he called out when he opened the door—and then he would make a beeline straight for the icebox and the coldest bottle of brew (there was usually a frosted amber bottle near the back)—because Prohibition, he always said, only served to make him thirstier. But tonight Henry was standing in the hallway as he entered, right before him, and when Tom Hailey saw him there he did not make for the icebox, he did not say, *Anybody home?* He froze, mesmerized. The cigarette hung from his lips for a moment, and then it fell to the wooden floor, still smoldering.

"Henry?" he said.

He couldn't believe his eyes.

"I spent a lot of time in front of the lamp today," Henry said.

"I can see that," Tom Hailey said carefully. "I see."

He approached Henry slowly, studying him as though the possibility existed that it wasn't him at all. He ran his index finger down Henry's cheek, and then looked at his finger. Nothing. The tip of his finger was white as snow.

He smiled, and when Henry saw him smile, a smile grew on his own face as well. This was something he hadn't experienced in a long time: someone he wanted to make proud.

"So—you want to see for yourself, little man?" Tom Hailey asked him.

Henry nodded. "I think I do," he said.

Tom Hailey couldn't take his eyes off of him. "Wow," he said, over and over again. "Wow." Then: "Where's your father?"

Henry pointed to their room. The door was closed.

"What's he doing in there?"

"He won't look at me," Henry said.

"He won't look at you," Tom Hailey said, softly, kneeling, and he pushed the hair back from Henry's eyes. "Well, your father is an emotional man."

"He's a drunk," Henry said. "He's my father, but he's a drunk who's given up on his life because of all the bad things that have happened in it. I'm not going to do that."

Tom Hailey smiled. "No," he said. "I can see that you're not."

"He doesn't like me this way," he said. "But I don't like him the way he is, either. So we're even."

"Sounds like you are," Tom Hailey said, and then he stood and ripped the newspaper from the toaster, the closest reflective surface he could find. In it Henry saw his face for the first time in a week, pinched and distorted in the smooth, curving surface, like in a fun-house mirror. He had turned brown. Henry Walker was brown.

"There's just one more little thing," Tom Hailey said. He found a pair of scissors in the kitchen drawer, and cut Henry's hair until it formed a little black helmet on his head. The effect was perfect.

"What've you done to my boy?" Henry's father said, appearing behind them.

"It's what we all agreed to," Tom Hailey said. "I know it's shocking. I'm a little shocked myself, but—"

Henry's father rushed at Tom Hailey, flailing. He had never been much of a fighter. Tom Hailey took Mr. Walker's arms and pinned them to the side of his body and held them there against him, almost in a hug, until all the fire inside of him died, doused by his own tears, breathing and shivering.

"He's not even my son anymore," he said, crying now. "He's somebody else. My son is gone."

And this was true. Henry knew this was true. Henry had gone, had left himself entirely. The boy he now was—*Bakari, from the darkest Congo*—looked at Tom Hailey and

[Illegible.]

The next morning, they had yet another wonderful breakfast. Henry had learned to overlook the ashes in his eggs, had even come to believe Tom when he said they were good for you. His father thought it was pepper.

After they ate, Tom Hailey clapped his hands together twice, as though he were doing an illusion of his own. "Time to see how we fare," he said, "in the real world. Throw on a coat, because it's cold out there."

"Outside?"

All of a sudden Henry's heart began to race like a car engine, and Tom Hailey started tapping his knife against the table, matching its rhythm.

"Don't worry so much, Henry," he said. "It's going to be fine."

They were a strange trio, two white men with a young Negro boy. There had been a snowfall overnight, and against that backdrop Henry appeared even darker. No one passed them without giving at least one long and puzzled stare.

"Good," Tom Hailey murmured beneath his breath as they walked. "This is very good indeedy."

Henry's father coughed. "Where are we going?" he said. "It's cold as a witch's teat."

"There's a place," Tom Hailey said, smoking. "Three or four blocks from here. The first test. See how little Frankenstein here fits in." And he rubbed Henry's furry head. "I kid," he said. "You know that, right? I kid."

Five blocks later, they stopped on the corner across the street from a park. As though they were walking backward through time from block to block, everything changed, office buildings became apartments, and apartments small houses, small houses with tiny lawns, well kept but deteriorating, as if from the inside out. Everybody here was black now. Everybody. Some men wrapped in blankets shivering in doorways, some shoveling the snow from their walks. But the looks they got were the same.

A black woman who must have been about fifty in a blue cotton dress and a dark shawl walked past them. She was underdressed for the weather—who wasn't, these days?—but she was walking fast, probably on her way to someplace warm.

"Excuse me," Tom Hailey said. She stopped, a bit reluctantly, and gave the white man a hard stare. As if she'd had conversations with men who looked like Tom Hailey and they hadn't gone well. But she lost the look quickly.

"Yes sir," she said.

"This boy," he said, pushing Henry forward a little. "He's lost. All turned around. Says he lives near here, but he's not a hundred percent sure. Do you know him?"

She gave Henry a long look-over. "I don't think I do," she said.

"Look again," Tom Hailey said. "Just want to make sure."

This time she stared at Henry for such a long time that both of them—Henry and Tom Hailey—thought she'd seen through the guise. But no: she smiled. "I'm sorry," she said. "Sorry."

Tom Hailey kept walking, and Henry and his father followed. There was a park across the street. The park had a swing set and a slide and a rope to climb on. It was clean, but even from here Henry could see the rust on the swing set's metal poles, and when one of the kids swung really high, the entire set shook, looked like it was about to pull itself out of the ground. Six or seven kids there, playing. All of them Negroes.

"Go on," Tom Hailey said.

Henry looked up at him. Not at his father, who was hanging a step or two back, but at him.

"Go on and play," he said.

"With them?"

"Sure, why not? They're no different from you. Not really." He winked.

"By myself?"

"I'll go with you, son," his father said. But Tom Hailey laughed.

"And how's it going to look if you go with him? White man with a little black boy. How is that going to look? The idea is to see if he can pass. Period. That's it."

Mr. Walker didn't have an answer for that. "But that's how it's always going to look," he said. "Today, tomorrow, and the next day. It's going to be the same then as it is now, if you keep this up."

Tom Hailey didn't say anything, because he had already thought of this.

Henry's approach was slow, and cautious, but he was no slower or more cautious than any new boy would be in a place he'd never been before. Mr. Walker and Tom Hailey watched him go. Henry turned around once and waved, and they waved back, and he did not look back again. A wrought-iron fence surrounded the park; Henry pushed the gate open and walked toward the boys. They were tossing a ball, one to another. Henry looked more closely and saw it was a snowball, packed hard, and the game, he could tell, was to see who would be the one to break it first. They were laughing. They looked to be about Henry's age. Henry walked closer. He knew they knew he was there, but they made like they didn't notice—until he entered the sphere of the circle itself and stood there for a moment, but only a moment, and then the snowball came to him.

It was the first time he'd played with anybody except Hannah in years.

Tom Hailey and Mr. Walker watched, the snow falling on their hats, their shoulders.

"We need to talk, Mr. Walker," Tom Hailey said without looking at him, without taking his eyes off of Henry.

"I know," he said.

"You do?"

"I do," he said.

"And you understand, it's nothing personal. It's business."

"Sure."

"But it's just not going to work out," Tom Hailey said. "The three of us. It's just a business thing."

"To you," Mr. Walker said. "Not to me. To me it's something different."

"I know that. But it's still a business thing."

Tom Hailey took a wad of money from his coat pocket and placed it in Mr. Walker's hand. It was a lot of money. You could see the lump it made on the outside when Henry's father stuffed it into his pocket. Then Tom Hailey gave him his card.

"Call me," he said. "From time to time. I'll let you know how we're doing. And if things are going well, there'll be more where that came from. I could wire it to you or—"

"I don't want to talk about this," Mr. Walker said.

"Fine, then," Tom Hailey said.

"I want to say goodbye," he said. "Can I at least say goodbye to my son?"

Tom Hailey didn't say anything. He didn't shake his head, he didn't wink, he didn't shrug. He pretended he hadn't heard this, and he stared straight ahead, his eyes focused on the distance, and when he looked back to where Mr. Walker had been standing, he was gone.

The snow began falling harder now. The snowball had broken, and so they had to make another. And another. The tossing soon turned into a real snowball fight, and Henry gave as good as he got, and they were all laughing. Henry was having such a good time, he didn't even think about what a good time he was having. He was just having it. The snow fell quickly. Within minutes, the park was wholly white, every inch of it. Henry had never seen so much snow. But then the wind began to blow, and the temperature suddenly plunged, and as the other boys ran off for a warmer spot, Henry instinctively followed, but they disappeared into the blizzard, and he stopped, lost now himself.

That's when he saw Mr. Sebastian. Through the sheets of snow raining down on him and on everything around him, he saw Mr. Sebastian across the park. He was waiting for him, waiting for him the same way he always had, sitting in the same chair, wearing the same clothes, as if he were still sitting in Room 702. And even in all the whiteness around them, Mr. Sebastian glowed even whiter—hardly a color at all, it seemed now, but more the absence of it. With a curling finger, he invited Henry closer. *I have her,* he said. *What was yours is mine now. I'll show you. Come here and I'll show you, Henry.* Henry walked toward him, but with each step Mr. Sebastian seemed to fade a little farther away. Henry started to run, then tripped over something and fell face-first into the snow. He picked himself up and kept running, but the snow came fast and the wind hard, tearing through the illusion that was Mr. Sebastian. By the time Henry got there, it had completely disappeared. He'd thought this would happen. If there was one thing Mr. Sebastian knew how to do, it was how to disappear.

But then, who didn't these days? It seemed to be a power shared by everybody Henry knew. First his mother, then his sister, and now—he was sure of it—his father. The moment he left them and set out on his walk toward the park, somehow Henry had known that he would never be seeing his father again, or not for a really long time, so long a time as not even to matter. This was, as they say, in the cards. He turned around once, for a last look, but not again: one last look was enough. The list of lost things was getting longer and longer, and perhaps that explained why this loss didn't feel as bad as the others—didn't really hurt so much. There were losses that made you heavier and losses that made you lighter, and this loss made Henry light. On the way back to Tom Hailey's apartment that afternoon, Henry was almost floating, as if the world was opening up to him through the aperture of his father's absence—a new world, all bright and shiny.

Tom Hailey draped his arm across Henry's shoulder, and like this they walked silently through the snow. "What say we get something to eat," Tom Hailey finally said.

Henry nodded. "Sounds like a good idea."

And they walked until they found a place where a white man and a young black one could eat together.

It took some time.

Henry Walker. I daresay we will never see h—

[Journal entry abruptly ends.]

The Ossified Girl's Song of Love

May 29, 1954

Closer. Come closer. I can't talk much above a whisper anymore, but I will tell you what I know.

He never loved me, I know that. By the time we met, it was too late for both of us: Henry had no more love left inside of him, and though my heart still beat as soft and warm as any woman's, the rest of me had hardened almost entirely into stone. By the time we met, my arms and legs didn't move, and my mouth only enough to chew, swallow, and smoke. My food was brought to me. Before Henry came, this was a chore shared by everyone. I receive two meals a day: one in the morning and one in the evening. I was a burden, and I remain one. I'm the very definition of the word, and yet no one complains. I'm lucky to have this family. But when Henry came, he took over the duties all by himself. He fed me every day, both meals, for years. We talked, and that was more pleasant. But it was just as pleasant not to talk, to be together in our own silence, something we created together. He never loved me, but I do think he was quite fond of me. I think he saw beneath my carapace to who I was, as I saw beneath his. This is what love is, of course, this second sight, this spyglass to the soul. But what if there's nothing there to see? If the heart has died, withered, and hardened? Then you might as well be blind.

In the morning, he brought me eggs, sausage, toast, and coffee, same as you'd get in a fine hotel. At night, it might have been anything—an infinite menu limited only by his imagination. It was always a surprise, and always a surprise worth waiting for. He covered the plate with an old golden cymbal from Dirk Mosby's drum set to keep the warm in. Henry was a thoughtful man. If, before he came, my eggs had gotten cold, if the bacon was hard and crunchy as my fingers would have been, if the milk had been spoiled—I never said a word. Never. *Take your givens, Jenny,* my mother always said, and I always did. But he knew how to treat a lady. Even an ossified one.

He brought me everything: food that fed my body, and words that fed my mind. I think I was the only one here he could really talk to. He had other friends, yes, because Henry was friendly. Or he tried to be. But our time together was special. He told me things he never told another living soul. The three or four years preceding his arrival at the Chinese Circus were lost to him, his memory clouded by grief and regret and whiskey. But everything before that he knew by heart. By the time we met, I was as rooted as a tree, but the stories he told of his life moved me. As if I were lifted from my spot in an airship and sent on a trip around the world, rising into heaven and plummeting into the depths of hell. When I closed my eyes, I saw it all. His life followed an unalterable path, there was no changing it, try as he might. He was one person who became two. We were his last hope. People are weak in the eyes of the gods. The goddess of necessity, Themis, brought forth three lovely daughters who were known as the Fates: Clotho, Lachesis, and Atropos. Life is woven by Clotho, measured by Lachesis; finally, the thread of life is cut by Atropos. They laugh at our feeble attempts to cheat them, because they always prevail. What happened to Henry is what happens to us all. But there has been no fate like his in a thousand years. It's as though he fell from the pages of a story into our new, plain world. I think Henry Walker is a hero, a tragic one. The only difference between a real hero and a tragic one is that the tragic ones live through their losses, and Henry lived through them all. His sister, his mother . . . How he kept breathing is a mystery to me.

No one listens to me. It's impossible: my voice is just the echo of a whisper. You have to be quiet in a quiet place and really want to hear. There's no one now who wants to do that, but I like the sound of my voice resounding in my head. But it's Henry's voice I hear most of all.

It's not the number of losses but their size that counts. A little girl cries when the fish she wins at the ring toss dies before she gets home, and we can count that on the tally sheet, if you want to. But a boy whose mother dies before his ninth birthday, whose luminous sister is stolen from him before his eleventh, and whose father falls into the hopeless arms of death and lies there dying a little bit every day in plain sight of his son and the world—these are the real losses, the ones that tear into the body and bleed the soul. Henry wasn't the kind of man to count them, but that's why we have friends. They count our losses for us.

I'm a fool for love stories, though. Stories that begin with a gaze across a room and end in a clinch—I can't get enough of stories like that. People think they only happen in books, but that's not true: they happen every day. I've seen them happen myself. From my perch on the stage, leaning upright against the wooden planks like a corpse on display, I've seen boys in coveralls, girls in calico hold on to to each other as they never have before. Love is sometimes born of fear, and that's what I provide. Even though I can't move, even though there is nothing I could do to harm them and they know it, I think I am the scariest thing some of these people have ever seen. I'm the draw here, really. Strongmen are a dime a dozen, and the bearded lady? Please. When the crackers file in and stand six or seven deep, they are lining up for me, to touch me, to see if I'm for real. They have to figure I'm not, and they figure I'm not until they touch me. And then you should see them draw their hands back! As if they'd touched fire. This is where love is born. A girl falls into the arms of her date. She gasps, then grasps his hand. Some nights, I'll gaze across the crowded room myself with nothing but love in my eyes—my eyes the only part of me that's moving—until they settle into the gaze of a terrified young man, and I'll give him the silent word: *Touch her. Take her hand. Love her for the rest of your life.*

In the end, Henry was a man with two stories: one story was about revenge, and the other was about love.

I liked the love one.

Her name was Marianne La Fleur. He called her *Mary*, or *Mary the Flower*, or *My Flower*, or *Marry Me, My Flower*. She was white—and so was he, the day he met her. He had been mostly white for several years by then. But from 1933 to 1938 (a mere boy of twelve to a young man at seventeen), he was a full-time Negro. Tom Hailey thought it was important for him to stay black, because there was no telling what might happen when they were least expecting it. The worst things always happened when you were least expecting them. Henry had a busy schedule, but there were weeks here and there when they had no shows whatsoever, and Henry wanted to see himself the way he used to be, just for a day or so. But Tom Hailey wouldn't have it. Tom Hailey was always looking at the bigger picture. What if someone saw him on the street somewhere and somehow recognized him—*Bakari, from the darkest Congo*—who was now

Henry, from the whitest Albany? It would ruin everything, and no one wanted to ruin everything. So Henry stayed black. He stayed black for so long that even after he stopped taking the medicine his skin maintained a shadowy cast, not white or black but a dusky gray, not purely one thing or another. But that was later. For most of his teenage years he stayed a Negro.

For five years there was nobody quite like him. He traveled across the entire country—New York, St. Louis, San Francisco—and everywhere he went, crowds thronged to see *Bakari, from the darkest Congo.* They thronged to see him burn a hundred-dollar bill and make it reappear. He did things with eggs no one had ever seen before, and they thronged to see that as well. Tom Hailey masterminded Bakari's progress from a near creature to a real boy, or one who was almost real, not being Henry. America watched him become an American. They watched him learn our customs, our language. Newspaper articles were written about him.

Bakari speaks!

"I bring to you the African magic," he says in halting English
to resounding applause!

Every show, he learned a little more of the language. "Tonight," Tom Hailey said, "instead of eggs, use baseballs. And when the third one disappears, say, *Strike three, you're out!* Give it a little accent, of course. A little of that African thing you do so well."

Soon he was conversing. The evolution in his style was, for a while, a sort of national pastime, until the time came when he became too much like us, almost exactly like us, and interest precipitously waned. Other African magicians—real ones—caught our imagination, and Tom Hailey thought it was time for Bakari to return to the Congo.

This is when Bakari became Prince Aki de Rajah, a Hindu fakir.

It was 1937. He wore a purple turban and spoke in an East Indian accent. In this incarnation, his skin was two or three shades lighter. Tom Hailey had become adept at modulating skin tone. His mother had always wanted him to become a doctor; instead, he became Henry's private chemist. It took a subtle combination of pigmentation pills and light. He printed up a new set of cards that read *Dr. Tom Hailey*. He was quite pleased with himself.

As Prince Aki de Rajah, Henry became a mentalist. He told fortunes. He seemed to know the future. Before the show, Dr. Tom Hailey would collect questions from the audience and communicate with Henry in code. Most of the questions centered on the same things: money, health, and love. Before Henry took the stage, Dr. Tom Hailey would ask an audience member a whispered question, as though he were just making conversation—"How long have you been married?"—and would communicate this to Henry (watching from backstage) by scratching his elbow, or patting his knee. And when the question was "Will my wife and I remain happy?," Henry could answer, "The next seventeen years will be as happy as the first seventeen," shocking the audience with his vast knowledge of their private lives. There was nothing, it seemed, he didn't know.

But his most famous trick was called the Mango Tree. He had a small wooden box, about four feet high, covered with a cloth. Into this he laid a little earth, and on top of the earth he placed a mango seed. After a few seconds he removed the cloth and there was a little mango tree, about six inches high, its roots in the earth he had placed in the box. Then he draped the cloth over the box again, and when he removed it there was the mango tree—but this time three feet high and a half-foot in diameter. No one knew how he did it—except, of course, for the white magicians, who were performing the same trick. But no one seemed to notice them, because they were not Prince Aki de Rajah.

He was Prince Aki de Rajah for the next two and a half years. And who knows how much longer he would have stayed that way, had it not been for a tragedy, a tragedy born of desire.

For Tom Hailey was—as he would tell you himself, given half the chance—a dyed-in-the-wool breast man. When he looked at a woman, he saw her breasts and little else. Little else even mattered to him. He called them *balboas*. Henry had no idea where such an expression might have come from. But a night wouldn't pass, as both of them peered through curtains at the crowd assembling for the show, when Tom Hailey wouldn't point, then lean down and whisper in Henry's ear: *Look at the balboas on that one!* Henry would look at them and nod; he didn't know what else to do. (Henry, it should be said, was not a breast man; Henry was not, nor did he become, the type of man who separated and segmented woman into smaller parts. When he loved a woman he loved all of her, every inch, from the nail on her big toe to the last hair on her head. Even I knew that—I, whom he never loved.)

Through the course of the show, Tom Hailey surveyed the audience for balboas adequate to his longing. The plunging sweetheart necklines popular in the late 1930s were a gift from the gods; cleavage sang a siren's song only he could hear. The chest that rose and fell with every breath like an ocean's wave was the place he yearned to rest his head that night. He closed his eyes and imagined their secret nipples, the *X* that marked the spot on the map of his desire. He was like a drunk or a junkie: he *had* to have them, and he had to have more of them, always more. He had always liked them big, but over the years he had to have them bigger, and then bigger still. Eventually they had to be outrageously huge, huge in a way other men might find distasteful, or even freakish. Brassiere-challenging balboas. No teardrops or heart shapes for Tom Hailey: he demanded the mythic breasts of yore, breasts that in the wrong hands could be deadly, smothering, breasts that only he could handle, that only he could appropriately love. Breasts that cried out for him to love them.

Some years ago, he discovered and introduced himself to a certain pair. This was Cincinnati, 1939. Henry and Tom Hailey came through Cincinnati often, because the Rajah was popular there. There was also a surprising fecundity of humongous balboas. *Must be something in the water,* Tom Hailey mused with a sigh. *How I envy the children here, suckling at their mama's teat.* Henry had just turned eighteen a week before. Tom Hailey had stuck a candle in a muffin and sung him the song and said, *I know exactly what I'm getting you for your birthday. I just don't have it yet.* Henry said he was happy to wait. *That's what I like about you,* Tom Hailey said. *One of the 247 things. You're happy to wait. Good things come to those who do.*

The good thing came in the middle of a hot Cincinnati night.

In the darkness of sleep, Henry heard laughter, a commotion, something being knocked over and broken, and woke when a light edged harshly beneath his eyelids.

"Wake up, Rajah," Tom Hailey said, shaking him by the shoulder. The first thing he was able to focus on was Tom Hailey's big ears, which appeared to flap before his eyes in the dreamy delirium of sleep. "I have your present."

That's when he realized someone else was there as well: he heard a women's lilting giggle coming from somewhere beyond the door.

"Who's out there?" Henry said, before Tom Hailey placed a hand over his mouth and whispered: "Remember," he said. "You're still the Rajah." And he winked. "Got it?" Henry nodded. "And if she's cold at first, don't worry. When a cold mama gets hot, she sizzles!"

His breath wafted on a magic carpet of gin, a smell Henry had known all of his life. But it was different, for while his father drank in sadness, Tom Hailey drank in joy.

"Who is it?" Henry said softly.

"Just a girl," Tom Hailey. "A girl who wants to see your mango tree. Rajah!" he said, quite loudly this time. "Allow me to introduce to you one of your biggest fans." He winked again, as if to say, *Biggest: get it?* "Bess. Come on in, Bess."

She appeared at the doorway of his bedroom, a woman Henry recognized from earlier that evening. *Balboa alert!* Tom Hailey had said, pointing her out from behind the curtains. "Face like a horse, but from the right angle you can make the face disappear. I'll show you how one day."

She did have something of the equine about her: large teeth, a nose in which the nostrils were most predominant, and big brown eyes on either side of her face, bright-red lips. But the rest of her was all udder. She looked at Henry with the beaming, vacant expression of someone meeting a star. Then she glanced at Tom Hailey, who gave her a reassuring nod, and she approached the bed where Henry lay.

"Prince Aki de Rajah," she said, and bowed, as if before royalty. "It is my utmost pleasure to meet you."

"With emphasis on the pleasure." Tom Hailey could not stop winking. Then to her: "His English is getting better, but he still doesn't understand a lot." Then to Henry: *"Kubu mufti. Kubu ma june-ko."*

Bess Reed sat down on the edge of his bed. He wasn't wearing a shirt, and he pulled the sheet up to cover his chest. But she pulled it down. "Me, Bess," she said, pointing to herself. "Okay?"

Henry nodded.

His chest had been turned the same color brown as his face, and Bess appeared entranced by it. She touched it and laughed again. She looked back at Tom Hailey, who was now standing just inside the door. "You sure this is okay?" she said.

"Never been surer of anything in my life," he said. "Where he comes from, it's a tradition. Eighteenth birthday. He has to become a man or there is great shame attached. He has to wander in the jungle for a week or something, showing penance."

"We wouldn't want that," Bess said. She held Henry's face in her hands the way a mother would.

Tom Hailey met Henry's horrified stare with a compassionate smile. "Don't worry, son," he said. "It's all going to be fine. Better than fine. Bess will treat you special. Now, I guess I should make myself scarce. Unless you need me for something."

"We're okay from here, aren't we, dear?" Bess said. "But maybe you want to help me with my clasp?"

His eyes lit up. "Gladly," Tom Hailey said. "Oh so gladly."

He took off her dress and took his time about it, and Henry and he both watched as she came spilling out of her brassiere. Henry thought they would never stop, and Tom Hailey wished they wouldn't. When they did, Tom Hailey turned off the light and left.

The next morning, breakfast was unnaturally quiet. Tom Hailey spread jam on his biscuit, and surreptitiously watched Henry hungrily put away his eggs—scrambled with cheese.

"You okay?" he asked him.

Henry kept chewing, and didn't lift his gaze from the plate. "I'm okay," he said.

Tom Hailey smiled, and winked, and they never spoke of the encounter again.

So it would come as no surprise that Tom Hailey was with a woman the night he died, one he'd eyed peering from behind the curtain as she sat there rapt by the Rajah's performance. Her name was Muriel Szakmary. She'd been in the second row, accompanied by a girlfriend, whom every few minutes she would elbow excitedly. Muriel was just his type: not particularly attractive, but not without her own peculiar charms. Two of them. Tom took her out to dinner, and as he gazed at the voluptuous paradise across the table, a piece of half-chewed steak fat lodged in his throat. He choked on it, and collapsed right there in the restaurant where he was eating. Henry was already back in his hotel room, reading, so he wouldn't know for several hours that he had lost yet another father. And more.

For when Tom Hailey died he took the secret of his pigmentation process with him. Henry tried to replicate it for the funeral, but he took too many pills, and on the morning of the service he was a Negro again, and as a Negro was not allowed to attend the funeral. He was not allowed to attend the funeral of the man who had become his father and saved his life. The man who had made him what he was.

Slowly, over the next few weeks, he became white again, or whitish. He never completely returned to his natural skin color. He didn't know what that was, though: it had been so long since he'd seen it. It had been so long since he had been himself, he had no idea who that might be. He went back to playing three-card monte. He looked at every man who paused before his table, at his skin, waiting for one of them to be Mr. Sebastian. And one of them was—Henry knew it—but Mr. Sebastian knew better than to show his face, knew how to transform himself into someone completely different. Much like Henry himself. He was there and not there, always.

Henry made enough to rent a room on the second floor of a spinster's house—a woman who might have been his mother's age, if his mother were alive. She was a quiet woman, but she liked to sit with Henry and watch him eat. She said, "You have such good manners. The way you hold your knife and fork, always spread your napkin on your lap first thing. People don't have good manners these days. Not anymore." He knew nothing. He was lost in the world. It was as though he were being born all over again, and had to learn, from

the beginning, simply how to be. But he remembered this much—
how to hold a fork and knife.

Luckily for him, there was a war. World War II. Henry enlisted into
the infantry immediately, and became a member of the Twenty-
second Infantry Division, stationed in France. France! He had always wanted to go to France. His sister had, too. She showed him
pictures of Paris from one of the travel magazines she found in the
trash. But she never got to go there, and he did.

The war made him happy. It's where he made his first real
friends—Charlie Smith, Dayton Mulroney, Mookie Marks. Each
had his own talent: Charlie played mandolin, Dayton spoke French,
Mookie sang like a bird, and Henry, of course, had his cards.
Throughout the vicious campaign that took them across France and
finally to the Battle of the Hürtgen Forest, they fought and slept
and ate together. Other units had singers, musicians, and overedu-
cated French-speaking soldiers. But theirs was the only one with a
magician. It was so beautiful there, Henry thought it would be a
good place to die.

But he didn't die. He had a number of opportunities to die, but
he lived through them all. None of them died. Though countless
men were killed, burned to death, blown into pieces by panzers,
the four of them escaped every confrontation unharmed—without
a scratch on them. Their crazy luck was attributed to Henry and his
magic. Henry did a few card tricks in foxholes, and once made a
grenade disappear, so they knew he had skills. But Mookie Marks
believed he had special powers that protected them, and he told
people stories he was said to have experienced firsthand, most of
which he had made up out of whole cloth. It was said that Henry
could change a bullet's path with a whisper. That he could make
them all invisible with a sigh. All around them bombs exploded, but

none could penetrate the shield Henry had created to surround and protect them.

One day, during a break in a firefight, Henry and Mookie were smoking, waiting for something to happen. Charlie was showing Dayton a picture of his ex-girl back home, Katie Baker. He called her that even though that wasn't her name anymore. It was Katie Lasker, because she'd married somebody else. He still liked to look at her picture. It was like this sometimes. Terrible end-of-the-world noise and fire, as if all the evil of the world were focused on you and you alone. Then quiet. Time for a smoke.

Henry turned to Mookie. "Stop saying it, Mookie."

"Stop saying what?"

"About the magic. About the 'magic powers' protecting us from the Germans. People are talking. I don't like it."

"But it's true," Mookie said. "You're like our guardian angel. Except you're not an angel. You're a man, right here with us. And you can *shoot*. Better than an angel, if you ask me."

"I'm not a magician, Mookie," Henry said. "I can play around with cards is all, stuff like that. I can't do anything, you know, like that. *Nada.*"

In France, during World War II, Henry Walker tried to become someone different, someone new. But it wasn't working out.

Mookie laughed. "Remember that time you read my mind?" he said.

"A lucky guess."

"And how many times have you, you know, made those eggs appear, from nowhere? Good eatin' they were, too. And you can make a pack of cigarettes rise off a table, no strings attached. Crazy stuff, Henry. So don't be so bashful. You got us covered. I love you for it."

Charlie said, "Me too. I love you. With all my guts."

The sound of a rifle shot soared from nowhere into nothing, and the three of them sighed. So it began, again.

"I've never seen you miss," Charlie said, gently kicking Henry's rifle with the toe of his boot. "Never. You've killed more Germans than Eisenhower."

"That's not magic," Henry said. "That's hatred."

"I hate 'em, too, but I miss sometimes."

"Not Germans," Henry said, and he stared Charlie down. "I don't hate Germans. I hate one man. The Germans, they're just practice for him."

"What the hell's that supposed to mean? I still think—"

"You can think what you want to," Henry said, as another shot, then another, whizzed past above their heads. "But I don't want you talking about it anymore."

"No more talking," Mookie said. "For you. But it's true and you know it."

Mookie picked up a handful of mud and tossed it into Henry's face. He shook his head. "What's the big deal either way? I mean, if it helps me to believe it, if it helps me feel less like I'm going to die any second, what's the big deal?"

Henry only looked at him, the mud as he wiped it from his cheek turning half his face black. "No big deal, I guess," Henry said. "No big deal at all."

"It is a big deal, though," Charlie said.

"It is," Dayton said. "Life is a big deal. Staying alive. That's important to me. And I want to thank the man who's making that happen. Thank you from the bottom of my boots."

"You keep yourself alive," Henry said. "Not me."

Charlie turned to Henry and said, "I'll prove it."

They were all leaning against the wall of a trench. The Germans had them blocked on two fronts; they were far outnumbered. Once the shooting began again, in earnest, it felt the same as it had before, as if it would never stop. The sky seemed to be raining bullets. Birds trying to fly high above the terror below were killed anyway, and their limp bodies fell into the trench and bled on their boots.

It was into this hailstorm of certain death that Charlie confidently stood. He smiled, arms outstretched, proud and cocky, illuminated by the sun.

"Here I am, you fucking asshole Germans!" he cried. "Shoot me if you can! Kill me! I dare you to even try!"

He stood there for a good five seconds before Mookie and Henry hauled him back in by his ankles. "You stupid fucking idiot," Henry said.

But Charlie was laughing. So was Dayton. Mookie looked at him, then at Henry, quiet amid the hellish clamor.

"There's not a scratch on him," he said. "Not a scratch."

"Like I said," Henry said, "it doesn't matter to me. Say what you want. If it helps."

Word of his powers spread from soldier to soldier. It was said he could make tanks disappear, turn bullets into feathers, and read the minds of the enemy. Some said the success of the invasion of Normandy was in large part due to him.

By the time the war was over, Henry Walker had become the most famous magician in the world.

But this is not the story I meant to tell.

I used to read novels, when I could still turn the pages. The best ones always started talking about one thing and, almost without your knowing it, would switch to another. Or the author would say, *I'm going to tell you about this one thing,* and proceed to tell you about something else entirely. This was always the kind of book I liked. They seemed more like life, the way people will start off with every intention of going to the store but end up in the park, or dig a hole to plant a tree and end up finding a buried treasure. Intentions appear to be the most fragile things in the world. The story I meant to tell was the one explaining why Henry Walker never loved me. He never loved me. And it's not because he still loved Marianne La Fleur, because he didn't. It was because she failed to love him.

So the war was over, the troops had returned. Though welcomed by a thousand cheering Americans as their ship docked in New York Harbor, like so many others Henry came home to no one. The Gershwins wrote about it. *They're writing songs of love, But not for me* . . . All of Henry's war friends, though alive, disappeared into the fabric of the country, never to be seen again. Dressed in his army green, Henry walked through the music, noise, and confetti, duffel bag over his shoulder, invisible without even having to try to be. In his heart he wished the war could have gone on forever. He had made himself new there, but, coming back, he felt old again, the same. He was in the same place he was before it began.

He thought he could get in an hour or so of the monte before lunch.

Then he heard his name.

"Henry?"

He stopped, turned, saw no one.

Walked on.

"Mr. Walker!"

Someone knew his name, and nothing could have shocked him more. That someone was a small man in a double-breasted herringbone suit, a gray felt fedora. He was carrying a thin leather briefcase in one hand and waving excitedly with the other, pushing toward Henry through the crowd. Henry assumed that he was in some kind of trouble, that his old life had caught up with him, or he with it. This man had discovered the past and was suing him for—what would it be? Pretending to be a Negro? Faking a fakir?

It couldn't be good, whatever it was. So Henry turned away, and walked faster.

The man fell into step right beside him, but, being a foot shorter, he had to take two steps for every one of Henry's. He was almost running.

"Kastenbaum," the man said. "Edgar Kastenbaum." He stuck out his hand, and Henry ignored it, kept walking, but with absolutely no idea where he walking to. Already this Kastenbaum was breathing hard, and sweating. But he was still right beside him.

"I prefer 'Eddie,' " he went on, smiling, "not 'Ed.' 'Ed' to me always seemed so, I don't know, *grown up.* So serious. My grandfather was an Ed, *is* an Ed. The Lord gave him seven smiles to use over the course of his life, and he never used them up. My father inherited them and has stored them away for safekeeping. To me that's an Ed. An Eddie, on the other hand, has a side to him that's funny and fun-loving—*twenty-three skidoo,* to coin a phrase. So call me Eddie. Or Kastenbaum. If you ever lose your temper with me—and I'm sure you will, it happens to the best of us—you can call out—angrily—*Kastenbaum!* It sounds better. And I'll call you Mr. Walker. Or the Great Henry. Though I'd like to think of something more eye-catching. Or ear-catching, as the case may be. Any ideas?"

Henry kept walking, and looked down at the diminutive Eddie. "Any ideas?" Henry said. "Ideas about what?"

"I imagine you had a lot of time to think about it, on the voyage home. Welcome home, by the way."

Henry stopped and looked at this man, and this man in turn stopped and seemed quite relieved to be able to do so. "Home?" Henry said. "I don't even know what that word means." Even with the sun out, the city was a gray, monstrous, ugly thing. He couldn't see himself becoming a part of it. But then, he couldn't see himself becoming a part of anything.

"Would you like a cigarette?" Kastenbaum proffered a pack. "I don't smoke them myself, but I keep them for those who do."

"Listen, I don't know you," Henry said. "And I don't know what you're talking about. Either you're completely insane or you've got me confused with someone else. Now, if you'll excuse me, I need to find a job."

"Why?"

"Because I enjoy eating food and sleeping with a roof over my head."

Kastenbaum held up the briefcase. "But I already have a job for you," he said. "In fact, I have a hundred."

"A hundred? What do I need with a hundred jobs?"

"Dates," he said. "Performances. Magic performances. You're booked through August."

"What could you possibly mean?"

"You're famous, Mr. Walker," he said. "Surely you know that."

Kastenbaum knelt, right there on the sidewalk, and neatly flipped the golden locks of his briefcase open. From it he removed a sheaf of newspaper clippings, which Henry began to leaf through, one by one.

"There are twenty-three of them," Kastenbaum said. "And I'm sure there were many more."

"They're . . . all about me," Henry said.

"That's right."

"But—" He thought of Mookie and his mouth, and Charlie, and all the men he had lived and fought with over the last four years. He knew how it had happened.

"Who are you?" Henry said, hoping for an answer, a real one, something that would relieve him of his confusion.

But it didn't come. Kastenbaum stood tall, and stuck his chest out proudly. "I'm your manager, Mr. Walker."

Now it was Kastenbaum's turn to walk, and Henry, pulled along by the powerful undertow of this mysterious man—as well as plain old curiosity—followed.

"Where are we going?" Henry asked him.

Kastenbaum looked straight ahead, toward the future, and smiled. "Your office, of course."

On the way there, Kastenbaum gave him the lowdown, how word of his magical exploits had traveled from division to division, battalion to battalion, by boat, plane, and submarine, back to the shores of America itself. He was hot. He was very hot. He was on fire, he was so hot.

"And there's only one rule in show business," Kastenbaum told him. "And that rule is to strike while the iron's hot. I saw an opportunity for you to capitalize on your success overseas. I couldn't contact you, of course, so I thought it best to proceed on my own."

"You mean for *you* to capitalize," Henry said.

"Don't blow a fuse," Kastenbaum said. "Mutually beneficial relationships are the best relationships."

"I don't want a manager, Mr. Kastenbaum."

"It's too late for that, Mr. Walker: you have one."

"Well, you're fired."

"Strictly speaking, since I was never really hired, it would be impossible for you to fire me. We never signed a contract. And if there's one rule in show business, without a contract you've got nothing." He gave Henry a moment to become completely confused. "I also feel it's precipitate to reject something before you know what it is you're rejecting. Give it a moment. We're here."

They had stopped in front of a four-story brick-and-glass building on Bridge Street. A sullen building, more depressing than imposing. All the windows were dark and soaped over. Where the doorknob should have been was just a hole. To the left a dead bird lay decomposing in the alley.

"It was the best I could secure with the funds available to me at the time. Think of it as temporary. Meanwhile, we can fix it up."

Henry sighed.

"Come on," said Kastenbaum.

Henry took one step up the landing and looked up at the number on the building, painted in black above the doorway.

"It's 702," Henry said.

"That's right—702 Bridge Street. Commit it to memory. Is there a problem?"

Henry was frozen, staring at the numbers. "No," he said, in a low whisper. He sounded like he was talking to himself. "I'm fine."

Three flights of wooden stairs, unlit—an ascent into darkness. They passed the dark doorways of Moody's Rubber Supply, Swinburne's Novelties. Finally to a plain door fronted with clouded glass and, beyond it, a very bright light. The light radiated from it as if behind that door were the sun itself. As if God lived there.

"After you, boss," Kastenbaum said, opening the door.

Henry let the door swing open and the light fall over him. He stood there as if transfixed by a vision. Or visions. The office was indeed brightly lit, but this was not where all the light was coming from: shoulder to shoulder, lining the walls of the Great Henry's waiting room, were fifteen of the most beautiful women he had ever seen in his life. Blondes, brunettes, redheads, with legs that never seemed to stop, and balboas—oh, the balboas. He knew Tom Hailey was scratching at his coffin now, trying to get out, so he could share this view of the skate-arounds with his former employee.

He looked down at Kastenbaum, who had already learned to anticipate the next question. "They're here for the audition, boss," he said.

The audition? Henry thought. But he knew not to ask for a clarification, knowing that one would be forthcoming, and soon.

"You'll need an assistant, of course," Kastenbaum said.

"Of course."

Henry smiled. Kastenbaum smiled. It was impossible, but true: ten minutes off of the boat and they had become something like best friends. Bob Hope and Bing Crosby. A pair. Sometimes these things happen in a moment. Such was the case with them.

"You have that contract handy?" Henry said.

"Right here in my trusty briefcase."

"Show me where to sign."

And they walked through the beauty of the waiting room into another, smaller room—Henry's office—and closed the door behind them.

I don't know why it brings me such pleasure to imagine these women lining the walls of his office, like books on a shelf. They're the opposite of what I am: if they're the books, *I'm* the shelf. I should hate them for being who they are, or myself for being me. But I don't. I see them as Henry must have seen them—as a gift. A sign of life. Harbingers of good things to come. I can't hate them. What would the world be like without them? And what would they be like without me?

Henry had never had an assistant before, unless he counted Tom Hailey, who filtered through the audience before a show obtaining the knowledge Henry would later insert into his predictions. But he couldn't count Tom Hailey. In a way, Henry had been *his* assistant, a product of his indefatigable will to create the illusion Henry himself became. Without question, Tom Hailey had always been in charge. He hated him, of course, but he loved him even more; everything he was and everything he wasn't was because of Tom Hailey. His first life ended when Hannah was taken, and there was

no reason for him not to believe that, without Tom Hailey, the rest
of his life would have been no more than the elaboration of that
ending. Tom Hailey had taught him the single most important
thing he had ever learned: adaptation. That's what it's all about.
Adapting is the secret of survival. Without that, without the willing-
ness and ability to change, nothing would be alive at all. So Henry
became black for a while, then a shade lighter, and now he was
white again. But he would gladly have turned green if it meant he
could linger in the heart of his own waiting room forever, just gazing around him at the women there. According to Kastenbaum,
though, he had to send them all away. Except one.

"We have to do this *now?*" Henry said. He sat in what Kastenbaum had pulled back and almost ceremonially dubbed "his chair,"
a high-backed, unevenly swiveling executive's chair with the stuff-
ing pouring out of its seat. Still, it was the most comfortable thing
his rear end had known in years. The walls of the office were bare
brick.

"We have to get right on it," Kastenbaum said. He tapped on his
watch. "Time waits for no man. You don't hear time saying, *I'll wait
for you up here at the corner.* Nope. Waits for no man."

"But," Henry said, "can't they stick around for a while? We
could all just go out for a nice dinner or something."

"Sounds like fun. I'm sure they'd enjoy it as much as you would.
But I've made calculations." He looked at his watch, a Bulova.
"And if we don't start now, there's no way we can put a show to-
gether in time."

"How long do we have?"

"Six weeks," Kastenbaum said. "Forty-two days."

Six weeks? Henry had never put together a show of any kind on
his own—six weeks seemed impossible. But then it was as if the
spirit of Tom Hailey himself appeared behind his fancy chair and
squeezed his shoulders and said, *Do you think that's what a fish thought*

when he realized he had to grow feet to become a mammal and travel on dry land? Sure. But he did it. That fish grew feet and he did it.

Henry shrugged his shoulders and sighed. "Let's begin," he said.

One by one they came, and one by one they were sent away. Like this:

"And your name is?"

"Victoria Harris."

Hair falling to her shoulders in waves, lips decorated in a patriotic red, green eyes, long lashes, and breasts seemingly ready to bust through her bra's harness. Henry couldn't help thinking of Tom Hailey and Lauren, his secretary. Henry had walked in on them once in Tom Hailey's office. Lauren was splayed across the top of his desk, and Tom Hailey was mauling her as if he were a carnivorous animal. She appeared not to mind Henry's presence in the least, and Tom Hailey didn't stop. Henry remembered the cigarette burning in the ashtray.

"And you're interested in becoming a magician's assistant," said Kastenbaum, who asked the bulk of the questions.

"Oh, very much!" She was an eager one. Overeager, possibly.

"What experience do you have in this field?"

"Well," she said, "none, per se. But I've been an assistant to someone all of my life. How much different could it be?"

"Would you be comfortable onstage, before hundreds of people, many of whom will be looking right at you? At least at parts of you." Kastenbaum darted a playful glance at Henry.

"I like being admired," she said. "Before the war, I modeled nylon stockings. I wanted to go back to it, now that we have them again, but there are other girls now. Younger ones."

"Thank you, Victoria," Kastenbaum said, making notes on his

legal pad. "I think that's everything. We have your telephone number. We'll be in touch."

"I'm single," she said, looking at Henry. "If that makes any difference."

"What difference would that make?" Kastenbaum said.

"For traveling? I'd be free to travel. I'd be . . . free." She kept her eyes on Henry.

"Wonderful," Kastenbaum said. "Thanks."

She left. After the door clicked behind her, Kastenbaum slowly began nodding.

"I liked her," he said. "She had a spark. And her, um, particular attributes would have the men in the audience gazing her way. And their wives distracted by their husbands gazing her way. You call that misdirection, right?"

"Right."

"So?"

"She's nice," Henry said. "And very nice to look at. But no. I don't think so."

"You don't think so?"

"No." Henry sighed. It felt as if he'd just crawled out of a foxhole, and now here he was rejecting a series of gorgeous women who only wanted to work beside him, disposing of rabbits and birds and being cut in half. There'd been women, lots of them. French, German. One from a country he'd never heard of. But the rooms they were in were always too dark for him to see them that well. He liked it the way it was now, with the lights on. "Just no," he said. "She doesn't work for me."

Kastenbaum appeared depressed for a moment, but rallied just as quickly. His emotions bounced like a rubber ball. She was the tenth girl they'd seen that day.

"Okay, then," he said. "Let's get the next one in here." He looked down at his sheet and smiled. "This can't be her real name," he said. "Can't be." He rose, almost laughing, stuck his head out the door, and called her name. "Marianne La Fleur, please."

Henry knew she was the one the moment she walked in. He told me this exactly: *The moment she walked in, I knew.* I said, "Because she reminded you of Hannah." I said she must have had the same blond hair or the same blue eyes, the same luminosity, someone so bright he would have to turn away from her to get any sleep at all. This Marianne would have to be a grown-up version of the girl he had been looking for since she'd been taken. Not looking the way the police had looked, for a few pointless weeks—Henry looked for her the way you look at a landscape and think, *Something's missing.* Her absence was everywhere. And I thought he must have found it in Marianne La Fleur.

"No," he said. "You're exactly wrong."

"Exactly wrong?" I said. "How can you be exactly wrong?"

He told me how.

Marianne La Fleur was dark, inside and out. Her name was the only bright thing about her. Her black hair, contrary to the style of the period, appeared to have been given only scant attention with a brush, and grew past her shoulders with no apparent intention of stopping. She was the kind of woman whom it was impossible to imagine ever as a child, but who must have been born just as she appeared before them that day, her round chocolate-brown eyes not sparking but smoldering, and her wrists so thin he could hold one in his hand like the stem of an umbrella. She didn't smile. Little about her was even female; she had done nothing to herself the way the others had, nothing to make her seem more attractive than she actually was.

This, I asked Henry, *this is what you fell in love with?*

So?

The Great Houdini was killed by a sucker punch in the stomach, he replied. *Some things are impossible to understand.*

. . .

As Kastenbaum was about to begin the Q and A, Henry raised his hand. "I'll take this one," he said.

"Sure," Kastenbaum said. "Sure."

"So, Miss La Fleur," Henry said, trying to keep his voice from shaking. "You have some familiarity with magic?"

"I do," she said. Henry and Kastenbaum leaned in closer: they didn't hear her. "I do," she said again, this time with a little more volume.

"Oh. Well. That's good, isn't it?" Henry looked at Kastenbaum, surprised: she was the first who did. The others were just applying for a job, any job. "Experience," Henry said. "Good."

But Kastenbaum scowled. "And what would that be exactly?" he said.

"Well, I'm a bit of a magician myself. Not like you, of course. But a bit of one." She stared at Henry for a beat, directly into his eyes. "May I?"

"Please," Kastenbaum said. "By all means."

"I'm going to pick a number between one and ten," she said. "What is it?"

Henry shrugged. He looked at Kastenbaum. "Three?"

"Yes," she said. "Three."

Henry laughed. For the first time in a long time, he laughed. "Well done," he said.

"Thank you."

"But that's not *magic*," Kastenbaum said. He looked at Henry. He didn't like what was going on here. "Had you said 'nine,' she could have said yes as well. We have no way of knowing."

"Not knowing," Henry said, nodding. "That's what magic is all about."

She was hired on the spot.

. . .

That night, Kastenbaum warmed the stool of a bar until he fell off of it, drunk; cracking his head against the concrete floor sobered him a little. A couple of sailors lifted him up and showed him, gently, the way out, and he thanked them, and stumbled down Broadway, lost in the night and the neon glare, in the laughter and song that filled the city these days. But Kastenbaum was not laughing. He was not singing. He was spent. He had lived a lifetime in one day. It was remarkable, actually. Everything had gone exactly as he had planned—and it was, admittedly, a crazy plan; everything about it was. But it had worked! If there was one rule in show business, he thought, it was this: no risk, no reward. And he had risked every-thing. Every penny he had in the world, his entire future. First, there was the rent for the office. Henry's apartment was expensive, as was the equipment he had purchased, all from money Kasten-baum's father had loaned him. He had booked performances. He had even had some very nice stationery made, raised black letters on linen paper: *Edgar Kastenbaum, Manager.* He had gone to the docks to find his first and only client, Henry Walker, and he had found him, and through equal amounts charm and sensible persua-sion he had convinced Henry to throw in his chips with him. Charm and persuasion: he had it. But also belief. Belief in himself. If he believed in himself, he felt he could do anything. His father always told him the sky was the limit if he simply believed in himself. How many times had his father told him the story of his own life, his slow and steady rise from the son of a simple farmer to the largest distrib-utor of tulip bulbs in America? How he had made his way from the bottom—from *below* the bottom, in fact, since there is nothing lower than being the son of a farmer with no farm—going door to door, block to block, town to town, until the name of Orwell Kastenbaum became the single most trusted name in tulips. WE SELL KASTEN-

BAUM TULIPS! The signs were everywhere. Tulips! Tulips, he said, put a roof over your head, they put shoes on your feet, they feed you. The water flows from the spigot because of tulips. Who would have ever thought of it—tulips? It was insane. *I was insane,* his father would say. Mine was a crazy dream—but what dream *isn't* crazy? Can a dream be a dream and be sensible? *No.* A sensible dream is a plan. Men like us dream, and our dreams come true because we believe in ourselves. *Go!*

Thus was Edgar Kastenbaum launched in flight from his father's nest.

And everything had gone exactly as planned (halfway through the afternoon, he was already looking forward to the stories he would tell his own son, were he ever to have one)—until Marianne La Fleur walked into the office and Henry Walker hired her. Who knew such a thing could have happened? He had thought—assumed—that he and Henry were on the same page, at least as far as what constituted true female beauty. He thought every American male had pretty much the same ideal—the Vargas Girl. Sly, sultry, sexy. Ready for anything. Made you drool just to think about. A magician's assistant was a woman men adored and other women hated. She had to be as beautiful as the magic was incredible! Though she did nothing other than stand there and hand the master whatever gaffed instrument of magic he requested, and sometimes float and sometimes get cut in half, a magician with a plain assistant was no different from a man with an ugly wife: not only was it hard to look at the woman, but you wondered about the man who would have her.

Marianne La Fleur was not ugly, though; she was something worse. She was scary. Or no—haunted. She was a haunted woman about whom, when you looked at her, you would wonder, What *happened* to her? Whatever it was, it must have been something terrible. She was odd, and everything she did was odd. Even when she blinked, she blinked slowly, as though a lot of thought went into it, as if she wanted you to know that she was blinking *for a reason*. Ask her a question, and there was always an uncomfortable pause before she replied. Even the simplest question. *How are you?* One, one thousand; two, one thousand; three. *Fine,* she said. One, one thousand. *How are you?* And the way she dressed. Her clothes had clearly belonged to at least one person before her, if in fact they belonged to her at all: she could have stolen them off of a clothesline on the way into the interview. The top was too large and frilly (her chest was painfully flat, almost nonexistent), the skirt tight and plain, and the heels of her shoes—her old black leather heelless shoes—were edged in mud. Where had she come from? Kastenbaum imagined her growing from the soil like a plant, or a weed, and then pulling herself out by the roots. And now she was the assistant. Henry was captivated by her for some reason Kastenbaum could not begin to fathom.

But, walking home that night, he continued to believe in himself. Like his father, he was a leader, a captain, the kind of man you'd want at the helm when the water got rough. Perhaps Marianne La Fleur would not sink their ship. He wasn't sanguine about it, he wasn't sanguine at all. But there was nothing he could do. He had to carry on.

The days passed quickly. The first show, at the Emporium, was now only two weeks away. Henry and Marianne had been preparing all this time. Kastenbaum had invested in all the latest equipment: half a dozen false-bottom boxes, invisible string, mirrors. There was also a top-quality and very expensive revolving wheel of death (Henry had learned to throw knives while in the army), which, because of its large size, Kastenbaum stored in one of his father's warehouses. And there were various experimental electrical devices to spice up what was, admittedly, a generic routine. Kastenbaum looked forward to watching them explore and experiment with all of this. But Henry insisted on practicing with Marianne in private.

"That's ridiculous, Henry," Kastenbaum had said. "I have to know what's going on."

"Why?"

"Because I'm the *manager*, that's why," he said. "The front man. I'm the guy who sells you. If there's one rule in show business, it's that the manager has to be part of the routine. The invisible part. Behind the scenes, you know."

"It sounds like there are a lot of rules in show business," Henry said.

"There are," Kastenbaum said. "And I'm not telling you half of them."

"I understand," Henry said. But Kastenbaum could tell he was only getting lip service. "And as soon as we can show you, you'll be the first to see the routine. But there's a process, in the beginning, something that has to happen between the magician and his assistant. In private. A relationship has to be established. Marianne will have to know my thoughts, and I hers. A mere glance her way, and she'll have to understand what she needs to do. If I give her my left hand instead of my right, that will mean one thing instead of another. If I smile at her, there will be a message concealed therein. The same with her. She has to have a sense of how things are going. If she glowers at me, even briefly, that will mean I have to pick things up a bit, do more to keep her attention—their attention, I mean. The audience. In other words, we have to be two halves of the same person, and that entails a period of privacy and closeness in order to create that reality. Of all the things an audience experiences at a magic show, that one thing alone, the relationship between the magician and his assistant, cannot be an illusion."

Kastenbaum didn't say what he was thinking, which was that this did not sound so much like the relationship between a magician and his assistant as it did the relationship between a man and his lover. But he couldn't say it, because he was on thin ice already: he could tell by the way Henry glanced at him, or glowered, and the way he smiled, or mostly didn't.

As Kastenbaum turned to leave, Henry grabbed his shoulder, stopping him in his tracks and turning him back to meet his gaze. "This is going to be great," Henry said. "It's going to be the greatest show in the history of magic. Every magician in the world will hear of it. Every single one. He'll know I'm here. He'll know I'm back. He'll know—"

"Who is 'he,' Henry?"

"What?"

"You said, 'He'll know I'm here.' Who is this 'he'?"

Henry shook his head. "Nobody," he said. "He's nobody."

Kastenbaum, of course, had assumed correctly: Henry wanted to be alone with Marianne La Fleur because he was in love with her, and because he wanted her to be in love with him. Kastenbaum, it would turn out, was correct about everything, always. It was his talent and his curse. Even then, he knew that they were doomed, that Marianne La Fleur would bring both of them to their knees. But Kastenbaum was Henry's Cassandra: as much as he believed in himself, he himself was never believed. He felt his father's spirit—though his father was still alive and living only two miles away—always hovering there above him, grading him as he had when Edgar was a child, quietly but sternly shaking his head, urging his son onward toward that bright star of success. But all Kastenbaum could see was darkness.

It would be nice, I think, if there were something inside of us like a string pull on a lamp that automatically clicked ON when we were loved by someone else. It would be nice if love had a certain and automatic return.

One night, in a deft mix of business and pleasure, Henry set an entire table while Marianne watched—china plates, shining silver, crystal wineglasses—out of thin air. Then lamb chops, carrots and peas, a loaf of bread (warm), and a bottle of 1897 Madeira, which he opened, somehow, with one pass of his right hand. Dinner was served.

He pulled out Marianne's chair, and she floated across the room to sit in it. She didn't actually float but only seemed to, her feet never appearing to touch the ground beneath her long kitchen-peasant skirt. Finally arriving, she gave him her version of a smile.

She didn't say a word about what she had just watched transpire.

"Well," he said, seating himself and placing the cloth napkin carefully in his lap. "What did you think?"

"About . . ."

"Dinner. The way it was produced. I think I'll call the act 'Ambrosia,' because ambrosia—"

"The food of the gods," she said. "I know. And I thought it was very fine."

Any other woman—any other mortal, for that matter—would have been astounded beyond measure at what he had just done. The fact that she wasn't—though immensely disappointing—was also oddly attractive. He was in love with the only person in the entire world who was not and never would be impressed with his magic.

She ate. For a few moments they didn't speak, the clattering of Henry's fork and knife against his plate the only sound.

Then Henry coughed. It was one of those coughs that started small but soon became impossible to stop. It went on until his face turned red and he gasped for breath.

For the first time that evening—for the first time ever, possibly—

Marianne gazed at him with what looked like a real human concern. "Are you feeling all right?" she asked him.

He nodded. "I must have gotten something stuck in my throat," he said. "But it's fine now."

"You're sure?"

"Of course," he said. "Not to worry. I'm a little tired. The first show is three nights away. And I won't even let Death stop me from doing it."

"Certainly not Death," she said.

He smiled. He began eating again, as did she. She kept staring at him, though, studying him, until he became unnerved by it.

"Is there something you want to say to me?" he asked her.

She shook her head, slowly, her face so pale now it seemed to disappear.

"The peas are perfect," she said, bringing three or four of them to her mouth, like eggs in the nest of her spoon. Henry watched her every movement. She was like a poem. There was nothing extraneous about her. She seemed to consist of only what was necessary for life and no more. If he could just look at her as she lived her life—as she read, slept, breathed—he would be a happy man at that moment. He felt it was all he needed.

Then, like a sudden clap of thunder, someone began to bang at the door.

"Henry! *Henry!* Let me in."

It was Kastenbaum. Henry sighed. "I'm not going to let him in," he said.

Marianne brought her napkin to her mouth, pressed it lightly against her lips, shook her head.

"No," she said. "Do. I'm tired. I think I'll go to bed."

She slept in the small guest room, which had once perhaps been a maid's quarters. There was room for a bed with a single mattress, a wooden table, a lamp, and not much more. But it appeared to be enough for her.

She stood. And though they had never kissed or even brought their bodies close to one another in an embrace, they looked at each other like lovers for whom it would be days, maybe months, before they would see each other again.

She went to her room and gently closed the door behind her.

Henry stood and went to the door. "Kastenbaum," he said, opening it. Kastenbaum flew in. His hair, usually brushed straight back and well oiled, with a natural if discreet part right down the middle, now fell into his eyes, which were mad. He strode from one end of the apartment to the other, from the dining area to the makeshift staging area in the back. He looked derisively at the materials he had purchased and thought of his father—his father, who would insist on being paid back for it all.

"Where is she?" he said.

"You'll keep your voice down," Henry said. "She's asleep."

"Exhausted from the many hours of preparation, no doubt."

"I asked you to keep your voice down."

"No you didn't," Kastenbaum said. "You *told* me to keep my voice down. You *ordered* me. Some partnership this is. You're a despot, is what you are. King Henry the Ninth."

"You're drunk," Henry said.

"Drunk?" Kastenbaum said. "Drunk? This is not drunk, my friend. When I'm drunk, I can neither walk nor talk. I can't open both eyes at the same time. I forget my name and my reasons for living. But a martini or three can give a man the confidence to say what he should be able to say when he's completely sober, if in fact he's a man at all."

"And what is it you needed three martinis to say to me?"

Something in Kastenbaum seemed to focus then. He finally had a sense of where he was. He looked at Henry, at the cornucopia on the table before him.

"I haven't had dinner," he said. "May I?"

Henry nodded. When Kastenbaum had started pounding at the

door, Henry had had a forkful of lamb on the way to his mouth, but had set it down to answer it; Kastenbaum picked the fork up and completed its journey. He closed his eyes, suffused with joy: this was exactly what he needed.

But something happened. After a moment or two, he stopped chewing. His eyes opened. He frowned. And he began to pull something from his mouth. Henry couldn't tell what it was, and neither could Kastenbaum, but that of course was the idea. It was invisible. It was an invisible string, magical debris, a long string that kept coming and coming and coming until Henry began to laugh. Kastenbaum couldn't help it: as mad as he was, he laughed as well. Kastenbaum had a high-pitched squealing and joyous laugh, like a baby's; it was impossible, hearing it, not to start laughing yourself. And so Henry laughed even harder, and soon they were both laughing so hard that they had to sit down at the table or they would fall onto the floor, literally weak in the knees. After a minute of this, the laughter inside of them was gone, all used up. They felt empty, as if they would never laugh again for the rest of their lives.

Kastenbaum placed a pea on the stem of a fork and launched it into the air by quickly depressing the prongs. It arced beautifully, right into his mouth. Seeing this, Henry remembered why he had loved Kastenbaum, almost from the moment they met.

"Do you know what the first rule of show business is, Henry? Any idea at all?"

Henry shook his head. "I never do."

"It's *trust*," Kastenbaum said. "The first rule of show business is trust. I have to trust you, and you have to trust me."

"I trust you, Eddie," he said. "I trust you completely."

Kastenbaum looked at Henry directly. "Well," he said, "that makes one of us."

Kastenbaum began tapping the fork on the edge of the table, steadily, like the ticking of a clock.

"You can trust me," Henry said, placing his hand on Kastenbaum's to stop the tapping. "We're in this together, Eddie, all the way. Without you, I'd have nothing."

Kastenbaum smiled, or tried to. But it was stillborn, dead on his face. "That's just it, Henry," he said. "You don't *have* anything. Neither of us has anything. Not yet. Your first time out, we can sell the show on anticipation alone. The Patriotic Prestidigitator. They love that hokey crap. But you got no track record, just this crazy story you brought back with you from the war. You're perfect now, golden. But that only lasts until the moment you get onstage, and the lights go up, and they see you, and every single body out there has two eyes, believe me: one wants to see you succeed, and the other wants to see you crash and burn. You don't get many chances to fail in this business, Henry. There're too many people in line behind you."

"That doesn't sound like a vote of confidence," Henry said.

Kastenbaum stood and walked back toward the staging area, where all the gaffs were arranged in a mysterious order down the middle of a long table. "Didn't know I got a vote," he said.

"And what's that supposed to mean?"

Kastenbaum picked up what looked like a full glass of water and turned it over; nothing came out. "I haven't even seen the show, Henry," he said. "I don't know what I'm selling—*who* I'm selling. What I'm going to see. You're going to open to a full house and every reporter in the city without another living person having seen what you're planning to do."

"I want to surprise you."

"I don't like surprises."

Henry looked away. "Eddie," he said. "About the show. It's a little . . . different."

Which was the last thing Kastenbaum wanted to hear. "A little different than what?"

"A little different than everything," he said. "Not exactly what I thought we'd do. But I try to keep myself open to change. To the life of it. You can't force these things. You have to let them grow. I don't know, Eddie. I like it, but—it's a little off the beaten path."

"All the more reason to show it to somebody," Kastenbaum said. "Somebody like me. So we can package it. So we can tell them what they're going to see before they see it, so they won't be too surprised when they do. This business, it's all about fulfilling expectations. Tell 'em what they're going to get and then give it to them. That's it! But if they come expecting to see a rabbit and you show them an elephant—I don't care how big it is, Henry—they're going to be disappointed. Little girls are going to be crying, and their mothers are going to ask for their money back, because they expected to see a rabbit and you showed them—"

"I get it," Henry said. "An elephant. Don't worry on that score. No rabbits. No elephants, either."

"It's like this," Kastenbaum said, picking up a deck of cards from a table with unnaturally high legs. He shuffled them and blindly removed a card from the middle. Without looking at it he said, "What card am I holding?"

Henry didn't blink. "The three of hearts," he said.

Kastenbaum smiled. "See? I love it."

"Why?"

"Because it's always the three of hearts with you." Kastenbaum slipped it back into the deck and sighed. He shook his head and looked at his friend. "You're not going to let me see it, are you?"

He knew the answer, but he had to ask.

"No," Henry said. "I'm sorry, Eddie. But I'm not."

"Can you at least tell me why?"

"You know why," he said.

"Ah," he said. "Of course. Marianne."

"Marianne. She brings a special . . . quality to the show. It's not something I can really describe, and if I could, if I tried to, I honestly don't think you'd like it."

"Why?"

"Because it violates the first rule of show business," Henry said.

"Which first rule?" Kastenbaum said.

Henry thought about it. "All of them," he said.

After Kastenbaum left, disconsolate, Henry washed the dishes and put them away. He wished he knew a way to make the dishes disappear, but he didn't; he had to wash them all himself. After this, he went to the far end of the living room, where he and Marianne practiced, and reviewed in his mind the order in which everything would occur, the things he would say. He had it memorized—every beat, every breath.

He turned off the lights, but before heading to his own bed he looked in on her. He gently pushed open her door. Moonlight shone through the window and brushed against her cheeks. Her long black hair was splayed wildly against her pillow, as if she'd been thrashing in her sleep. But she hadn't been, Henry knew that much, because he watched her like this every night, and she never moved, she barely even breathed. It was as if she had truly given her waking hours everything she could, every ounce of strength and will and energy, and now she rested and became (and only I, of course, would think of such a thing) much like me: frozen in her place. Some nights he even touched her, he held her hand, he placed his palm against her face—and still she didn't move. Tonight he sat beside her on the edge of her bed, and he leaned down and kissed her on the cheek, much as he had done to his mother on the day she died.

. . .

So no. He didn't love me, and I never expected him to. I never expected him even to *want* to. Believe it or not, there are men who have wished they could, who hear me talk, who see the spark in my eyes, who like my sense of humor—some men have wished I wasn't made of stone. They wished they could hold me. They wished I could hold them back. Still not love, maybe, but a wish for it, which is pretty good for a gal in the state I'm in.

But Henry could only love one person at a time, and when he did it was with everything he had. The kind of love that believed the world existed solely to provide a backdrop for their lives. This is how he had loved his mother, then Hannah, and finally Marianne. And when there was no one left to love, the same energy and passion fueled his hatred. And he hated the same way: one at a time, Mr. Sebastian being the eternal unlucky recipient. By the time he got to me, he had nothing left at all.

The morning of the day of the show, Kastenbaum awoke with a vision. It wasn't a dream, because it happened in the moments just after awaking, when you're not in one place or another. In the vision, he was sitting in the front of the Emporium, which was packed, dressed in his tuxedo. He was glowing with a smile so large his face could hardly contain it. And he was clapping wildly, as hard and fast as a human possibly could. But he was the only one. The rest of the audience didn't move. They might as well have been dead.

This is when he noticed that the stage was empty. No one was there. No one ever had been.

He stopped clapping, and it was silence all around.

Finally, his father walked on from the wings. He stood before them all.

"Please accept my apologies," he said. "This has been a greater failure than even I imagined it would be. As I'm sure we all imagined it would be. Stand up, Edgar," his father said, looking at him now for the first time. "Please, stand up."

Reluctantly, Kastenbaum did. He turned to look at the audience members behind him and saw that all of them had only one eye, planted like a Cyclops's in the middle of their heads.

"Let's give a big round of applause for the man responsible for this fiasco," his father said. "My son."

And his father began clapping. But he was the only one; the rest, the one-eyed audience, remained still, looking at Kastenbaum, as if trying to puzzle out how one man alone could have achieved the distinction of being such a monumental failure. His father continued clapping until Kastenbaum couldn't take it anymore. He took a knife from his pocket and hurled it at his father, and it headed straight for his heart. His father stopped clapping and watched the knife's approach without alarm. But Kastenbaum held his breath. The one-eyed audience did, too. As if in slow motion, they watched the knife's progress and gasped as it approached its target.

But it passed right through him, as though he were made of dust, and fell harmlessly to the floor behind him. The audience burst into applause as his father took bow after bow. He winked at his son and spoke so only Edgar could hear him.

"Now *that's* how it's done," he said.

As the audience filed into the theater on opening night, Kastenbaum couldn't help staring at their faces, confirming the presence of two eyes on each of them; he felt less uncertain about things when everyone did. One man had a patch, though—a war injury, he told Kastenbaum, who stopped him to ask about it.

But Kastenbaum wasn't himself. He wasn't even sure who he was supposed to be. The confident and outgoing businessman who had collared Henry Walker at the docks that day was no longer a part of him. It was as if that spirit had fled. The realization that everything he had hoped for and planned for—his entire future— was resting on the success or failure of one night overwhelmed him. He had trouble breathing and, getting dizzy, had to retreat to his seat. He'd wanted to see his father come in. His father had said he would come, but there was doubt in his voice. *Never been a big fan of the magic shows*, he had told Edgar. *Your grandmother became a spiritualist because of them, you know. She had a séance every Friday. The dead are the most garrulous people you're likely to find.*

Eddie never saw him.

There was no introduction for Henry, no music, no bold and foggy entrance. At just past seven, the lights went down suddenly, and a moment later, he walked out onstage. Kastenbaum had to admit, Henry looked phenomenal, every inch the master magician he was purported to be. He had the face for it: so solemn and serious, sturdy, drawn, and handsome. There was not an ounce of fear in him, or none that showed, at any rate: Kastenbaum knew there was plenty inside.

After the applause subsided and all was silence, he spoke.

"The art of illusion," he said, his voice ringing to the very back of the theater, "is an entertaining pastime." At this, a dove flew from his empty hand and, as it flew above the front rows, turned to a shiny golden dust that sparkled, flying like snow onto the heads of the very rich. "We could spend the night doing just that." He stepped to one side and behind him revealed that there were two of him there, and with another step there were three. With the snap of his fingers, his creations disappeared. Kastenbaum swore every last person there gasped. It must have been done with mirrors; Henry had a lot of them. But what did Kastenbaum really know? Thanks to Henry, nothing. "There is a greater magic than that," Henry said. "And we know what that is. It is the magic of love."

A light slowly began to bleed into the darkness on the other side of the stage, illuminating Marianne La Fleur. She looked ghostly there, standing alone so far away from Henry, draped in her long white gown. Henry looked the part of the perfect magician, but she was no assistant. This is when the last scrap of hope within Kastenbaum's heart began to disappear. This is when he knew that, whatever expectations the audience brought with them, no matter how grand, they were not going to be fulfilled.

"Love," Henry said, taking a step toward Marianne, who appeared not to notice him at all. "If we only understood how it worked. For surely it's a trick, an illusion. Can anything so wonderfully powerful, so mysterious, so beguiling, be real at all?"

Henry produced a rose out of midair—an old trick, hardly even worth doing. But then, as if he were catching butterflies, his other hand snatched at the air, and each time it did another rose was in it, until he held a dozen.

"Love must be real," he said. "It hurts too much not to be."

Those sitting in the front rows were the first to see it—the blood, dripping from the palms of his hands. The women covered their eyes. Those in the back rows leaned closer in, to be sure that what they thought they were seeing they actually were.

Kastenbaum held his breath.

"Thorns," Henry said, as the blood dripped onto the stage. Each drop, as it splattered there, evaporated into a tiny cloud of smoke. Then the little clouds came together and gathered into the shape of a heart. Henry blew on it, and the smoky heart traversed the stage toward Marianne, dissipating completely just as it reached her. The roses themselves turned to dust in his hands.

Kastenbaum watched Marianne. She paid very little attention to the heart coming toward her, and when it evaporated merely shrugged her shoulders—if, in fact, the almost imperceptible upward movement of her shoulders constituted a shrug. What kind of goddamn assistant was she supposed to be? She was doing absolutely *nothing*. This was the idea, of course, Kastenbaum got that. But why? Henry was right: he was violating every first rule of show business there was or ever had been, every first rule he could think of or even make up. And where were the props he had invested so much of his money in? Where was the reflecting table or the ghost machine? *Where was the revolving wheel of death?* He had spent weeks tracking one down and had spent over two hundred dollars on shipping alone. The day before Henry's ship docked, Kastenbaum had spent a hopeful night drinking by himself, spinning the wheel of death, and launching the long silver knives it had come with. He got pretty good, if he did say so himself. He couldn't wait to see what Henry, a true artist, would be able to do with it. One of the stories that had made its way into the *Herald Tribune* concerned the night he had dispatched three Germans with one knife—and one throw. The wheel's absence here was an affront to Eddie's every sensibility. It angered and saddened him. He slipped deeper and deeper into his seat.

Henry stared across the expanse of stage toward Marianne, who continued to ignore him, and who actually seemed unaware that she was onstage at all, that hundreds of people were watching her as well, waiting for her to do *something*. An assistant was supposed to be charming, cute, peppy, with a nice set of knockers and healthy gams. But it was hard to tell if Marianne had a body beneath her ghostly-white gown. And if she did, who would want to see it? Something Henry had done with the lights made her seem slighter and grayer than she ever had before, the rings beneath her eyes darker, as if, like the Cheshire Cat, she was going to disappear. But instead of leaving behind a smile, all she would leave behind were those rings.

"No," Henry said. "Love is not magic—at least, not when love goes unreturned. This is the sad situation you see before you tonight. Is this not something all of us, at some point in our lives, have experienced? Have we not, at some point in our lives, been on one side of this story or the other? It's enough to drive us insane. It's enough to make us do things we never thought we were capable of. To capture the one we want—any way we know how."

He swept his arm through the air, and the doors of the cabinet beside Marianne flung open, apparently by themselves. Marianne didn't move. Kastenbaum wasn't sure how Henry had done this. He moved up in his seat a little to watch more closely. It was a large, plain, oaken cabinet, half a foot taller than Henry. From where Kastenbaum sat, it appeared to be approximately three feet deep and five feet wide. The audience, finally, seemed intrigued. With another sweep of the arm, Marianne floated—as she always appeared to float—into the cabinet, and the doors shut quickly, and for the first time Henry crossed to her side of the stage—not to open the doors, but to lock them. He clamped the huge silver lock onto the doors and sighed.

"Now she is mine," he said.

There was a smattering of applause, but most of the audience were still too befuddled to respond. Plus, if Henry opened the cabinet and Marianne was not there—well, did he think they had been born yesterday? He had not even shown them the inside of the cabinet, or the back, or the bottom. Most magicians took the trouble to do this, at least. Had he done this, they would have had more reason to wonder why she was gone, if indeed she *was* gone, when he opened the doors again, if indeed anything interesting was going on here at all. Her disappearance could be ascribed to any number of things, and therefore it was decided—silently, by the entire audience—not to appreciate this clearly banal effort.

But this is not what happened.

"She is mine," Henry said, "but it's impossible to own a woman as if she were an object—a thing, like a painting or a chair. When you do this, when you make this mistake, when you hold a woman captive against her will, the woman has no choice . . . but to die."

As he said this, the lock fell off, the cabinet doors swung open, and Marianne's lifeless body came tumbling out. The way her body fell—that was the thing. It appeared that she had to be unconscious, for she had absolutely no will to break her fall at all. This time, the gasps from the front rows were the least of it: there were screams, horrified screams. One lady in the very first row left her seat and fled the auditorium. She would later say she could see Marianne's eyes as she lay there on the stage: they were open, but blank. There was not an ounce of life within them.

Henry knelt, and held her body in his arms. He cried.

"I think . . . I think she is dead," he announced. "I have killed her by keeping her against her will. Is there a doctor here? Someone who can verify this for me, for all of us? Verify that this is not some paltry trick but true, that my Marianne is truly dead?"

There was a bit of a commotion then as three men stood and rushed to the stage. This was no longer a magic show at all: a woman's life was in danger—or, worse, over. Kastenbaum wondered at first if the doctors were plants, and had there been only one of them he would have been suspicious—but *three*? One had white hair and a handlebar mustache, and Kastenbaum recognized him as being somewhat famous in the city; the other two were younger, clean-shaven, and very nicely dressed, serious with their spectacles and wet, combed-back hair. First one and then another took Marianne's wrist, felt the artery at her neck, and another placed a mirror before her mouth, to see if she was breathing.

She wasn't.

They stood back, all three of them, stunned. The doctor with the mustache looked at Henry and then turned to the audience, and announced in a deep voice that carried all the way back to the last row, where Kastenbaum was seated, "This woman is dead."

Goddamn it all! Dead! Could things get any worse? No. When the assistant dies, you really have to mark that as the lowest even this show could possibly go. This was going to be one for the history books. In the future, people would look back to this show at the Emporium, magicians and the general public alike. *The Tragic Death of Marianne La Fleur, and How One Promising Magician's Career Died with Her.* Or something like that. Edgar Kastenbaum himself would be but a footnote in the story, though he would end up being equally dead, career-wise. He would be left with nothing. As he watched the doctors slowly leave the stage, he wondered if, as manager, he bore any liability for this tragedy, if, in fact, he should leave town right now. He looked around him: women were crying, sobbing into their sleeves, mascara running down their faces in a ghoulish, garish way. But he felt nothing. Not for Marianne La Fleur, at any rate. Her death had its good points, to be honest. If only it hadn't happened onstage.

And so the show, inasmuch as it was one, was over. Much of the audience were standing now, putting on their hats and coats, and some had filed into aisles and were wandering away when they heard Henry say, *No.* He said it softly at first, but the plaintive, quiet sadness of the word was heard by everybody. Then he said it again, louder this time: *No!*

Everybody turned.

Henry stood above her still body. One of the doctors approached, and took his arm to comfort him. But Henry shook it off.

"I cannot allow this," Henry said. "If my love can kill her, my love can bring her back to life."

"Mr. Walker," the doctor said, "we've had an ambulance called. It's best, I think, if we—"

Henry lifted her slight, limp body in his arms. Her long black hair fell across him like a shawl as her head leaned back at the unnatural angle of the dead. The audience watched him, bewildered and beguiled.

"You cannot watch this," he told them. "Love—true love—is private, between two people and two people alone."

And with Marianne in his arms, he stepped inside his cabinet.

The doors closed.

And they were gone.

How many minutes passed before Henry and Marianne La Fleur reappeared was a subject of intense speculation the next day, in the newspapers and on the streets of New York. Some said five minutes, others said ten, and still others said that it was only a matter of a moment, and that it only seemed longer because they could not wait to see what happened next, like children waiting for Christmas.

However long it was, they waited. Those who were still seated didn't speak but sat silently, staring at the cabinet. Those who had been leaving stood still in the aisles. A man had taken a dead woman into the cabinet. This was an idea that was impossible to grasp, something the mind was not prepared for. Add to that the fact that they had paid for the privilege of watching it, and the dark absurdity of it all left them reeling, then and later. Especially later.

However much time had passed, the door of the cabinet finally opened, and Henry Walker stepped out of it—alone. He looked drained, bloodless. His tuxedo was drenched in sweat. He turned his face away from the stage lights when they hit his eyes, as if he'd been in the dark for hours, and lightly tripped over a raised board in the floor, barely able to gather himself before he fell. Whatever had happened inside the cabinet, he looked like he had only just survived it, but was able to draw himself up as he approached the very edge of the stage and looked into and past all the strange and silent faces.

"Love," he said to them, "conquers all."

He turned then, lifted his arms in a flourish. And—behold—out she came.

Marianne La Fleur was alive.

She walked—floated—until she stood beside him onstage. He took her hand.

And he kissed her. Not a small kiss, either. For kisses on the stage of the Emporium in front of five hundred people, it broke the record.

The next morning, the *Times* would say that half of the women in the audience fainted; Kastenbaum knew this was a huge exaggeration. But he did see quite a few of them fall, like retiring marionettes, some caught by their husbands, others disappearing into the aisles between the seats. Kastenbaum himself felt the sensation of his heart stopping. He saw his life flash before his eyes, and it only took a second.

Henry had brought Marianne La Fleur back to life.

I should have quit smoking when my right arm dried up. I knew it was happening (my left arm was already glued to my side), and so I tried to position the right so it would lie across my lap, appearing natural and relaxed. I had a rideboy tie it down with a sash, and it was that way day and night. But my body had other ideas. My right arm is now extended straight ahead, and my hand is slightly open, as if waiting for someone to shake it; for a quarter, people can. Second only to striking a match on Agnes the Alligator Lady's leg, shaking my hand is the most popular blow-off we offer.

I should have quit smoking then, but I didn't. Nic, who does the takedown, has a son too young yet to be of much help around the place, so he works for me now, since Henry's been gone. He's only seven. He's a small boy with thick glasses and bangs cut an inch too high on his forehead. He lights the cigarettes for me and brings them to my lips. He doesn't talk much, which is fine.

But Henry liked to do this for me when he was here. He talked quite a bit; he needed me for that. He would light the cigarette, inhale once, and then give it over to me, and when I'd had my drag he'd take it back. We would share, the way lovers sometimes do. He didn't smoke himself, but could blow smoke rings, then shoot an arrow of smoke through the rings, and then capture all of the smoke in his hand and turn it into another cigarette, which made me smile. My only trick was smoking at all. The smoke crept from my mouth and floated up across my face like a veil. Then Henry would blow it away. I felt his breath across my face, his lips as close to mine as one lover's are to another's.

In the days following the resurrection of Marianne La Fleur, the entire city talked of little else. A woman had died and been brought back to life. When such a thing happens, is there anything else *to* talk about? As with the most remarkable events, even those who hadn't been there could narrate the entire show as if they had been. Every newspaper carried stories about it, and, like Amelia Earhart almost nine years before, it was all people talked about. A noted spiritualist maintained that the great number of women fainting could be attributed to having "some small portion" of their lives stolen from them and given to Marianne La Fleur. Investigative reporters dug into her background, only to find that there was none. Even Henry Walker, who had achieved his fame during the war, did not appear to have existed before it. Everything about them was mysterious and compelling.

Kastenbaum, for his part, was ecstatic. Advertising like this was priceless. He felt as if the gods had been watching, and, just as he was about to crash and burn, had snatched him back and given him everything he had ever wanted. He was a new man; he felt, in fact, that he had finally become one. He had put all his eggs in one basket, and the eggs were fine. Better than fine—they were golden now. *He* was golden. When he visited his father, as he did briefly the next morning, it was as an equal. People noticed, too. The way he held himself, the bounce in his step. He had even become, in his own mind, a handsome man. A tiny man, slump-shouldered, a bit of a nebbish: that Kastenbaum was dead. The closest he had been to a beautiful woman in his life was during the interviews for Henry's assistant, and he had fantasized about every one of them. But it was more than just wishful thinking now. Now these women did not seem beyond him. He felt he could have anyone he wanted. Walking down the street, his pronounced and bouncy gait and long strides turning heads, he thought, *This is why we are alive, to feel like this.*

He had discovered the secret of existence. The secret was success.

He let Henry sleep in the day after the show. He had to be exhausted. He and Marianne La Fleur had disappeared immediately after the performance; there were no curtain calls. The audience was too stunned to applaud, as if what had happened was beyond applause, as if applause would have somehow diminished it. He hoped that Henry hadn't taken it the wrong way.

But Henry seemed fine. When Kastenbaum arrived, around eleven o'clock, Henry was still dressed in his midnight-blue silk bathrobe, holding a cup of coffee. The shades were drawn. It looked and felt like night in there. Marianne was nowhere to be seen.

"Where is she?" Kastenbaum asked him. "The little starlet."

"Still sleeping," he said. "After what she went through last night, she'll probably sleep all day."

"I thought she had it the easiest of us all, actually," Kastenbaum said. "You really did everything. And I was out there dying myself until you pulled it off. Congratulations, Henry."

And he hugged him. It was a bit awkward; Henry didn't hug him back. What shocked Kastenbaum was how cold Henry felt.

Looking up at his friend, his eyes adjusted to the dark now, Kastenbaum struggled to remember Henry as he had been only a day before. He looked twenty years older today, all the blood drained from his face, and his eyes—once so bright, so green—appeared dim and gray.

His voice shook as he spoke. "I suppose it did go well," Henry said. "All things considered."

"Well? It went *amazing,*" Kastenbaum said. "You were right not to tell me about it, because I would have gone absolutely insane. But you pulled it off, and I'll never doubt you again, my friend. Never."

"It's good to know you were pleased."

"But you have to tell me now."

Henry looked at him. "Tell you what?"

"How it was done, Henry. I have to know. Give me the lay. I didn't make this trip for a biscuit."

Henry turned away. "Don't ask."

"How could I not? Everyone in New York wants to know. You won't tell them, of course—and neither will I—but as your manager, and friend, and whatever else I am, you have got to tell me. It's eating me up inside."

Henry was about to speak when Kastenbaum raised a finger. "My first guess was that the doctors were plants. That's the obvious thing. But there were three of them—three!—and then, in the papers this morning—I'm sure you saw it—they're the real thing. They have offices. They have *degrees.* So my second guess—okay, bear with me—is that Marianne naturally has such a low pulse—she's some kind of freak, I mean, just look at her—that without a stethoscope a doctor would be unable to detect it. Then I thought, A pulse is a pulse, they'd find it. So my third—"

"You can stop," Henry said.

"Why?"

"Because you'll never guess."

"I have thirteen guesses, Henry. I bet one of them—"

"Not if you had a hundred," Henry said. He sighed, and wandered into the living room, almost disappearing into the darkness. He fell heavily into the couch and shook his head. "And you don't want to know, Kastenbaum," he said. "You think you do, but you don't."

"Really? And why don't I?"

"Because, even if I told you, you wouldn't believe it."

"Really?" Kastenbaum said, laughing. "I'm no greenhorn in the world of magic, Henry. You know that. I researched all the tricks and read up on the history. I probably know more than you. Have you ever even heard of Alexander the Paphlagonian? Didn't think so. What about Jacques de Vaucanson? I even got pretty good with the knife-throwing, if I do say so myself. The ins and outs of this and that—and I realize how complicated the entire process can be. The only thing I wouldn't believe is if you told me she really *did* die and you really *did* bring her back to life—*that* I wouldn't believe, because that is impossible. But anything else . . ."

Kastenbaum's voice softened and drifted into silence as he stared at Henry's ethereal face. Because Henry wasn't smiling; he was as far away from a smile as a man could possibly be.

Kastenbaum knelt before Henry and looked at him dead-on. "Henry," he said. "Please don't. Please don't try to tell me that."

Now Henry did smile. "Okay," he said. "I won't."

His hand shaking, he grasped his cup and brought it to his lips. He tried to look away, but Kastenbaum wouldn't let him, moved to pin him again with his gaze.

"Henry," he said. "Don't kid a kidder. I'm not some *rube*. I'm the guy . . . I'm the guy who made this happen. You *owe* it to me. Seriously. Now, I'm going to sit here and look into your eyes, and you're going to tell me how you did it."

And it was as if their eyes were the only things in the room, glowing, floating in the ether.

"A long time ago, I took an oath," Henry said. "A blood oath. I took it from the devil himself. I swore never to reveal the secret of any illusion or even to speak of magic to one who is not learned in the dark arts, one who has not taken the magician's oath. I swore never to reveal the source of my magic or speak the name of the magician who taught me, or to perform any illusion to a nonmagician without first practicing the effect until the illusion is perfect; otherwise I would lose all that I had gained. I swore not only to practice illusion, but to live within it, to seem but not to be, for only in this way can we fully partake in the magical world. As the blood of the magician and his apprentice are one, I swore these things now and forever. Part of him is in me, Kastenbaum."

"The devil," he said.

"That's right," Henry said. "The devil himself. That's why I cannot tell."

Kastenbaum thought Henry might have gone insane—the way he spoke now, the way he said the words as if he were reading off an old piece of paper in his mind.

"Henry," he whispered.

"But I will tell you," Henry said, "because you're the only friend I have in the world."

"Thank you."

"Her trick is dying, Eddie, and my trick is bringing her back."

And Kastenbaum believed him.

Henry explained it this way. Marianne La Fleur lived as close to death as anyone possibly could. It wasn't an illness, however; it was a state of being. She could float between the two worlds freely, as easily as moving from one room to the next.

But it wasn't always voluntary. During the course of a day she felt its pull: death was the undertow of her life. *Watch her when she blinks*, he said, *this is when it happens.* Not every time, but Henry had seen her simply blink, and then struggle to open her eyes again. She used every ounce of energy in her living soul to bring herself back. *That's why she looks the way she does*, he said. It was a constant struggle. She went to sleep not knowing if she'd be able to crawl back up the steep and rocky pit she fell into during the night. The only thing between her and dying forever was her dreams, because she dreamed of life. These were what brought her back, and every morning she felt as if she had been thrown ashore again by a surging wave.

"How long has she been this way?" Kastenbaum said.

"From the very beginning of her life. Her mother died giving birth, and she never completely escaped death after that. Death was born with her, clung to her like a scent forever, her original smell."

"I see." Kastenbaum surprised himself by not being surprised. Marianne had always looked dead to him, or half dead at least; it was why he had been so against hiring her in the first place. All those other women—they were so alive!

"So, if she can die and then come back," Kastenbaum said, "what is it you do?"

Henry smiled and shrugged his shoulders. It was as if he couldn't believe it himself. "Sometimes she needs a hand up."

"Go on."

"It's all about time," Henry told him. "The longer she's dead, the harder it is for her to come back. To do the trick—for her to lie there onstage, while someone from the audience came to determine the truth of her condition—she's already too far gone to come back on her own."

"So?" Kastenbaum said.

Henry's eyes disappeared into the darkness. All that was left was his voice. "She showed me how," he said. "I can go there myself."

Kastenbaum shook his head: this story was exhausting him. "Wait a minute," he said. "You're telling me that you die, too?"

"No," Henry said. "I don't think so. But I can go there, wherever it is, and find her. I don't know where it is, or what. It's a kind of between place, and she's in there floating, and I can see her, and I think, *Marianne*. That's all I do. Think, *Marianne*. And the moment I do, she comes back. We both do. And that's when we come out of the closet."

Henry went into the other room to look in on Marianne—for obvious reasons now—and Kastenbaum broke his hard-and-fast no-drinks-before-noon rule and poured himself a tumbler of Henry's bourbon and drank it straight. He waited for it to go to his brain, warming the blood there.

Henry shut her door softly behind him. "She's fine," he said.

"You were gone awhile," said Kastenbaum. "I didn't know if you were taking a little trip. You know. To the other side." He was kidding around, or trying to at least.

Henry didn't answer him or smile—he had become so serious over the last few weeks—but looked at Kastenbaum's glass and the bottle beside it.

"Early for you, isn't it?"

"You broke your rule and I broke mine."

"I see," Henry said. "Well, I think I'll join you."

But just as he was pouring the bourbon, someone began rapping at his door. Henry set the bottle down.

"I'll get that," Kastenbaum said. "Why don't you turn a lamp on? It's pitch-black in here."

Henry turned a lamp on and stood behind Kastenbaum as he

opened the door. It was an old man. Or he seemed old. But as Henry studied him, he realized the man couldn't have been much older than Henry was himself. He wore an old suit made a long time ago for a much smaller man. Sad red eyes sank into his face as if they were trying to burrow beneath his flesh; his skin was peeled and chapped and cut by the cold. Even his whiskers appeared unable to find the strength to grow; they edged his face like metal filings. Shrouded in a light gray film, a mantle of dust. For the first time in years, Henry thought of his own father.

"Are you . . . Henry Walker?" the man said nervously, turning his head to one side like a dog waiting to be smacked.

"No," Kastenbaum said with a laugh, taking a step aside.

"I am," Henry said.

"The magician?" the man said. "Henry Walker the Great?"

"That's right," Henry said.

The man stared at Henry, his eyes almost sparkling. "Henry the Great," he said.

The man stood there, as if uncertain how to proceed.

"Can I help you?" Henry said.

"I hope so," he said. "Dear God, I hope so." He paused. "I heard about what happened last night," he said, taking a moment to breathe after every word. The elevator had been broken for some time; the trip up the stairs was a long one. "I didn't go myself, sorry to say. But I heard about it. I read about it in the papers, and everyone is talking about it, as you must know."

"Thank you," Henry said, although this seemed wrong to say.

The man brought his face close to Henry's and whispered: "It was a miracle, wasn't it?"

"It seemed so," Henry said, "and that's all that matters."

"But it happened, didn't it? It *did* happen."

"What happened, happened."

The man was getting more excited now, breathing heavily, his head bobbing up and down. Wild-eyed, a crazed smile on his face, he leaned in even closer. *"You brought her back to life,"* he said. Henry looked back at Kastenbaum. "You brought her back to life, didn't you?" the man said again.

Henry nodded. "I did," he said.

Finally, the man appeared satisfied, as if he'd heard what he came to hear, and Henry hoped he would turn and leave. But he didn't. Instead, he motioned to whoever was around the corner to come forward.

There were two others. One was a large man Henry guessed to be in his twenties, but the other was just a boy, very thin and small, with a white and pockmarked face. They were carrying something wrapped in an old tan blanket, one of them holding it at each end, and the moment he saw it Henry knew what it was. So did Kastenbaum.

They set the body on the floor.

The older man knelt and gingerly pulled back the blanket. The dead woman's eyes were open, and her thinning brown hair was brushed back, as if she had been made pretty for this appointment. She may have even had a bit of fresh makeup on as well. Her coat was buttoned from top to bottom. Her long blue dress had slipped upward, revealing her ankles, and the old man lovingly patted it down.

"Last night," the man said, gently brushing back a stray hair from her face. "It happened last night. There was nothing we could do. Couldn't get any medicine—don't have a doctor. Couldn't take her to a nice place either, you know the way they have them—sanatoriums, they're called."

"She—"

"Consumption," the man said. "TB."

Henry knelt to get a closer look. He was dizzy. As much as the man had reminded him of his father, the woman just that much reminded him of his mother, and the days of standing before the window, watching her die. It was like he was back there again, a boy, and Hannah standing beside him, still a little girl.

"Please," the man said. "I can't offer you any money. But our prayers will be yours forever and a day, and there is nothing like that power on God's green earth."

"Except yours," the little boy said. "Your power."

"That's right," the man said. "Except yours."

Kastenbaum stood behind Henry, stunned into a frozen silence.

"Bring her back," the man said. "Please. She's the boy's mother. Look at him. He's too young to be without his mother. He needs her. So do we all. She was—everything."

The family waited in holy silence for Henry to work his magic. But he didn't move. He couldn't. He looked at each of them. The big man began to cry without making a sound, the tears streaming down his face like rain. The old man touched his wife's face and gazed into her eyes, and the little boy blinked and blinked but didn't take his eyes off Henry, not even for a second.

Henry shook his head. He tried to speak, but no words came when he opened his mouth. There was nothing to say, nothing to be done. Then, with one final glance at the body on his floor, he walked away, into his own room, and closed the door softly behind him.

The family watched, not without hope, even now. They thought this might be a good thing. This was part of the magic, surely. He was going to get the wand, or the potion, or the crystal ball—whatever it was he used for this, for the bringing back of the dead. They were certain of it.

They waited there, in complete silence, each as still as the dead woman herself.

They waited there for a long time.

"Where is he?" the old man said. "What's he doing?"

"You should go now," Kastenbaum said.

"Go?" he said. "But the magician—"

"He's not coming back," Kastenbaum said.

But this didn't appear to make any sense at all. "Not coming back? Are you sure?" the man said.

Kastenbaum nodded.

The old man looked at his son. The boy was kneeling beside his mother, running his fingers through her hair: it was he who had made it so nice. "I see," the old man said, but it was clear that he didn't see, couldn't understand how things had resolved in this way. Nothing made sense anymore. "So I don't know what to do," he said. "Should we leave her here?"

"Leave her?" Kastenbaum said. "On the floor? In the middle of the room?"

"In case . . . in case he changes his mind."

But Kastenbaum shook his head and shut his eyes, tight. He couldn't bear this a moment more. He only wanted a drink now. He only wanted these people to go, so he could have a drink. But still they didn't move. Nothing was happening the way they had imagined it would: Kastenbaum would soon know exactly how they felt.

"Then what should we do?" the man said.

She seemed small, the man's wife, she seemed to shrink as he looked at her. Perhaps her soul had been standing by, hoping for a miracle itself. But now it was gone.

"She's dead," Kastenbaum said. "Bury her."

Kastenbaum returned to his office, and he splayed himself across the top of his cold metal desk and looked at the water-stained ceiling. He'd never really looked at the ceiling like this. His eyes not moving from it, his left hand pulled open the top drawer and blindly removed a bottle of scotch. He dipped the bill and cringed and then began talking to himself, something he did on occasion.

"Marianne La Fleur lives as close to death as anyone possibly could," he said. "She isn't sick; that's just how she is. She can float between one world and the other like moving from one room to the next. Where's she go? A kind of no-man's-land, and she's in there floating, floating in the darkness, and he can see her, and he takes her hand, and that's when she comes back. That's when they come out of the closet."

He gave it a moment to settle, the meaning of the words, the echo of Henry's story, until his fermented brain could assess them.

"Bunk," he said.

It was bunk. Henry was trying to work him with the Chinese angle. It was a trick. That's what magic *is*, tricks, tricks made to look like they weren't, tricks too tricky to be tricks at all. And that's what a magician is—a fakeloo artist, nothing more. The floating woman was all wires, artfully placed, with that U-shaped bar at one end doing the heavy lifting. The Suspended Head—all mirrors, placed at angles. It wasn't magic—it was geometry! This was a new one, sure, but the history of magic is all about the new becoming old, and becoming old quick. Eventually everybody would be doing the Dying Girl. They'd figure it out, and soon people would be coming back from the dead all over the place.

Henry took him for a rube the same as anybody. That's what hurt. That's what hurt like a dull knife, ripping open his chest. He had wanted—needed—this business. He had needed it bad. But more than that—a secret he kept from everybody but himself—he had wanted a friend.

He fell asleep in the office, and didn't wake until the next morning, when the telephone began to ring.

.   .   .

It was a call from the office of Jason Talbot, from the Virago, in Philadelphia. His secretary with the smoky voice: "Mr. Talbot, I have Mr. Kastenbaum on the line." The Virago was an important tour stop. The New York press traveled west as far as Philadelphia, but the Philadelphia press traveled as far as Ohio, and they needed that, a stepping stone for their journey across America, and then— who knows?—the world.

"Thank you, Miranda," Mr. Talbot said. He cleared his throat— Talbot woke up with a cigar in his mouth—and without a hello or how-are-you started in. "I read the *Times*, Kastenbaum."

"Yes sir. A nice piece, I thought."

"Nice piece," he said—or was it *Nice piece?*, like a question? Kastenbaum couldn't tell at first. "It wasn't completely clear to me what happened there. I was hoping you could set it up for me. Far as I could tell, your Henry Walker has an assistant. She dies. Then he brings her back to life. End of show. Does that about cover it?"

"Yes sir," Kastenbaum said. "Just about. It's pretty amazing, sir. Doctors from the audience—real doctors—they come up and examine her, and they pronounce her dead on the spot. Then, miraculously, life returns. Nothing like it's ever been done."

Talbot laughed. "Not hard to see why, is it?"

Kastenbaum stifled a yawn. He was having trouble being awake in the world. "Sorry?" he said.

Talbot exploded. Kastenbaum had to hold the phone away from his ear. "*Who* wants to see a *show* like *that?*" he bellowed.

"Who?" Kastenbaum said. "Who? It was huge here, Mr. Talbot. People loved it. People love magic. They eat it up."

"I'm one of them, Kastenbaum. I love magic. Disappearing doves. Floating women. Blindfolded knife-throwing on that, that—"

"Wheel of death," Kastenbaum said.

"Wheel of death. Exactly. But death *itself*? Kastenbaum—according to the *Times*, she doesn't almost die. She *dies*. She actually dies. And you want twenty large for the pleasure? That may be a New York show, Mr. Kastenbaum, but it's not a Philadelphia show. People here aren't ready for something like that. *I'm* not ready for something like that."

"Mr. Talbot, please—"

"He was a war hero, Kastenbaum. I assumed he would trade on that. Defeating Hitler with a magic spell or something—I don't know. That's his audience. Not some dead-girl mumbo-jumbo. It's scary, is what it is, Kastenbaum. It scares *me*! If that's what he has in mind, we can't have him here. No sir. Not now and not ever."

"You're making a big mistake, Mr. Talbot."

"Yeah? I don't think so."

And with a click the line went dead. But Kastenbaum held on to the phone for a long time, the receiver pressed against his ear, until the operator took the line and asked him if he'd like to make a call.

After that, the cancellations began to pour in. New Haven, Boston, Scranton, Burlington, Richmond, Washington, D.C. They all had their own reasons. In Boston it was religion ("I suppose this makes Christ just another magician?"). New Haven was more practical. They wondered: if she *didn't* come back to life, if something went wrong, what then? What would they do with a dead woman on their hands? Kastenbaum tried to tell them it was just a trick, a trick like any other, but when they asked him how it was done, he had to tell them that he didn't know, the fucking magician's creed and all that. Richmond said it was just unseemly, pure and simple. Not family entertainment, which is what they were looking for. And Scranton—Scranton said that unless he ditched the girl and came up with something more traditional, something patriotic, they didn't want him. Period.

Before lunch he had fielded nineteen such calls—every date

they had but one. That last cancellation came by telegram. He read it, finished off his bottle, and summed the morning up. "I'm screwed," he said.

It was the truth.

By three-thirty, Kastenbaum was very drunk, very, very drunk, but he had enough self-reflection remaining to realize that he was drunk and that he had been drunk for a while, seriously juiced anyway, that probably since early yesterday morning he had not stopped being drunk at all. Then he began to wonder if he had been truly sober—even for a few minutes—for the last whole week, and for the last few weeks before that. Had he, in fact, been floating on a light mist of alcohol for all that time? Yes, he had. And who knows? Not really knowing what it was *not* to be snockered—it was possible he had been for years. Which explained every dunce move he'd made his entire adult life, all his stupid ambition.

Came from a bottle.

This wisdom in hand, he made his way to Henry's, a path he knew by heart.

"You're drunk," Henry said.

Kastenbaum smiled, swaying. "Drunk?" he said. "I am indeed. I'm over the edge with the rams. What's your excuse?"

Because Henry, at least through Kastenbaum's glazed-over eyes, did not appear to be doing so well himself. He was worse than he was the day before. Gaunt and trembling, a stranger to sleep, sick to his very bones. In his undershirt now, and the black suit pants he wore onstage, he looked like a street bum on a bad day. Kastenbaum tried to not think about this too much.

He stumbled in, doffing an imaginary hat as he did so, and

looked with a feigned curiosity all around the room. "Still asleep, is she? Or—God forbid—dead? If it's the latter, I'll be glad to wait while you go catch her. Take your little trip into the netherworld. Before it gets too crowded with the big tour groups and whatnot."

Henry didn't think this was as funny as Kastenbaum did. Kastenbaum got a good laugh from it, at least, and kept laughing for a while. Then he stopped, and gave Henry a closer look. His face was somber and lost; his eyes were so dark they looked bruised, the whites of them red, as if they were bleeding. Henry loomed over Kastenbaum. He had always been taller, but now he appeared gigantic, like a tree, and Kastenbaum wasn't sure why, whether it had more to do with how drunk he was or how sober Henry was. Perhaps all of this was an effect brought on by the alcohol, inasmuch as there was more inside of him now than ever.

"So what's wrong, Henry? Spill the beans."

Henry almost smiled. "We're a pair, you and me," he said.

"I thought so, too, once."

Henry wandered aimlessly through the living room as he spoke. "You found me," he said. "You found me when I needed finding. It didn't take a minute for you to become a friend—my friend. And I hope you always will be."

"That warms my beating heart, Henry," he said. "But that's not how it is anymore. It's all about Marianne now. Tell me any different and I'll know you're lying."

"No," Henry said. "You're right. It is all about her now."

Kastenbaum approached the liquor stand, where he gave the scotch a loving look. There wasn't enough left in the bottle to make a difference. Without turning around he said, "It's over, Henry."

"What? What's over?"

"Us. This. Everything. We've been canceled. Believe it or not, no one wants to see Marianne die! At least no one wants to pay us for the privilege. Nobody. You name the place, we're not playing it."

When he turned around to look, he saw Henry's expression hadn't changed. No shock, no sadness, no nothing. It was as if he didn't have any real feelings anymore.

"Okay," Henry said. "Okay. Yes. I think so, too. In fact, I was going to tell you the same thing."

"Really? And when were you thinking you'd tell me?"

"Today," Henry said. "I've known for some time but didn't want to admit it, to believe it. But there's no escaping the truth now. I . . . we can't do this anymore. Every time I catch her, she's farther and farther away. One day—"

"Let me guess: you won't be able to."

Henry nodded. "There's more to it, Eddie," he said, "things I didn't know when we started all this. It's about saving her. Every time I go there, to get her, every time, I have to give up a part of my own life. That's my ticket in. I get closer to my own death every time."

"You look nearly dead already," Kastenbaum said.

"I know," he said. "I have to stop. You have to help me."

And, against all of his better instincts, Kastenbaum suddenly became hopeful again. Hope: he'd never thought he'd know it again. "Yes!" he said. "Yes! That's what I'm talking about! By all means I'll help you." He slapped his friend on the back. "Of course! We can go back to the old tried and true! *Real* magic. The rabbits and the mind-reading and the—the— That's what you mean, isn't it? I should get on the horn to everybody right away. I think we can pull this thing out of the ashes after all."

But Henry shook his head. "I can't put together another show," he said. "Not with Marianne the way she is now. It's all very . . . all very tenuous. She needs my complete attention."

"But I thought—"

"I have to devote myself to her if I'm to have any chance at all."

"Chance for what, though? You're not making sense, Henry."

"To keep her here," Henry said.

"But if she's sick, she needs a doctor. A real one."

"You don't understand!" Henry grabbed him hard by the shoulders and shook him. Kastenbaum tried to turn out of his grasp, but he couldn't—tried to because, for the first time since he'd known Henry, Kastenbaum was actually scared. He was scared of Henry. Henry had lost his mind.

He brought Kastenbaum close to him, still tight in his grip. Their bodies touched. Henry whispered in Kastenbaum's ear. "You don't understand," he said. "You don't understand the forces out there in the world conspiring to destroy us. The *evil*. It's no Sunday-school story, Eddie. Evil exists. It's real. It lives. And it has a plan. I know the plan because that's all I've done my entire life is study it, to try and *understand* it. And I think I have. I think I have."

Kastenbaum's breath came shallow now. He didn't blink. *Remain still*, he thought. *Disappear.*

"It's all very simple, Kastenbaum," Henry said. "His plan. He takes the weakest of us first. That's where he starts. That makes sense, doesn't it? The weakest of us. Women. The weak sisters, right? Women are, they're weak, because they *feel* things so deeply. This is how he takes advantage of them. And once they're gone, the strong, no matter how strong they are, they become weak as well. And one by one this is how he gets us all. All of us. *Unless we fight him.* Unless we make a stand. Unless we say, *No. No, no more.*"

"No more," Kastenbaum said in the same deep whisper. "No more! There. I said it."

Henry released his grip and stood back a bit. "I can't die, Eddie. Not yet. I have my own plans. This is why I need your help."

"Of course, Henry," he said, backing away. "Whatever you want."

Henry took Kastenbaum by the hand and led him to the bathroom. They both stood before the mirror, and they looked at themselves in it. Then Henry opened the cabinet and removed a can of shoe-black from it. He unscrewed the can and picked up the brush and began applying it to his face, strip by strip, until he was entirely covered in it, until he was black, completely, and the whites of his eyes shone out from the blackness like little beams of light.

Kastenbaum felt as if he had entered another world. What was happening? He couldn't speak, and he had no idea what he would say if he did.

"Evil always wins," Henry said. His voice was low, strained, guttural. He sounded as if he were possessed. "Eventually, evil wins. We fight it because it's the right thing to do, but in the end we'll always lose. Always. Because, to be good—truly good—there are rules, we have rules inside of us, rules we have to follow to be that way, to stay good. And evil can do anything it wants to. It's not a fair fight. Together, though, you and me, maybe there's something we could do. Something we could do—not to stop it—but at least to slow it down."

Kastenbaum backed away from Henry until he was in the hallway, and then farther, back into the main room. Once there, he felt that he'd escaped something, that only now was he safe. His breath came fast and deep. He waited, but Henry didn't follow him, and after a few moments it was clear that he wasn't coming out again at all. Eyeing the scotch again, Kastenbaum began to find the little puddle at the bottom of the decanter more appetizing. He slipped the cork out of it and threw back what little was there. It was the hint of something beautiful, like walking into a room and hearing the last few notes of a song.

How many sons had to make an appointment to see their own father? If there were others, Kastenbaum didn't know them. He imagined sons who could waltz into their father's office anytime they wished and their father would be pleased to see them. But a long time ago, probably around his tenth birthday, his father had changed their relationship from something filial to purely business. The senior Kastenbaum was no longer really his father. He was a future employer, and his son a future employee, and as such there were rules to follow, there were ways to be. His father could see him at three o'clock on Thursday. Tomorrow. This would give Kastenbaum time to clean himself up.

In the small, lonely chair before his father's great mahogany desk, Kastenbaum Jr. explained to Kastenbaum Sr. the chain of events that had inevitably led to the colossal failure that was Henry Walker. His father listened passively, betraying not the smallest interest, even when his son told him the nature of Henry's trick and insisted that it wasn't one at all. This was all business to him.

When he finished, his father nodded.

"That's a pity, Edgar," he said. "You were so hopeful early on. Too hopeful, perhaps. But the higher we go, the harder we fall."

"I know."

"Slow and steady wins the race."

"That's what you always say."

There was just the slightest bit of sniping evident in this last comment, but enough for a father to notice, and take umbrage.

"Well, I'm disappointed," his father said. "That goes without saying, of course." *But of course you had to say it*, his son thought. "This was going to be that foray into the business world which would prove to me and to everyone within the organization that, other than simply being my son, you were the right man to sit in this chair after I abandoned it. I hate nepotism. It's not fair to others, who work so hard regardless of their last name. But I'd be disingenuous to suggest that I shouldn't give you a leg up. I'd have to. It gets your foot in the door, but what you do once you're in the room—that's what matters."

"I know," his son said. "I know."

His father picked up his pipe from the small brass stand where it was resting and tapped it, lit it, and engaged himself in one of his interminable thoughtful pauses, looking away toward the heavens as if he were having a conversation with the Lord Himself, the results of which he might share with you in a moment. "We both know what this means," he said.

"Yes. But I think I should be given another chance," Kastenbaum said, interrupting his father before he said what Eddie knew he was going to say, because once he said it there would be no going back.

His father thought about it. He sized up his son with his small-eyed stare. "From what you've told me," he said, "the girl appears to be the problem."

"That's right."

"And Henry is an artist. Artists don't make practical decisions. That's not their job. That's yours, isn't it?"

"Yes," Kastenbaum said.

"Then I don't understand the problem."

"I've come to you for advice, Father," he said.

"And I'm giving it to you."

"What?" he said. "I don't understand."

"The girl," he said. "You need to deal with her. Talk to her. Make her see the damage she's causing. I'm sure she'll understand." Kastenbaum nodded. "Do your job, son. That's all I can tell you. Do your job."

His father looked at his watch. The meeting was over. His father stood and shook his son's hand the same way he had shaken the hand of the last man who had come into his office, the same way he would shake the next.

Kastenbaum knew what he had to do.

.   .   .

It was, if he did say so himself, a brilliant plan. He was pleased with himself, so pleased that, once he had gotten back to his lonely office, he poured himself a scotch and threw it back with a sailor's gusto. He called Henry and told him he had an idea. What he needed was an alarm clock, one of the new ones, a Big Ben. Instead of staying up half the night, he could set it to ring on every hour, and every hour he could wake up and check on Marianne. Henry enthusiastically agreed: this was exactly what he needed! He said he would leave immediately to purchase it.

Kastenbaum waited for a few minutes and called again. It rang and rang, but eventually Marianne's voice was on the other end.

"Hello?" she said.

"Marianne?" he said. "Kastenbaum here."

"Oh. Hello, Edgar."

"I hope I didn't wake you," he said.

She didn't answer this. "Henry's gone," she said.

"I know," he said. "He asked me to call. There's been a change of plans. He wants us all meet at the warehouse."

"There's a warehouse?"

"Where we store all the equipment," he said. "The equipment we've yet to use."

Where all the unused magic equipment was in storage, gathering dust, costing money he no longer had. Just the thought of it made him angry, resentful. But he tried to bottle that up for now.

"It's just around the corner," he said. "On Sixth."

"I don't know," she said. "Where is Henry?"

"He'll be there," he said. "Trust me."

The warehouse was a city block long and wide; their magic equipment took up only one small part of it. The rest of it was crowded with old metal desks and wooden chairs and cartons full of old tulip bulbs that for one reason or another were no good, things not quite discarded over the years from the many offices of his father, saved here because there was always a use for something, even when it wasn't clear what that use would be. Kastenbaum's paraphernalia had been stuck in a dark and musty corner somewhere near the back.

He met Marianne at the corrugated metal door and, after heaving it open, led her inside. It was difficult for him even to look at her now. Like a ghost, he thought, the image of a woman, hardly real. Dead already.

"Henry," she said, "is here?"

"Not yet," Kastenbaum said. "He will be soon. Meanwhile, why don't we take a look at all of our wonderful mechanisms? You haven't seen them all. I think you'll find them fascinating."

As they walked through the aisles, past empty bookcases and three-legged tables, Kastenbaum pulled the strings that led to the lights far above them, small isolated bulbs that created almost no light, only another shade of darkness. He glanced at Marianne. He couldn't tell whether she was already suspicious or merely confused. She walked so slowly, and looked around her wide-eyed, like a child in a museum.

"I always get lost back here," Kastenbaum said, trying to engage her in pleasant conversation. "It's a labyrinth."

"Where is Henry?" Marianne said, and this time he did hear a little bit of fear in her voice. It didn't surprise him: he was a little scared back here as well.

"On his way, I'm sure."

She stopped. "We should go back," she said. "We should wait for him outside."

As she turned, he took her by the wrist and held her—too hard. He hadn't meant to hold her so hard. The thing was, he had almost had too much to drink. He had never had too much, but he had often had almost too much, and this was one of those times. He was a little lightheaded, a second or two behind the moment.

He let her go, and apologized with a smile.

"We're here."

He pulled another string, and as their eyes adjusted to the shadows cast by the gray light, all the implements of pleasant deception appeared before them. There was something magical in just gazing at them, Kastenbaum thought, and he realized, possibly for the first time, the real reason he had found Henry when he arrived here, back from the war. It was of course a business decision, and, had things gone differently, would have been a mighty good one. But it was more than that. This access to another world was what he was after—the quality that comes from knowing something only a few people in the world know, these secrets of dissimulation. Knowing them meant he was special, and he felt special being surrounded by it all. This was the great trick, after everything that had happened to him: Kastenbaum, for a moment, was actually happy.

"So—what do you think?"

Marianne looked around her, her face betraying not the least emotion. "This is what Henry was going to do," she said. "What you wanted him to do."

"But he didn't," he said, forcing a smile. "He didn't. I don't know if he's ever actually worked with props this large, this advanced. I know for a fact he never had a Pepper's Ghost. Only a few people have that."

Marianne didn't appear particularly interested—she seemed so soulless now, so empty of everything human—but Kastenbaum didn't care. He carried on.

"It's complicated to explain. But, basically, it projects the image of a ghost on a stage, where it interacts with live people. Very real-looking, very believable."

He wanted to keep it friendly. He didn't say, *You would be perfect as the ghost.*

He walked over to a small wooden table, tripping over a cord, righting himself.

"And here, this is where, if he had wanted to, Henry could be headless."

This caught her eye. "Headless," she said. "Why—"

"Not literally. Mirrors is all it is. Very simple, but very effective."

"Henry's not here," she said softly. She sounded resigned.

"Patience," Kastenbaum said. "There's one more thing I want to show. It's over here, in the corner."

He took her by the arm again, this time more gently, and led her to the edge of the light. They stood for a moment in silence, staring.

"What is it?" she said.

"It's the wheel," he said. "The wheel of death. Right up your alley, isn't it, Marianne?" For the first time, a stingy bitterness crept into his voice. An accusation. "I thought you might like it."

Now she knew. She must know. The way she looked at him, at the wheel. So dark and hopeless. She almost smiled. "The wheel of death."

"Go on and look at it," he said. "Please. Come a little closer."

She did. She floated slowly across the concrete floor and she touched it—the dark, splintered wood, the metal cuffs, the outside circle of the wheel itself. She moved from side to side, and then, with more strength than he thought she had, she turned it. It made a single revolution. "I don't understand," she said.

"Then let me explain," he said, and he stood alongside her before the wheel. "There are four clamps. Two high, two low. That's where you—the magician's assistant, I mean—would put her feet and hands. So your arms are angled out across the wheel, your feet twelve inches apart or so. Then we *turn* it"—and Kastenbaum gave it a heave—"and as the assistant goes round and round, Henry—or the magician, whoever he is—throws knives at you. Or not you, really, but at the wheel. It seems very dangerous, but a good knife-thrower doesn't have a problem hitting the spaces around the girl. It's easy." Kastenbaum laughed, shrugged. "And that's the trick."

"But it's not a trick," she said, gently touching one of the metal clamps. "It's skill. It's a true aim."

"Exactly."

"And so it's possible—mistakes can be made."

"It's possible. But—"

"There is a chance," she said. "You put yourself in his hands, and it's up to him whether you live or die."

"Yes," he said. "I suppose that's true. It's up to him."

Marianne had not taken her eyes off the wheel. "I want to see what it's like," she said.

"What it's like?" Kastenbaum said. He hadn't expected this. "You mean—"

"Put me on the wheel," she said.

"Of course," Kastenbaum said, quickly regaining his composure. "I mean, why not? Just step up here . . . That's right . . . Now raise your arms a bit, so they're perpendicular to your body, near the holds. That's right. That's good—there."

And he snapped the clasps shut. First the ones on her wrists, and then the larger ones that held her ankles down. "That feel okay?"

"Fine," she said.

"Good," he said. "Good."

"Now turn it," she said.

He laughed. "Turn it? Are you sure?"

"I'm sure."

"It might make you a little dizzy."

"I think I can endure that," she said. "Please, turn it."

He did, and Marianne began going in circles, slowly at first, but, after a second push, faster, round and round, three, maybe four times. Then it slowed, and stopped. It was weighted to end where it began, with the assistant's head at the top, feet at the bottom.

Kastenbaum watched the wheel slow to a stop, and once it had, she looked at him with the realization he'd known she would come to sooner rather than later.

"Henry's not coming, is he?" she said.

Kastenbaum shook his head. "No," he said. "He's not."

"Why is he not?" She had never spoken in a softer voice.

"I just wanted to talk to you, Marianne, alone. I just want to *talk*. Henry never would have allowed that. And I wanted you to see all of this, everything that's possible for us, for Henry. Everything he has at his disposal."

"I see," she said. Her wrists shifted in the holds. "But now, after this—"

"He'll fire me," he said. "Not that it matters, as things stand now. But that's what I wanted to talk to you about."

"All right," she said. They locked eyes.

"I want you to leave," he said. "I want you to go."

This didn't seem to make sense to her. "*Go?* Go where?"

"It doesn't matter," he said. "Just . . . away. I'll give you money, enough to go anywhere. Wherever you'd like. Even Europe."

Marianne's breathing came quicker now. "Please let me down," she said. "Let me down now."

"Of course," he said. But as he walked toward the wheel and reached for the clamp around her left wrist, he stopped. He looked at Marianne; he had never been so close to her, and now that he was, saw that there was something really beautiful about her. She looked like a young girl. Her skin was completely translucent. He could see the dark-blue veins in her neck and cheek, the small black dots within the green of her eyes.

"Edgar," she said. "Unclasp me. Please."

But he didn't. She needed to hear him first.

"It's very important to me that you do this, Marianne," he said. "Not just for me. But for all of us. Henry isn't well, and he won't get well until you're gone. He'll lose everything because of you, and I know you don't want that."

"Let me down," she said.

"Will you leave?"

"Edgar—"

"You *must* go!" he said, his rising voice echoing throughout all the huge, empty warehouse. When he heard the sound of his voice come back to him, he realized just how much anger and grief had been stored up for this moment. It was powerful. "Why do you want to ruin everything? Henry wants to save you. But no one can save you. No one can save anybody else; we have to save ourselves. I don't think you want even that, though. I don't think you want him to live his own life. I think you want him to keep trying to save you *forever*, over and over again, until both of you die. Isn't that right?"

"*No*," she said softly, but adamantly. Even when she screamed, she whispered. Then, in the matter of a moment, she seemed to change her mind. "You're right, Edgar. I'll go. I'll leave. You can have him back. Now let me down."

But Kastenbaum shook his head: he knew she was lying.

"Why have you done this to us?" He moved closer to her, and as he brought his hand close to her face, realized he was shaking. He was scared of her, he had always been scared of her, and only now, with her arms and legs attached to the wheel, could he hazard this intimate approach. "Henry talked to me yesterday about evil. About all the evil in the world. And he didn't say this, not in so many words, but I think he was talking about you. I think that's what you are. Pure evil. I just don't think Henry can see it."

"Henry chose me," she said. "Out of all of them, he chose me."

"He made the *wrong* choice. All this"—and with his arms out wide, he indicated all of the wonderful magic things around them— "all this we could be sharing with the world if he'd only picked someone else, any one of those sweet, luscious, vibrant young women. I don't know why you were even there. Do you?"

The question seemed to draw her back, as if she really had to think about it. She looked at Kastenbaum, but then, as if she were unable to identify him, looked away. "No," she said. "But there must have been a reason."

"Where did you come from?"

He was close enough to kiss her now. But her lips didn't move, she didn't answer, it was as if she wasn't listening at all. Though Kastenbaum glared at her, she was almost invisible now: his eyes seemed to pass straight through her. There was nothing there anymore, nothing inside of her. She had given up completely. She stared past Kastenbaum, into the darkness of the warehouse behind him, as if she could see something there. But there was nothing there to see, nothing.

"You're killing him," he said. "You're *killing* him."

And with this he spun the wheel. She turned once, slowly. Then he spun it again, harder. This time she went around a little bit faster. He spun it again and again, and with each revolution he said, *"Go,* Marianne. Leave us!" And then, "Leave us to our lives!" He was becoming increasingly desperate each time, but each time she said nothing, even after the fifth, sixth, and seventh times. She acted as if it didn't matter anymore, as if nothing mattered. And he supposed nothing did. He knew she had to be dizzy now, because he was dizzy himself, watching her. He was out of his head. His hand brushed against his pocket, and he felt it there, like running into an old friend: his bottle. He took it out and drank from it. He felt it in his blood, the elixir. The inside of his skull hummed with a pleasant buzz that soon turned into a roar. All he could do now was watch her revolve, and he stood there doing just that, not really knowing where to go from here.

This is when he saw the knives. They were on a wooden rack

behind a box against the wall. He moved the box for a better look. There they were, all of them, so bright, so silver, they created their own light. There were about a dozen of them. Some were very small, but, one by one, they graduated in size until the last one, which was like a saber, which looked as if it could slice somebody right in half. Kastenbaum wasn't even sure he could lift that one, so he picked up one in the middle of the rack. It was half as long as his arm. A meticulously detailed scene was inscribed on the handle—a picture of Abraham, about to slice off his son's head. Kastenbaum looked at it for a long time, because it was so beautiful, and she watched as he looked at it, as the wheel kept turning around. It kept turning for an impossibly long time.

He walked away from the wall and stood before the wheel in the small gray pool of light beneath the bulb. He knew how to throw a knife. He had been throwing them for years, ever since he saw Thurston do it when he came to town one night in 1934. This is what got him interested in magic in the first place. Thurston was amazing. Amazing! He was not known as a knife-thrower, but, like all masters of art, he could do it when he wanted, and that night he had. His assistant had been blindfolded, and he threw knife after knife at her, and she walked away, as beautiful and perfect as she had been before the heart-stopping demonstration. Kastenbaum remembered waiting for him at the stage door in the alley after the show. He waited until everybody else gave up and left. It seemed to take forever, but Thurston did come out. Kastenbaum was nervous, but Thurston was quite kind. Thurston took his big black hat off, smiled at the boy, and said he would answer one question. Any question the boy had he would answer, but then he had to go. Kastenbaum of course had a hundred questions; he had a *thousand*.

As I did. When Henry came here, a black magician who wasn't even black, who seemed to come out of the ether itself and then disappear right back into it, I had a thousand questions, too. The difference, the difference between Kastenbaum and myself, is that I had a chance to ask them, and every day I did, I asked another and another and another, and that's how I pieced together this story. I have no idea how much of it is true, but that hardly matters to me. I learned *his* truth. That's how I know he never loved me, and how I know it had nothing to do with me or the great stone object I have become. It was him, all him. How could he love me after all of that, after his mother, his father, his sister, and then, finally, this? I had a thousand questions, and I asked them, and he answered them all.

But Kastenbaum only had the opportunity to ask Thurston one. So he asked the first one that came into his head. *Throwing knives*, he asked his hero. *Is there a trick to it?* And Thurston smiled. He placed his big black hat on his head and said, *Oh yes, son, there's a trick to it. You have to want to miss.*

The Lost Years

Henry knew the way by heart, but it was the only thing left in his life he knew that way. The road snaked up a wooded hill, past eucalyptus trees and magnolias and a grove of mulberry. Blackberry bushes grew wild along the side of the road. No easy passage here, not now. Years ago, long before Henry came, it had been a road for horse-drawn wagons, but it had never really been widened for the automobile, especially for one as large as Henry's, a bright-red Buick Eight. If another car had met him going the other direction, one of them would have had to veer off into the overgrown meadow and wait for the other to pass.

But there were no other cars. Henry was alone. Such a tall man, his knees knocked against the steering wheel, and his head brushed the roof. It was as if he had grown up without a sense of dimension relative to the rest of the world; he was always either too big for it, or too small. And after he had been almost every conceivable color, all color seemed to have been drained from him now. You could look straight through him. Thirty years old. I've watched him grow into his sorrow, like a boy growing into his father's clothes; the day comes, and they fit.

It's hard, though, even for me, to remember him the way he was. Memories fade, older ones replaced by new. But I do recall him, at our parties, dressed in his little blue suit, telling all the guests what their names were. He knew everybody's name, and sometimes middle name, too. *Lloyd Carlton Krieder. Miss Abby Lynn Brown.* All our fine friends in their finery, my husband and I so proud. Henry carried himself, even then, like a leader. Looking at him, you thought, *There is the future.* None of this seems to matter now. What difference can it make to know things that no longer were? To know when it was better. To know that he was once a boy.

Everything had changed. The last time he was here, rosebushes bloomed everywhere, and as the winding road snaked up the mountain, the dusty pink petals paved the way: it was like leaving one world and going to another. Way back when, taking care of the rosebushes was one man's entire job. His name was Curtis. I'm sure Henry remembered him. He wore a green jumpsuit and a yellow cap, and liked to rub Henry hard on the top of his head every single time he saw him, and he would look toward the ground and, in mock surprise, say, *Somebody dropped a freckle!* Then he'd pretend to pick it up and place it back on Henry's face. But clearly Curtis wasn't here anymore; now the bushes grew wild and spindly, and the roses were dry and would have crumbled at his touch. The road itself had been washed out, by time and wind and rain. Henry imagined that, not so long from now, the entire road would vanish, and no one would know what was at the end of it. In fact, glancing in his rearview mirror, he could see the road disappearing behind him as he drove over it, rolling up like a carpet, not even there anymore.

He wondered if he would be able to find his way back out.

Before turning into the final bend, Henry imagined the hotel as he'd seen it last. It wasn't hard to conjure. There was something so fantastic about the place—its elegance—*timeless elegance* is how the brochures put it—and its unabashed siren call to those lucky few who could do with only the best, that it had etched its image on a special part of his mind reserved for splendor. Giant shrubbery groomed into the shapes of dogs and horses. Marble floors, gilded ceilings, staircases that seemed to lead all the way to heaven, the music, the laughter, the smell of beautiful women. And the unmistakable feeling that you were among the truly special people, the best of the best, the cream of the crop, even if you weren't cream yourself, even if you lived in the basement with the rats. The Hotel Fremont.

But that was a long time ago, and, like Henry, it had changed. The wondrous building of so many rooms stood like an ancient ruin crumbling into rock and dust. It was hollow and dead. Even the doors were gone. He parked his car at the foot of the stairs leading to the lobby, and began walking. He could see into every room. Within their darkness, he thought he saw someone, or something, vague and smoky shapes, shapes that drew back into the darkness as he approached, and then disappeared altogether. A cold wind blew from every room, and small dark birds made their nests in the windows. What had happened to this paradise? The same thing that happened in the first one, he thought: a great sin had been committed here, and God had sent the people away.

He took the back stairs up to the seventh floor. This was his old route, the one he used to take every day, ten times or more, with and without Hannah. As rotted as they were, and with every third or fourth slat missing, these stairs were as familiar to him as his own hands. The cool smooth of the railing. If he'd had a childhood at all, this was where it had happened, climbing and descending these stairs, hiding, and being found.

Room 702 did have a door, though, and it was closed. He raised his hand to knock, but paused. He didn't need to knock on this door. He knew who was on the other side of it, and the man on the other side knew he was coming. He had to. He knew what was going to happen before it happened, because he wrote the script. Nothing Henry could do would surprise him.

He opened the door, and there he was, Mr. Sebastian. There he was, sitting in the same big red velvet high-backed chair, dressed in his fine black tuxedo, in his shiny shoes, with his hair combed back, a smile on his lips, his face as deathly white as it had always been. He was the same, down to the quarter with the image of George Washington on it sliding through his fingers.

"Henry," he said. "Come in."

Henry didn't speak. What could he say? He found it hard to breathe, as if his chest were being slowly constricted. But he resisted. He fought past whatever it was—it may have been his own heart—and looked around the room. Nothing had changed here, either. It was as if maid service had only just left. The bed was neat, not a wrinkle on it, not a speck of dust anywhere that he could see.

Henry had brought a knife with him, small enough to fit in his pocket but sharp enough to kill. He felt it there, held it without seeming to hold it at all, as only a true magician can. It could fly from his fingers at any moment, as if on wings.

He locked eyes with Mr. Sebastian. Henry was fearless, the way men who have nothing to lose are fearless. "I'm going to kill you," he said.

"I know," Mr. Sebastian said, so cool. "I know. But not now. Not today. Later. Another place, another time. Today we have other business."

The quarter continued to slide through Mr. Sebastian's fingers, as if it had a mind of its own, as if it would continue its unceasing journey even if Henry were to sever the hand from his body.

Henry slipped the knife back into his pocket. "So you know why I'm here."

Mr. Sebastian gave him a patronizing smile. "Of course," he said. "The real question is, do you?"

Henry nodded, though he seemed less sure of this than his counterpart. "I want to see her," he said.

Mr. Sebastian feigned confusion. He wasn't confused, of course. He was never confused. But he liked to seem so. "Her?" he said. "*Her?* I'm not sure which *her* you mean."

It was then Henry saw a door in the corner of the room open. Henry had always assumed it was a closet. But it wasn't. It was the door to everything that wasn't this world.

And I came out.

He didn't recognize me at first, I could tell. That hurt my feelings a little bit, the way he looked at me, not knowing. All he saw was a woman dressed in the style of clothes women of a certain means used to wear—tight, frilly, and corseted. Her hair pinned back in a bun, her face a bit drawn and sallow. It had been a long time since he'd seen it. And yet—

"Mother," he said.

I let the word nest in my ears. "Henry," I said.

He wanted to come to me, I could tell. But there was not going to be any of that, and Henry knew it. He was not going to pass Mr. Sebastian's chair. We were so close, but we could come no closer.

"I started it," I said. "All of this. I'm so sorry, Henry."

"What do you mean?"

"Everything that's happened, and everything that will. I wish I hadn't died, that's all I mean. I think if I'd lived things might have been different." No use in saying any of this, nothing changed by it, but it had to be said. I had been waiting forever to say it.

"You were sick," he said. "There was nothing you could do."

"There's always something you can do when you're alive," I said. "I just didn't do it."

He shook his head and smiled, so forgiving, but I couldn't bear it another moment. I had to turn away. I covered my face with my hands and cried. There really was nothing I could do, nothing, and for a mother there's no worse feeling.

Mr. Sebastian was sympathetic. "Now, now," he said.

Then he looked toward the door, and Marianne La Fleur came in.

She seemed to float into the room, as dark and ethereal, as beautiful as she had been in life. The same. Restored, exactly as Henry wished to remember her. When they found her in the warehouse, this was not how she'd looked. She'd been decorated with knives from top to bottom. Not a single one had missed its intended target.

"Marianne," he said.

She simply looked at him with her sad eyes.

Now Henry wondered how many of the dead were back there. He wondered if Kastenbaum was there. Kastenbaum, the last of the long line of people he had known and loved and lived beyond. Kastenbaum had been put to death in the electric chair at Sing Sing, just a month ago. Henry had loved him once, even though he didn't fully realize this until after Kastenbaum was dead. Kastenbaum had saved him after the war, that day on the docks. Stepping off the boat, Henry had had no idea where he was going, what he would do with his life, and Kastenbaum had shown him a way. Reason enough to love him.

Henry waited, but Marianne didn't speak. He just wanted to hear her say his name. That was always the best thing, her voice softly speaking his name, not because it was his name but because it was her saying it. Mr. Sebastian seemed to be enjoying the moment, allowing them this impossible opportunity to look once again into each other's eyes.

"She's something, isn't she?" Mr. Sebastian said. "Not many like her. A real catch. Too bad about what happened."

Henry's fingers felt the outline of the knife in his pocket. It would be of no use to him here, he knew that, but it felt good to touch it, as if it might.

"Marianne," he said. Still she didn't speak.

The devil smiled. "And now for the star of our show. Are you ready? Introducing the lovely, the talented, the gone but not forgotten—the *never* forgotten—Miss Hannah Walker."

The moment between this mock introduction and her actual appearance seemed to last forever. Henry felt his heart beating. He felt it beating in his head, in his fingertips. And then she was there. She came with the small steps of a little girl unsure of her footing. She was nine years old. The hair so long and blond, the eyes uncluttered by experience, her wrists still so small he knew he could wrap his fingers around them almost twice. And so much more beautiful than anything he had ever seen before, he wondered how she ever could have existed at all.

She walked out into the room and stood beside Marianne. Then, hesitantly, she moved to stand between Marianne and me. I felt her little shoulder leaning against my hip. Hannah, my sweet girl, was a little nervous. She played with her fingers, looked at the floor, then back and forth between Marianne and Mr. Sebastian, as if she was not quite sure what to do, now that she was here. Then she looked at Henry and smiled. The moment she saw him she smiled, and what a gift it was for him to see it.

"You did kill her," Henry said to Mr. Sebastian, having known it all along but not as certain fact. "She's dead."

"Of course she's dead," Mr. Sebastian said. "This little girl is, anyway. How could you think, even for a moment, that she wouldn't be?"

Henry heard something in that: the devil's cunning words. "What's that mean?" Henry said. "This little girl is dead?"

Mr. Sebastian smiled, and then he almost whispered: "I'm not going to answer that. I'm cultivating an aura of mystery, you see. It's like magic: you don't want to give too much away."

Henry looked at Hannah, and she looked at him.

"Hi, Henry," Hannah said.

"Hi, Hannah."

She blushed. "You're so *big*," she said.

"I know. That happens."

She nodded, but this was news to her. "Oh," she said.

Mr. Sebastian removed his watch from his vest pocket and sighed. "Unfortunately, we don't have all the time in the world. Let's get this show on the road!"

Henry looked at Hannah, at Marianne, and at me, and then at Mr. Sebastian. "What do I do?" Henry said. "I don't know what to do."

"That's why I'm here," Mr. Sebastian said. "To tell you." He took a deep breath, and flattened the wrinkles of his pants leg with the palms of his hands. "Here's the deal," he said. "You get to take one of them back."

"One of them," Henry said.

"That's right," he said. "One."

"But I want them all," Henry said. "All of them."

"I know. That's the hell of it, Henry," he said, and playfully winked.

Marianne, Hannah, and I stood there on display. We all looked at Henry, and Henry looked back and forth at us. We could hear his heart beating. The sound of it filled the room.

"Only one," Henry said softly.

"Only one."

Henry paused, about to make the biggest decision of his life. He thought of Hannah at the window of my room, when he had lifted her high enough to get a good view of my death. This is the last time I saw my children, beautiful even through the milky panes. But at least I'd had a life, and Marianne had had one, too. Good lives? Not entirely. And deaths not to be envied.

But Hannah—Hannah's life had only just begun when she was lost to Henry. There had been almost nothing to it at all. And the truth, as anyone could have told you, is that he loved her best.

"Hannah, then," he said softly. "If I can only take one, Hannah."

I was happy with his choice. My heart broke—whose wouldn't?—but in the deepest parts of me, I was happy.

Not so Marianne. She closed her eyes to hide her distress, for, as close as she'd been to death, she had always wanted to live. She shook her head and looked at Henry, so sad.

And then we, Marianne and I, stepped back.

But Hannah stayed where she was. She looked at Mr. Sebastian, and then at her brother. She tried a smile, but she couldn't quite make one. A difficult moment.

"I don't know," she said.

Henry hadn't expected this. "You don't *know*?" Henry said. "You don't know what?"

She couldn't look at Henry now. When she spoke, it was in the smallest voice. "I don't know if I want to go," she said.

Mr. Sebastian's eyes widened in mock surprise. "Well, this is certainly an unexpected turn of events!" He looked at Henry. "I had no idea. I swear."

"Hannah. I can take you *back*," Henry said. "You can live. You can have a life."

"I *know*," she said. "It's just that I've been here so long, longer than I've been anywhere else. I guess—I think I'm just used to it." She smiled a little. "I'm not unhappy."

"But you're *dead*, Hannah," he said. "Dead."

She shrugged her shoulders. "So are a lot of people," she said. "But Henry," she said brightly, "what about Marianne? She hasn't been here as long. She's not so used to it yet. Take her, Henry. That would be the best choice, I think."

Henry couldn't believe this was happening. He was giving her life—and she refused!

Mr. Sebastian tapped a finger on his pocket watch. "We don't have forever," he said. He looked at Henry. "At least, you don't."

"Of course," Henry said, extending his hand. "Of course. Marianne, then."

And then she looked up at him with her dark eyes. But there was more life in them now than he had ever seen in them before.

"As your second choice, Henry?" she said. "The runner-up? No, Henry. I don't think so."

"But Marianne—"

She fixed him with a piercing stare. "I would rather be dead than go with you," she said.

Then he looked at me, the last in line.

"Mother?" he said. "Please?"

But I had already had enough of life. It would have been too hard for me to go back now. Even though I didn't say it, Henry knew. And the truth was, he didn't want me. He didn't need me, not anymore.

Mr. Sebastian sighed and shook his head. "I'm sorry, Henry," he said. "But maybe it's for the best. Everything happens for a reason. Let go of the past. Maybe that's the lesson here. *Let go of the past.* Forgetting is always better, especially when the only things you have to remember are sad."

And so Henry turned and left, he left us here, and he descended the stairs, and got in his car, and he drove down the roadless hill, past the crumbling roses and the eyes of all the ghosts who watched over him, and away from the Hotel Fremont forever, alone. I missed him already, but I couldn't watch for another moment. I closed my eyes, and I never opened them again.

Justice

May 31, 1954

My name is Carson Mulvaney, and I run a small private-detective agency in downtown Memphis, Tennessee. I come into this story late, but that's the nature of the business I'm in. I come into every story late; in fact, I'm usually the last one to appear. I'm the last person anyone wants to call, the last to be asked, *Can you help me?* And though I almost always say yes, the truth is usually no. I can't.

The sordid and often tragic events that occasion the request don't, as a matter of course, lend themselves to happy endings. Therefore, I think of myself not so much as *help* as a jaundiced light shed onto the darkness of someone's life. That being said, my work, more than anything else, is about love. Most people don't understand that. Maybe it's about someone who has chosen the *wrong person* to love, or about someone who has invested hopes and dreams with the *wrong person*, or about desire, which is not, in and of itself, a bad thing at all. But any of these can have negative results.

It's an unfortunate fact of my work and, I would have to say, of life itself, that only love can take us to the darkest places.

There are cases, such as this one, in which I'm asked to find somebody who is lost, or gone, or somehow misplaced in the rush of time and distance that comes between us all. I like these cases. This kind of case, more than anything else I do, is about love. Is there anything better than knowing someone wants to find you? Is there anything better than being found?

Well, yes.

This was my second trip to Jeremiah Mosgrove's Chinese Circus. The Korean War was winding down, atomic bombs were exploding in the Nevada desert, and I was on my way to a sideshow. I'd been hired to find Henry Walker and I had found him, a month ago. Normally, that would have been the end of the story—once is usually enough—but this case presented its own unique complications, and so here I was, back to find him again. I had something I finally needed to tell him.

The first person I spoke to was Jeremiah Mosgrove himself. He was an open-faced man with a large mustache who apparently ate well and, until I handed him my card, seemed happy to see me.

He looked at the card, at me, and back at the card. "Private detective?" he said.

"Yes sir," I said. "That's right."

He nodded, and studied the card again. He stifled a laugh.

"Is something funny, Mr. Mosgrove?"

"Oh no, not really," he said. "It's just that you don't strike me as the private-detective type."

I straightened my tie. "And what type do you imagine a private detective to be?" I asked him, as though this were the first time I'd encountered such a reaction.

He leaned back and forth in his chair, thinking. "You know," he said, "the big tough-guy type with the snappy rejoinders. The type who floats in on a breeze of alcohol and disappointment, a day late on his last shave, hardened and sad. Kind of like—"

"Humphrey Bogart in *The Maltese Falcon*."

He nodded. "Yes," he said. "Exactly."

I sighed. "That's a movie, Mr. Mosgrove."

"I'm aware of that."

"This is not a movie," I said.

"I'm aware of that as well."

His attitude implied that the distinction was unnecessary, that he knew as well as anybody what was real and what wasn't, in part, I'm sure, because that was his business: selling the unreal, the manufactured. He had to know the difference. But he was a victim of the ruse as much as the next guy.

I am not Humphrey Bogart. I have a slight, delicate frame, one you'd sooner associate with a pre-adolescent boy than with a forty-two-year-old man. A strong wind won't knock me over, but it can set me back a bit; if I turn my shoulder into it, though, I'm fine. I've never had it measured, but I know my head is small. My face, smaller yet, is crowded with everything one expects to see on a face, but again, in miniature. My eyes, nose, and mouth are tiny. But then, they have to be in order to fit there. I shave and bathe on a regular basis. I do both twice a day, once in the morning and once in the evening. And I have three cats—Howie, Joe, and Lou—who, when I'm traveling, I entrust to my neighbor Mrs. Lefcourt, who takes very good care of them, and brings in my mail, too.

So I'm a disappointment to many people who have expectations about who they'd like me to be. Believe it or not, I can be tough. I have even, on occasion, been known to utter the snappy rejoinder. I can be that man. It's a mask I wear, when necessary. Sometimes it's easier to conform to other people's ideas about you than to ask them to see you as who you really are.

"Good," I said. "Let me tell you why I'm here."

"You writing a book? The two-headed embryo is a gaff, by the way," he said, "if that's what this is about."

"It's about Henry Walker, Mr. Mosgrove."

Very quickly, Mr. Mosgrove lost his affectations and became attentive. He dropped the attitude and looked at me with a pair of sad eyes. "Has he been found?"

"He's not here?"

"No," he said. "He disappeared last week. No one knows where he went."

"No one?" I took out my pad and flipped through it until I came to the first clean page. "He didn't have any friends here? Anyone he might talk to?"

"I was his friend," he said icily. "He talked to me."

"But he didn't tell you anything? Plans, a desire to leave, or where he might go if he did?"

"Nothing like that," he said. "That's why I'm a little concerned. If he didn't tell me—"

"Is there anyone else he might have spoken to? Any other friends?"

Though loath to admit it, Mr. Mosgrove said he did.

I left to find Rudy, the Strongest Man in the Entire World.

The beguiling stench of spilled bourbon greeted me at the strongman's trailer door. I used my friendly knock, but he responded with a low growl. "Go away," he said.

I waited for a beat and knocked again. "Go away again," he said.

I thought about it. I didn't know how strong he was, but if he was half as strong as he sounded, he could break me like a fresh stick of celery. "I brought a friend with me," I lied. "The name Jack Daniel's ring a bell?"

"Two bells," he said. "Like a church. Go away."

"Rudy," I said, "I need to ask you a couple of questions. About a man named Henry Walker. They tell me you were his friend."

After this he didn't tell me to go away. He was quiet. Then I heard him lumbering toward the door. He opened it and stuck his head out—big and bald and angled like a square. I pitied his mother on the day he was born.

"Were?" he said. "What do you mean, 'were'?"

"I didn't mean anything," I said. "What do you think I meant?"

He thought about it. "That he was dead," he said. "That those greasers had killed him."

"Tell me about them."

"Three of them," he said. "Three greasers."

"Mind if I come in, so we can talk?"

"Well." He looked behind him. "It's kind of a mess."

"That's fine," I said.

He eyed me the way people had been eyeing me all day. "You're not a cop," he said.

"No, I'm not. Thank you for noticing."

With one last look, he disappeared back inside; I had to believe this was my invitation. Gingerly I followed him.

His place was not a mess. It was in a disarray so perfect it could only have been done by an artist. My mother had an expression, *A place for everything and everything in its place,* an adage I had grown to see the truth in. But nothing here was in its place. There was a plastic coffee cup on his pillow, and his pillow was on the floor. A preponderance of evidence suggested he dined on his bed. The refrigerator door was open, casting the sole light. I felt like I had entered the cave of an advanced prehistoric man.

I sat down on something that looked like a chair. "Tell me about the greasers," I said.

"You first. Why are you looking for Henry?"

"I've been hired to," I said.

"Really?"

"Yes, really."

"By who?"

"A family member," I said.

"Now I know you're lying," he said.

"Why is that?"

He found his bottle, grasped it with his giant hand, and thrust it into his mouth. He drank it, straight. In a heartbeat it was gone.

"Because he didn't have one," he said. "Everyone in his family is dead."

"Not everyone," I said.

He gave me a look I'd seen before, the kind of look preceding an outburst of violence. But sometimes it was just a look, and that's what I was counting on here. "You're confusing me," he said. "I hate it when people do that."

"Then let me explain," I said. "My name is Carson Mulvaney. I'm a private detective. Are you aware that Henry Walker had a sister?"

"Of course I am," he said. "He told me all about her. She's dead. Very dead. Dead for a long time."

"She seemed quite lively the last time I saw her," I said.

"What's that supposed to mean?"

"I'm working for her," I told him. "Hannah Walker is alive."

For the next minute or so, Rudy's eyes had that vacant expression usually reserved for corpses. I've seen corpses—well, one corpse. It was an old lady who'd crossed against the green. She never saw it coming. His eyes had that same faraway look hers did, as if he were trying to remember something he never would. The truth tore someplace deep inside of him apart. He looked up at me with eyes so small they were almost invisible beneath his Cro-Magnon brow.

"Jenny needs to hear this," he said.

"Of course," I said. "I'm willing to talk with anyone."

"And Jeremiah, too," he said. "And JJ, I reckon. They all need to hear this. Unless you're full of it. I hope you're not full of it, mister."

"I can assure you that I'm not," I said.

He gave me another hard look. "Then follow me."

I followed him. Through years of practice, he'd learned how to angle himself through his trailer door so that what looked impossible was achieved with some aplomb. He turned left and loped along the side of the trailers until we got to a small tent where, if I remembered correctly from the garish poster, Spiderella plied her trade. But she wasn't in there now.

"Go in here and wait," he said. "I'll be right back."

I did as I was told. He was gone for close to four and a half minutes, and when he returned he had something in his arms. It looked like a long chunk of petrified wood, until I saw it had a head. And feet. And probably everything in between. But the rest of it was beneath a blanket, and I didn't particularly care to peek. The only parts that moved were its lips and eyes, and I realized that, whatever else it was, the part I saw was alive, and that it was a woman.

"This is Mr. Mulvaney," Rudy said.

"Charmed, I'm sure," she said.

"Hey."

"This is Jenny," Rudy said. "She and Henry, they were pretty close."

"It's nice to meet you," I said, and I instinctively stuck out a hand for her to shake.

"Sorry," she said. "I don't shake hands. Germs." And she smiled.

A minute or two later, Jeremiah and JJ pushed through the tent's flap. Jeremiah I knew. He nodded in my direction. JJ was as taut and tight as a guy wire.

"Hello," I said. But they didn't give me the courtesy of a reply.

"So go on," Rudy said. "We want to hear this."

So I told them. I told them because I could see that, beneath each of their respective odd shells, some easier to see than others, they cared. There was a lot of love for Henry Walker in that tent. And I have a soft spot for people who love like that. They're as rare as ivory-billed woodpeckers, and just as beautiful.

I started my story.

I was between things when she called, though I can't point to a time I haven't been between things, or things have been between me and something else. I had spent a good part of the morning, as I did every morning, doing the crosswords, straightening the office, and waiting for the phone to ring, but when it did it never failed to make my heart stop. One never expects the unexpected. I tried to be the hopeful sort, but there was something about my office—a gray corner space toward the back of a three-story red brick building, reachable only via a creaky grilled elevator run by a blind man. This was the best I could afford. The darkness never failed to depress me. *I should get out more before the sun goes down,* I thought. But I never did.

I had the radio on all day. That's how I kept up with current events. The Rosenbergs were about to executed, Eisenhower was sworn in, and a flood in the North Sea killed almost two thousand people. Good to know.

At any rate, she called, I answered, and she asked me what I did. She had a sweet voice. I liked it quite a bit, the way her words felt in my ear.

"What do I do?" I said. "I'm an investigator. Exactly what it says in the directory." I could have been more polite, but I was having trouble with twenty-seven down: *Lost in quagmire.*

"A *private* investigator?"

"I keep things to myself," I said. "Yes."

"Because I'd like to keep this private," she said.

"From who?"

I wanted to keep her talking. With every word, her voice became sweeter, as though she were just about to launch into song. The kind of voice that made people happy. She had no real accent that I could glean. She was cupping a hand over the telephone; my years of experience told me that. I could picture her in her kitchen, alone, the telephone cord stretched to breaking. "It doesn't matter," she said.

So already I had a good idea where this was going. "You don't have to tell me. Husband troubles? You want to keep it private from him because he's keeping things private from you, and you want to find out what those things are. Such as where he really goes when he says he's going bowling."

She laughed. "No, nothing like that," she said.

"Did he tell you that?"

"Listen," she said. Now it was getting hard to hear her at all. Her voice didn't even qualify as a whisper anymore. Little sounds were carried on her breath, through the wires, right into my ear. So I listened hard. "Maybe we should talk, in person."

"I was counting on it. My office is on Third Street. I can meet you anywhere within walking distance."

"How far can you walk?"

"Not that far," I said.

"Because I'd like you to come here. I have a baby, and it's easier if I don't have to leave. Do you think you could come here? To Concord Heights?"

I said I could.

Concord Heights was a ritzy Memphis neighborhood of modest castles about six miles away. To buy a house there, you needed a lot of money plus a letter of permission from God. Only the best people lived there, which meant it was rife with all the known deadly sins, plus others they didn't have names for yet. A private investigator could make a good living off the peccadilloes committed in one square block of the place, and, regardless of what she said, I thought this is what I was in for.

I was wrong.

Mrs. Hannah Callahan was her name. Not Walker anymore. She looked like the kind of woman I could swear I'd seen before, just not in person. People like me don't meet women like Hannah Callahan: we see them on the covers of magazines. In other words, she was as beautiful as a summer's sky, a girl who could do more than stop traffic: she could stop a train. Blonde, skin like fine silk, and a body that made an hourglass look like half an hour. I stared at her for about a minute too long. She waited until I looked up and then asked me to come in.

"You didn't park on the street, did you?" she asked, peering out.

"I didn't park anywhere," I said. "I took the bus."

"The bus comes out here? I didn't know that."

I didn't tell her I wasn't sure my car could make it this far, but let her believe I was following her instructions: she didn't want anyone knowing I was here. I'd told her I understood. As necessary a part as I might play in this drama, I was, as I said, the undesirable part of it. Private means private; it also means secret, and sometimes it means dark. This doesn't do a great deal for my self-esteem.

"Would you like something to drink?" she asked me.

"A glass of water would be nice."

"Have a seat, then. I'll get it."

I watched her walk away. I felt as if I were seeing something I shouldn't. Beauty such as hers strikes a man that way.

I sat down in one of the plush wingback chairs. It was purple and made of a material that had no connection to nature at all, and made me think of yellow people in a big room with lots of sewing machines. The couch was the size of the average American car; they must have had the couch first and then constructed the house around it, because there was no door big enough for that couch to get through. Add to this a major chandelier, a painting of a dog with a rabbit in its mouth, and a bookcase full of real books. If these people worried about money, they only worried about how to spend it.

I heard a baby crying from one of the upstairs bedrooms.

She came back holding a little tray. On it were a pitcher, a glass, and a little bowl of ice. In the bowl of ice was a set of silver tongs she used to delicately remove three cubes from the bowl into the glass. Then she poured the water.

"I expected someone . . . different," she said.

"People do."

"Someone like—I don't know—Humphrey Bogart?"

"I understand," I said.

She blushed. "I guess that's just the movies," she said.

I nodded. I thought I would just let her talk about Humphrey Bogart until she got tired of talking about him. But she was all done.

She smiled. "You're wondering why I asked you here," she said.

"Yes," I said. I took out my pad and pencil.

I had a personal bet with myself that, no matter what she'd said on the phone, it was a cheating husband. But I lost.

"I want you to find my brother," she said.

I wrote down the word *brother*. "Okay," I said.

"Okay?"

"I mean, yes. Of course. I'll find your brother."

She sipped from her glass. She was having a Coke. "I didn't realize it was that easy."

"Well, either it's easy or it's not," I said. "Either way, I'll find him."

"How can you be so . . . confident?"

"I'm not," I said. "But if I said I couldn't find him, would you hire me?"

She smiled. "That makes sense," she said.

"But you're going to have to tell me some things," I said.

"Of course. Like what?"

"Things like his name, what he looks like, when you saw him last. If you know where he might be now, in a general sense. Anything, everything. The basic stuff."

All this time the baby had been crying. Not a blood-curdling yelp but a lament. A generalized discomfort. An existential moan. Hannah Callahan looked at me.

"He's okay," she said. "I mean, it's naptime. Deborah's off today."

"Deborah?"

"The nanny."

"Of course," I said. "I wondered where the nanny was." The truth is, I'd never been in the house of a family who had a nanny. I was moving up in the world.

"So," I said, "let's start with all that, and then we'll see where it gets us."

She looked away. "Unfortunately," she said, "I don't really know."

"Come again?"

"I can't answer your questions. I mean, I would answer them if I could," she said, "but I can't. I don't know."

Things tend to get more complicated the longer you stay in one place. I sighed. "Okay," I said. "But these, really, are the simplest questions I could come up with. My idea was to start here and then move into the more difficult realm of likes and dislikes, favorite color, vacation spots." I looked at her. "What *can* you tell me?"

"I'm sorry, Mr. Mulvaney," she said. "I'll tell you everything I know."

"Thank you."

She took another sip of Coke, set it down, and watched some of the moisture beads slip down the cool glass to the coaster.

"The thing is, we were separated when we were children," she said. "I haven't seen him since I was nine years old. I could tell you what he looked like then, but I don't think that would be a big help to you now."

I said it probably wouldn't.

She smiled. "But I do remember him. He had a long sharp nose, black hair. Tall, dark, and handsome, even as a boy. I would imagine he still is—handsome, I mean. Our father was."

"And your father?"

"Dead, I'm sure. Though I haven't seen him in as long, either. You know what it was like back then, during the Depression. People needed to make difficult choices just to survive."

When I was nine, I sold newspapers in a subway station. I waited there until my father got off the train. He was a drunk, and I had instructions from my mother to grab him and bring him home before he spent whatever was in his pocket on what he called his medicine. I thought about sharing this little story with Hannah Callahan, but decided against it.

"His name is Henry Walker," she said.

"Henry Walker?" I said. "The name rings a bell. A little one."

"Yes," she said. "He's a magician. Or was one. He was famous for a little while, after the war."

"Right," I said. "I remember." I wrote this down and looked at her over the top of my glasses. "You know, it's not very hard to find famous people."

"I know," she said. "But at the time—that was almost eight years ago—I wasn't ready. To find him. But I am now."

"Now that he's no longer famous."

She gave me a look, and nodded. "He seems to have disappeared off the face of the earth," she said.

"Well, that's a magician for you. Have you considered that he may be dead?"

"I've considered that."

"And?"

"And I don't care to believe it."

"I see. And if I find out that he is?"

"Then I will. Of course."

"He could have changed his name," I said.

"I imagine there are a lot of things that have changed," she said. She was sad now, and the sadness suited her. She was even more beautiful because of it.

"That's all I can tell you, Mr. Mulvaney. Do you think you can find him?"

"Of course," I said. I stood, and shook her hand. "And you're sure there's nothing else you can think of to tell me?"

"I'm sure," she said.

But even then I knew she was lying. I just didn't know how much.

To make a long story short, I found him. Not far from where we are right now.

When I'm successful, which I am about 50 percent of the time, I have a stock answer when clients ask me how I did it: *It wasn't hard, it wasn't easy. It's simply my job.*

But this was actually quite easy.

Some men have many lives. An insurance salesman in Ohio can just as easily sell widgets in Minnesota, and a widget salesman in California can just as easily sell cars in New Hampshire. But a man who has been a magician since the age of ten, stays a magician for the rest of his life.

A man like Henry Walker, I imagined, wouldn't stray far from the idea of who he was.

My first stop was a little organization called the American Traveling Sideshow Bureau. The bureau was one small office on a small street on the south side of Memphis, between Dexter's Pawn and Carol's Beauty Supplies. I walked in without knocking. The linoleum was cracked and scuffed, and the fluorescent lights flickered bare on the ceiling, and dust motes danced in a stray beam of sunshine that cut through the blinds. A framed certificate from an obscure university hung on one of the walls, but other than that they were bare. There was a desk against the wall, and behind the desk was Howard Spellman, who turned out to be the entire bureau. He wore a nice suit with a pocket watch and a bow tie, and he had a mustache that looked more like an eyebrow for his lip than anything else.

After looking at my card, he leaned back in his chair and stared at me for a moment, then another. He was sizing me up. "If you're here hoping to uncover the seamy underside of the sideshow world, you will have to spend some time in my company. For I have many such stories that go along just those lines. For instance—"

"I bet you do. But I'm not here for that," I said. "I'm looking for someone, and I thought you could help me. Do you keep any records, say, of past and present acts, or employees working with sideshows and circuses?"

"That's exactly what I keep," he said. "That's *all* I keep. As best I can. There's a large turnover in the industry. I maintain an exhaustive compendium related, of course, to sideshows. I know more about them, I daresay, than anyone you are likely to meet in this life."

"Why?" I said.

"I have a fascination with that world and the eccentricities that exist within it."

"I see."

"So how can I help you?"

"Henry Walker. He's a magician. Ever heard of him?"

His face beamed with satisfaction. He had always been the smartest kid in the room, the one everyone hated. "Of course I have."

"I've heard of him, too," I said. "But I'm looking for a little more than a memory. I'm trying to find out where he is."

"Then I can't help you," he said.

"But I thought you knew everything."

"I know everything there is to know. But no one knows that," he said, and lifted a pipe from its little golden stand. He filled it, tapped it, lit it, then blew a little smoke my way. "After the war he did one show—one. People still talk about it. Perhaps this is how you're familiar with him. I would wager that it is. He brought a dead woman back to life."

"A woman wants to find him," I said. "His sister."

He sucked on his pipe and sighed. "Then I wish I could help. I can't. I'm sorry."

What distinguishes good private detectives from those who are not as good is the second question. The second question is always much the same as the first, but different enough to elicit a different response. So I asked.

"You mean there's no Henry Walker working the sideshows, the circuit, anywhere, to your knowledge?"

"I didn't say that," he said. He felt something in his nose and gingerly picked at it. "There *is* a Henry Walker, who happens to be a magician, working in Jeremiah Mosgrove's Chinese Circus. How do I know? you might ask. I have a cadre of like-minded friends who live in various parts of the country, and they send me clippings, advertisements—that sort of thing. And I remember this Henry Walker because— Well, I would, of course. The name having been so famous."

"But I thought you said—"

"I did," he said. "But it's not the same Henry Walker."

"How could you know that?"

He liked this part—knowing so much more than I. He soaked up the moment before giving me the news. "Because he's black," he said. "He's a black man. Henry Walker was white."

I was confused. "So you're telling me there's this black man, a magician, who just happens to have the same name as another magician who was white? That strains credulity."

"Because you know so little of this world," he said. "The world of magic. Many magicians take the names of magicians who came before them. Houdini, for instance, stole his name from Jean-Eugène Robert-Houdin. Of course, Houdini was a great magician. This man, this Negro, is merely trading on the fame of a greater man who came before him. And he didn't even bother to add a syllable. Shows a lack of imagination, if you ask me."

"I was just going to ask you if that showed a lack of imagination."

"It does," he said.

He went to his filing cabinet and rifled through some papers before victoriously removing a page with a flourish. He looked at it. "Yes. According to this, the Chinese Circus was just in Tennessee, for a three-week stay. That was several weeks ago. I imagine they've moved on by now, farther south."

I nodded and stood. "Thanks," I said. "I appreciate it. You've been a big help."

That first time I came here, one month ago, it was just as the last families were leaving, and the circus was closing down for the night. I spoke to a woman; I believe her name was Yolanda. She was kind enough to tell me about a bar where Henry and the rest of them spent their time.

"What do you mean, the rest of them?"

"You'll see," she said.

It turned out to be a no-name bar off a no-name road that provided haven for all the misbegotten people a sideshow employs. Just a shack behind a stand of trees; the only sign it existed at all was the two lights peering out from between the pines and a couple of abandoned cars in a ditch beside the path leading to it. The lights were glowing yellow, like the eyes of a mad dog.

I walked in. I felt as if I'd come into an Elks Club meeting in progress (I'm a member of the Elks Club), but with several key differences. The barkeep was the Alligator Lady. She was serving a midget with one leg, a giant with two, and a pinhead with a hat on. Scattered around the room were the denizens of dark caves and unknown valleys and things that go bump in the night. They all turned to look at me when I walked in, and then went back to their beer, unimpressed. I didn't know how to take this.

And there was Henry Walker. Though he was hardly more than a shadow sitting alone at a table at the edge of the room, his face as black as the darkness he was hiding within, I knew it was him the moment I saw him.

I ordered two beers from the Alligator Lady. Then I approached him.

"Good evening, Mr. Walker." I set the beers on the table. "May I have a seat?"

He looked at the beers, and shrugged. "Sure," he said. "Have two."

He kicked a chair away from the table. I sat. But it didn't seem to make much of a difference to him. He didn't look my way once.

"This beverage is for you," I said.

"Beverage?" he said, and smiled. "That's a big word, Mr.—"

"Mulvaney," I said. "Carson Mulvaney. I'm a private detective."

"Ah," he said. It was as if he'd been expecting me. He drank the entirety of his beer in a breath. Then he looked at mine.

"I don't particularly like beer."

"Neither do I," he said.

Then he drank mine. He sighed, and his eyes took on a faraway look, an empty gaze. I knew that look. His mind was moving into a memory, where one more time we go over all our moves, the left turns and the rights, trying to understand how we got to this place we find ourselves in, how our lives ended up *here* instead of *there*. I could tell it didn't make sense to him, because it never does. Understanding what happened is one thing; why, another entirely. Not understanding *why* is what led to the invention of gods, in my opinion. But I had a feeling Henry Walker had not invented one yet.

"Are you going to take me in now," he said, "or do I have time to say goodbye? I have some friends I'd like to say goodbye to."

"Take you in?" I said.

But he wasn't listening to me. He laughed. "You know, for the longest time I haven't known."

"Known what, Mr. Walker?"

"Whether I wanted to be caught or not," he said. "Whether what I did was right or wrong. It was right for me. I had to do it. But it doesn't feel the way I thought it would. There's a code, isn't there? A code we have to live by if we're going to be a part of the civilized world?"

"I think so, yes," I said. "But—"

"The question is, what happens when you're not a part of it?"

"I'm afraid I don't know what you're talking about, Mr. Walker. I'm here because—"

"Please. Don't play dumb. It doesn't suit you. I'm talking about the man I killed," he said. "Mr. Sebastian."

My face stuttered. A face stutter happens when all expression leaves your face, and all you can do is blankly stare. I was being led into another story, one that, up until now, I had no idea was being told. But I felt I should play along. Thinking on your feet: the most important part of private detection. "Of course," I said. "Mr. Sebastian."

Henry fell in and out of the moment, at the mercy of any thought, any memory that happened to cross his mind. I see that look all the time—when you're talking to someone and you can tell they're not listening, that something else is happening, but it's only happening to them. This was Henry Walker. He was not really here.

"You must be very good at your job, Mr. Mulvaney."

"Yes. Well, I try to be."

He shook his head. "Linking me to the murder. Finding me here. It couldn't have been easy. You must know a lot," he said. "About me."

I nodded. "I know some things," I said. "I know, for instance, that you're not—how do I put this?"

"Black," he said. "That's how you put it, I think."

"Yes."

"It's not a big secret anymore," he said. "I'm careless, miss a spot occasionally. Anybody who cared to look, really *look* at me, could tell this is all a concoction. Shoe polish. But no one looks. When you're black—particularly here, in a place like Alabama—no one really looks long enough to see. It's a disguise," he said. "The blacker I become, the more invisible I become." He smiled. "But you see me."

I took out my pad and my pencil and turned the pad to the first clean page. "Perhaps you could tell me," I said, "how all this happened. This killing. I need to have notes to show my . . . superiors." I didn't know where this was going. But I wanted to go wherever it was and take notes along the way. Just so I could find the way back.

Then he said, "I would love to, Mr. Mulvaney. I'll start at the beginning."

"A good place."

He paused to breathe, to breathe deep, and to adjust himself in his chair. "I can sum up the whole story like this: I had a sister. Her name was Hannah. Our mother died. My father fell on hard times. He got a job as a janitor in a big hotel. A fancy place. Marble floors, high ceilings, the whole shebang."

"I get the idea," I said.

"Hannah and I had a lot of time on our hands. We were big explorers. We met some of the guests. Most of them were the nicest people you'd ever want to meet. But there was one, Mr. Sebastian—such a strange man. Everything about him was strange. He had a skin problem. Pure white, like he'd never been in the sun before, ever in his life. He scared me at first. But he was a magician, and that appealed to me. That's where I learned—that's when I started, because of him. I did everything he told me to. I even took the oath."

"The oath?"

"The magician's oath. Never to tell anyone what I'd learned or who I'd learned it from. And for a long time I held to it."

Something about this, how he looked away from my eyes for the first time since he started talking, made this seem like it was important to him. "Go on," I said.

"He taught me things," Henry said. "He was masterly. And I had a knack for it. Every day, I'd learn something new. It was a great . . . distraction. From my father, from my life."

"But then something happened."

"How'd you know?"

"Something always happens."

I looked down at his hands and at the quarter sliding through his fingers, back and forth. His fingers didn't look like they had anything to do with it at all. Like the only reason they were moving was to get out of the quarter's way. "He was playing me," he said. "Sebastian was playing me. All along, he was after my sister."

"That kind of man," I said.

"No," Henry said, holding me with his eyes. "He wasn't a man at all. He was the devil."

"The devil?"

"The devil himself. He took her. One day they simply disappeared. The police came, said they'd try to find her and all that, but she was the janitor's daughter, and how hard are they going to look for the janitor's daughter? And I couldn't tell them anything, what I knew."

"Because of the oath," I said.

"He mixed his blood with mine," Henry said. "I had him in me. I always have."

"You were a kid," I said, "you were scared," as if saying it would make a difference. But it didn't. My instinct told me that nothing would.

"All I've done my entire life is look for them," he said. He shook his head. "It wasn't the way a P.I. looks for people. I made it a part of my life. It was my calling. I've been around the world, Mr. Mulvaney. Across this entire country. Working. I spent World War II in France and Italy, not because I cared who won the goddamn war—I didn't—but because it was possible they were there. Maybe I'd see a banner with his name on it. *The Magical Mr. Sebastian!* Anything was possible. When I came back, I worked the auditoriums, the sideshows, under what feels now like a million different names, being a million different people, and never stopping, going every place there was a place to be. Everywhere I went, I looked for them. I asked people about him. I described him, his face, his skin."

"And?"

"I never found Hannah, because she's dead. She was dead a long time ago. Probably a week after he took her. So I was never going to find her, and I knew that. But I found him."

"And then?"

He smiled. He waved to the Alligator Lady to bring him another beer. "You know what happened then."

Henry Walker was one of the necessary people in the world. He was the guy the rest of us could look at and say, *As bad as things are, as low as I've fallen, as hard as this life is and will always be, at least I am not Henry Walker.* This is what I learned. If we're all born equals, whole numbers—and that is a shaky proposition in and of itself—Henry's journey through life was an exercise in subtraction. What did he have that wasn't eventually taken away from him? He was like a puddle in the sun: every day he became smaller and smaller, until he almost wasn't there at all. The only gift he ever got—his magic—was a gift from the devil himself—at least, that's who he thought he was. But even that was just a trade: Sebastian gave him magic and then took the one thing Henry loved. So, obviously, Henry had to kill him. It wasn't a decision. It was a fact of his life.

In that way I guess he was lucky. He had a goal.

He used to be a good magician, he told me. He used to be one of the best. But after Marianne La Fleur, after Edgar Kastenbaum, after he tried and failed one last time to make a real life for himself, I've found no records—newspaper articles, word-of-mouth, anything—to substantiate this. The problem was, he didn't know exactly who or what he was. Was he black, or was he white? Unable to choose, he could only be both. He was such a good magician he could play the same venue *twice*—once as a white man, the next as a black. Each time did an entirely different routine. His white performances were modeled on the early greats: Thurston, Kellar, and Robert-Houdin. The white Henry took his magic seriously and expected his audience to take it seriously as well. But his black performances were pure minstrel show. He'd learned how to play the fool, and he played it to the hilt, his big white eyes bulging like Ping-Pong balls from his night-black face, as if the tricks he did surprised even him. He called himself Clarence, the Demon Coon, when he was black, and, when he was white, Sir Edward Mauby, the Perplexing Prestidigitator, who wore a beard as an added disguise. But he really didn't need to. Henry, as himself, had only been seen once, at a single performance, when he'd raised Marianne La

Fleur from the dead. So he was one person, two people, separate but the same. This was the late forties—*the lost years,* he called them. He didn't use his real name again until after he killed Sebastian. Until he came to his final stop.

Clarence and Sir Edward toured America, looking for a man, a magician whom he knew only slightly, and whose real name he wasn't sure he even knew at all. He could only remember what the magician looked like: a slight man with a face so white it could have been painted on with chalk. Hard to forget that face if you saw it even once, and Henry saw it every day, suspended in front of his eyes like one of his own illusions. When he met people in the trade, he'd ask about him, if they'd heard of him, if he'd played there before, if they knew where he could find him. Henry described him for them. *My mentor,* Henry said. *Disappeared. I'd love to see him again, to thank him, for everything.*

But nobody knew him. Nobody had even heard of him.

Except one guy.

This guy, he wasn't even a magician. He was a truck driver. He hauled Ferris wheels for Barnum. He told Henry that one day he'd slipped off the highway for a little R&R and a maybe a cup of coffee at a local diner, where the coffee was better than what you'd get at the gas stations. He'd found a nice little spot called the Lou-Eze and sidled up to one of the stools when he noticed, down at the other end, a man doing magic tricks for a little girl. Seemed nice enough. The girl was with her mother, and they were both loving it, until the mother looked at her watch and said it was time to go. That was it. But he'd remembered because of the guy's face. He'd never seen anything like it. It was whiter than a bowl of flour. It was like his face was dead but the rest of his body wasn't. It moved, fully alive. Scary, is what it was. But the folks there seemed used to him, so the truck driver figured he must live somewhere around there.

And where would that be? Henry asked.

The guy thought about it until he was sure.

Indiana, he said. That would be Muncie, Indiana.

He seemed like a really nice man, the trucker said.

A large crowd had assembled for Henry's next show, but he himself would not attend. Was he supposed to be Clarence, the Demon Coon, that night, or Sir Edward Mauby, the Perplexing Prestidigitator? He couldn't remember. It didn't matter, because he would be neither of them ever again. His last performances had been disasters anyway: he had found himself, during the Mauby shows, slipping into Clarence, the elegant entertainer becoming his goofy, g-dropping, bug-eyed self. Or Clarence, who'd delighted thousands with his self-loathing antics, would suddenly become erudite and pensive. This bewildered Henry more than anyone watching. He had no idea what was happening to him. It was as if each of the characters he had created was more him now than he was himself. If Henry existed as himself at all, it was in the ever-shrinking gap between the two. But there was enough left of Henry Walker to abandon them both, and so, without packing a bag or leaving word with anyone, he drove off into the night bound for Muncie, Indiana. He was only doing what Sebastian had done all those years ago: disappear. His last trick, and his best one.

Muncie, Indiana, was fourteen hours away. Gasoline was an even thirty cents a gallon, and with twelve dollars and change in his pocket he had enough for his tank, some coffee, and a sandwich, with some left over. But he wasn't hungry. He only wanted to drive.

It was like he saw the town waiting for him at the end of an endless passage, the streets and houses almost too small to be seen at first, but steadily becoming defined as he approached. Every molecule in his body was drawn forward. A serious rain began to fall at dawn, the sky flooded, drops big as half-dollars, constant, intense. But even through this downpour he saw clearly in his mind the town up ahead. He could see the town, and the house in the town where Sebastian lived. A small white black-shuttered, not a lot different from any of the others around it except for the magnolia tree off to one side. It had a nice lawn, and a dazzling row of azaleas blooming beneath a bay window. A nice brick walkway off the concrete sidewalk lined with monkey grass, and a screen door between you and the front door, its brass knocker at eye level, and a mail slot halfway down. This is what was waiting for him. But Henry was ahead of himself, and so close to his own fulfillment it was easy to be, because who was going to let a couple of little things like time and space come between you and your destiny?

The rain would not stop falling. The two-lane blacktop disappeared beneath it into the generalized blackness of everything. Dim red brake lights on the side of the road looked like the eyes of feral animals, but were really only fearful travelers unable to move farther into the storm. But not Henry. He kept going. He could have closed his eyes and made it the rest of the way. Now he could walk through the door into the living room, and then into the kitchen, each a glowing testament to the American ideal, a corny commercial for cleanliness and order and normality, a variation on a familiar theme, comfortable and plain. This was the easy disguise his nemesis inhabited: respectability. But in his backyard you'd find the hacked-up remains of a dozen girls. On sunny afternoons his guests would arrive for tea beneath the big umbrella, and Mr. Sebastian would smile, knowing that death resided fourteen inches beneath their feet. The pleasure of the crime lived on in his heart, he was so proud, knowing he'd done it. He took full credit.

Henry saw all of this as he drove through the darkness of dawn.

The sky ran out of rain by the time he got to Muncie. Steam hovered above the baking streets like homeless ghosts. Muncie was a sweet little town. Perfect place to disappear. But Henry had found him. Henry would see him. *Something is seen not because it's visible; it's visible because it's seen.* Someone said that. It was the magician's creed.

Today Mr. Sebastian would be seen.

Henry drove directly to his house. Left, then right, then left again. He didn't ask directions. He didn't look in the directory. He didn't even have to look at the name on the mailbox to know where he was, because he knew the number: 702. It was as if he had been everywhere else and had come to the very last place he could be.

He didn't knock. Just walked right in like he'd been invited.

And there he was, Mr. Sebastian. Waiting. The same man, the same face, the same smile, the same chair. *The same chair.* How that could be, Henry didn't know. But it was. It was all the same, and for a moment Henry was a boy again, facing the devil for the first time. The only thing different was what he wore. The suit was gone. In its place was a knitted cotton shirt, white, a pair of blue slacks, and penny loafers. His new look.

"Hello, Henry," he said.

Henry didn't say anything. He just stared. He had a knife in his pocket, which he lightly felt with the tips of his fingers, a movement so small it seemed impossible to notice. But Mr. Sebastian's eyes fell there, and he pursed his lips, and the smile was different now. His face bore an expression of resigned disappointment. Even though he knew this was going to happen, he'd somehow wished it wouldn't. But now he knew for sure.

"I'm sorry, Henry," he said. "I want you to know that." His eyes seemed to hark back to everything that had happened. "Even though I wouldn't change anything about it, I'm sorry for the grief it's caused you."

Mr. Sebastian paused to give Henry a chance to respond. But Henry didn't say anything. "So—would you like to know what happened to Hannah?"

Now he did speak. "No," he said.

"I'll be happy to tell you," he said. "It's not a long story."

"No."

"Fine," he said, and shrugged. He looked around him, as if the conversation were losing some of its interest. "I think it would disappoint you anyway. Other girls—I have good stories about some of the other girls. But Hannah was an everyday experience in almost every way. Except, of course, for her hair. She had the most beautiful hair, didn't she?"

Henry remembered her hair. The thought of it now, and the thought that Mr. Sebastian had touched it, destroyed him. Before coming here, he had known that he would be destroyed—that they both would—but not so soon, not yet, and not by a memory. Henry felt his chest being carved open from the inside out. Then all feeling left him. The knife was in his hand. Mr. Sebastian's expression remained unchanged. There would have been a greater sweetness to it if Henry had surprised him, but this didn't change anything. "Think *Hannah*," Henry said. And, with all his skill and hatred, the two things he had been practicing all of his life, Henry threw the knife. It spun across the room almost too fast to see, and would have pierced the wall opposite had it not been stopped by Sebastian's heart. A perfect throw. Beautiful, the way everything perfect, even death, is beautiful. After all these hours and years, this took less than a second. The wound closed around the knife, and so there was only a little blood; Sebastian appeared unimpressed. He looked at it, then up at Henry, and smiled.

"You were a good student," he said, reading Henry's mind for the last time. "The best."

And he died.

Henry had entered the house white, but when he left it he was black, the color he would remain for the rest of his life.

Most people who become private detectives do so after a long stint with the police department or some governmental position. But I was drawn to it early and was never able to imagine myself as anything else. I loved school. When I was growing up, all I ever wanted to do was to study, to read, to understand. My parents worried about me, and I worried about them. I could see, by their example and the example of almost every adult I met, that once a boy became a man the search for truth was, for the most part, over. Only academics spent their lives worrying questions, learning, discovering new things. But most people—and my greatest fear was becoming most people—simply gave all that up, and lived happily ignorant of the world around them, of the people around them, even of their own husbands and wives: mysteries, forever and always. That's why I became a detective. I am always curious, learning. I am always figuring things out. There's something liberating about the truth, in and of itself. It's good news, even when the news is bad.

I told Henry that it was not in my power to arrest him. I told him not to flee, that it was possible an officer of the law would come soon and take him away to jail. It all depended on certain things, I said. He shrugged his shoulders. He had already given up.

I never told him about Hannah. I never told him that the sister he took for dead was alive and living two hundred miles away. I should've, but I didn't, and at the time I didn't know why.

. . .

I called ahead because she'd asked me to call ahead. She said that now wasn't the best time, but when I told her I had news, she was quiet for a moment and then told me to hurry. I suspected her husband would be home soon and she was still keeping secrets. Marriage is a beautiful thing.

She came to the door holding her baby. He looked at me suspiciously. Hannah smiled and asked me in anyway.

She looked past me. "You parked on the street," she said.

"This won't take long," I said. Though maybe it would, I didn't know. Say things with enough conviction and people tend to believe you. You can even begin to believe yourself.

We sat down in the same chairs we'd sat in before. There was a crib beside Hannah's chair now, but otherwise nothing at all had changed.

"You said you had news," she said.

"Did I?" I suppose I wasn't being very friendly, but I was never friendly when I learned that someone had been lying to me. When someone lied to me, I became more like the man everybody wanted me to be: Bogie. Marlowe. A tough guy. A man with snappy rejoinders. A man with an unconventional moral code who would break an arm to get the information he needs. All because I hadn't gotten what I'd asked for in the beginning. It was simple, really. All I wanted was the truth.

"Please. Tell me," she said.

"I've done a little research, Hannah."

"Of course. That's your job. That's why I hired you."

"About you, I mean."

This set her back a bit. Not far, but further back than I'd seen her. "Me?" she said. "Really?" She might as well have said, *Whatever for?* Her eyes were that big and surprised.

I gave her the cold stare. "Why didn't you tell me?"

She shifted the baby from one leg to the other. "I'm sorry—tell you what?"

"What *happened*," I said. "What really happened. You told me you were separated from your family when you were a girl. But you didn't tell me how."

"How?"

I stared at her until she relented.

"I didn't think that was important," she said. Another lie. It couldn't have been more obviously a lie if it had had a big flag tied to it with the words I'M A LIE written on it. "Not for what I asked you to do."

"That's the thing," I said. "I decide what's important. A girl is abducted, disappears, is figured for dead, but turns up in Concord Heights more than twenty years later living the life of Riley and never attempts to make it back to her own family? I'm no Einstein, but it sounds important to me."

I threw a copy of a newspaper clipping on the coffee table. I got it from an old friend at the AP who owed me a favor. The story was all there, just like Henry told it. The hotel, the city. The strange man. The disappearance. Everything.

But she didn't reach for the clipping. She didn't even look at it. She didn't have to, because she knew what it was.

"Why didn't you tell me this when you hired me?"

"I don't know," she said. But she knew. I could read her like *Ned's First Reader.* "I'm not hiding anything, Mr. Mulvaney. I asked you to find Henry, not to find out about the particulars of my past. What difference does it make?"

The baby began to cry a little, and she gave him a short, bumpy ride on her knee until he settled down.

"The truth always makes a difference," I said. "That's the business I'm in, Mrs. Callahan. That's all I'm after, the truth, and when I feel like someone is keeping it from me, I get angry."

"You don't seem very angry."

"Another part of my job I'm good at: keeping my feelings to myself."

She wiped the drying tears from the baby's face and then looked at me with the look I'd seen before, the look that says, *Okay, I give up now, this time I'll tell you the truth.* Of course, people usually lied again anyway. But I was ready to give her a second chance.

"What you have there," she said, "that story. That's not what happened. At least, not like that."

"Really?" I said. I picked it up, pretended to read it through. "Seems like a tough story to get wrong, you know?"

She didn't disagree. "Some of it's true," she said. "Just not all of it."

"Go on."

She stood and placed the baby in his crib. He mewled for a minute, but soon he fell to sleep. Hannah rested her hands in her lap and took one deep, preparatory breath.

"I was separated from my family," she said. "That much is true, as I told you. And I never saw my father or my brother again. That's true as well. But it wasn't an abduction, Mr. Mulvaney. It was—an arrangement."

"An arrangement?"

"I—we—didn't have the easiest life," she said. "I'm not whining about it, but that's true. By the time I was ten, my mother had died of TB and my father had lost everything. We had next to nothing. He got a job in a hotel. As a janitor. Can you imagine what that's like—to be a great man, only to have all of that taken from you and to end up . . . like that? He hated himself. He began to drink, a lot, and when he wasn't working he was drunk, and then he was working drunk. We hardly saw him but for dinner. By that time, it was as if he had died as well."

"That's sad," I said.

"It is," she said. "Henry and I were very close. Closer than close. He loved me *too* much, if such a thing is possible. I think he . . . I think he wanted to save me."

"Save you? From what?"

"The world," she said. "The world and all the bad things in it. And for a while I let him. But then something happened."

"What?"

"Two things. I realized he couldn't live my life for me. I don't know if I actually had that exact thought, but that's what it amounted to. After that, there was a distance between us. I wanted something he couldn't give me. We created new lives for ourselves. There was this dog—a stray. He just showed up one day, and I poured everything into him, my whole heart. He kept me alive somehow. Just taking care of him."

"And the other thing?"

She shook her head. "Henry seemed doomed," she said. "Even then. He wasn't someone you would tie your hopes and dreams to. But then he found something else, too."

"Mr. Sebastian," I said.

"Yes," she said. "Mr. Sebastian. That wasn't his real name, of course. He just called himself that to make him seem more—you know—*magical*. For Henry. He wasn't even a real magician. He was just a man who knew a few tricks. He was a salesman, actually; he sold soap, all kinds, even the fancy soaps the nice hotels had. That's why he stayed at the Hotel Fremont."

"A soap salesman," I said.

"Henry became obsessed with him, with learning all his tricks. He was in his room all the time, so much that even my father, as absent from our lives as he was, began to take notice. So he followed Henry one day to see where he was going, and after Henry left, after he'd gotten his trick of the day, my father knocked on the door, went in, and met this man. They spoke for a long time. That day, and every day thereafter for a week or so."

"And Henry?"

"He had no idea."

"Okay," I said. "Go on."

"Mr. Sebastian, as you call him, had made quite a bit of money. Even through the worst times, you see, people need soap."

"Okay," I said.

"My point is that through these conversations my father determined that Mr. Sebastian was a good man, that he had money, and that he had always wanted a family. At least a child all his own."

"So why didn't he have one?"

Hannah laughed, but it was a forced laugh, the kind you bring out when you can't find another sound to make. "A silly thing," she said. "He had this skin condition. He couldn't go out in the sun, because if he did he would burn, terribly. His face was so white it was—well—scary. Women weren't really drawn to him, you see."

"I understand," I said.

"The upshot of all this is that my father couldn't take care of both of us, Henry and me, any longer. He especially couldn't see a life for me, not the way things were."

Hannah paused, purposefully, giving me an opportunity to put things together. She played with her wedding ring, turning it back and forth in half-circles around her finger. I had put things together a minute ago, but I took them apart again, because I didn't like the way they looked. But there it was again. The truth.

"They worked out an arrangement," I said.

"Yes," she said.

"Which was?"

"He gave me away, Mr. Mulvaney," she said. "He gave me to Mr. Sebastian."

I shook my head then, not because I didn't believe her but because what she had just said was having trouble fitting into my brain. I had to shake my head to give it room.

"Your father gave you away," I said, as if by repeating it I could believe it, as if somehow it would make more sense.

She glanced at her sleeping baby, then back to me. "Yes," she said. "I wasn't abducted—I was adopted. He took me in, and I took his name." She smiled. "It wasn't exactly legal. There were no papers signed. I guess you would call it a gentleman's agreement."

"I'm not sure that's what I would call it. Gentlemen don't usually give their children away."

"Judge my father as you wish," she said, a bit haughtily for a woman who had once been traded like a baseball card. "But that's what happened."

"It must have been hard."

"It was," she said. "It was hard, at first. I missed my . . . first father. And Henry—I especially missed Henry. I couldn't imagine what he was going through. But then the three of us—"

"The three of you?"

"Mr. Sebastian, me, and the dog—Joan Crawford—we began to lead such a different life from the one I had known. A good life. He raised me as if I were his own. I can't imagine what would have happened to me had I not gone with him. I had a home, Mr. Mulvaney. I went to school. *College.* I don't think my real father could have managed that. So—yes. It's been good. Astonishingly good."

"Sounds wonderful," I said. I picked up the clipping. "But what about this? Newspapers usually don't make stuff up."

"My father did that, for Henry."

"For *Henry?*"

"He couldn't tell Henry what he'd done," she said. "That he had given me away to someone else. He couldn't live with Henry's knowing that. So he had the police come, and all the rest, so Henry could think . . ."

"That you'd been abducted, raped, and killed," I said. "He thought it was better that Henry thought that? What a dad."

"He was not a brave man, Mr. Mulvaney," she said. "My father did the right thing by me—by giving me a father to take his place.

I believe that with all of my heart. But he didn't do right by Henry. That's why I want you to find him. So I can tell him. I want him to know I'm fine."

And that was the part of this story that seemed so odd and out of place to me. She *was* fine. Anyone could have seen that. She was a beautiful woman who lived in a great house with her baby and a nanny and a husband who was gone all day working. She really did seem happy, and, after meeting and talking with Henry, I couldn't see how this made sense. How such a thing could be possible.

"So," she said, "have you?"

"Have I what?"

"Found him," she said. "Henry. You said you had news, and I thought that must be it."

The hope in her eyes could have lit the world. "I think so," I said. "Yes."

She was excited. "Really? Oh my. Really? Is he still a magician?"

I nodded. "Not a very good one," I said, "according to what I've gathered. But yes. A magician."

"Henry," she said wistfully. "You have no idea how many nights I've gone to sleep thinking of him, just wondering, imagining what it would be like to see him again. I so want to see him, Mr. Mulvaney! I have this family now. Not the kind I imagined I'd have . . . but it is a family. I want him to be a part of it. And we have money. I can help him if he needs it. He can live here with us if he wants to. But most of all I just want to tell him I'm alive. What's he like?"

"You got it right before," I said. "He's doomed."

Hannah was about to speak then, but she heard something. I did, too: a car in the drive. The car door opened, and closed. Footsteps, coming up the walk. She gave me the look, the looks-like-I've-been-caught look. A look I knew in eighteen languages.

"Oh dear," she said.

"He's not the violent type, is he? I can defend myself, of course.

I'm not as weak as I appear. But it would help to know whether I should get into a defensive posture."

She laughed. "No," she said. "He's not the violent type. I don't think I've ever even seen him angry."

"Really? Why all the secrecy, then?"

She stood and examined her beauty in a mirror. She wanted to make sure this man would see her at her best. "Because I didn't want him to think I was sad," she said. She turned to me. "He loves me so much. All he wants is my happiness. And I'm *not* really sad. I just want Henry to be a part of this."

"I should go," I said.

"No," she said. "Tell me more. He won't come inside for a minute anyway. He's going to turn on the sprinklers, then look over the azalea blooms. What he always does when he comes home."

I closed my pad and slipped it, along with my pencil, into my coat pocket. Then I looked at her, and I took a deep breath, one of the deepest I've ever taken in my life. I felt it in my toes. "Before he comes," I said, "there's something I should tell you. Two things, really."

When people say, *There's something I should tell you*, you know it's not going to be good news. She waited, standing still as a winter statue. "Hannah," I said, "Mr. Sebastian—or whatever his name is—he's dead."

"*What?*"

"He's dead. That's the first thing." I thought I should let that settle for moment before moving on. I did. "The second thing is that Henry killed him."

She looked at me now as if she suddenly recognized me as a stranger.

"It's a shock, I know," I said.

"Oh my Lord," she said. "More than a shock. It's the most ridiculous thing I've ever heard."

"Sorry?"

"Are you really a private investigator, Mr. Mulvaney? Because, if you are, you're the worst I've ever heard of."

"I may in fact be one of the worst," I said. "But sometimes, almost by accident, I learn things. I figure things out."

"Well, you haven't figured this thing out. Not that I ever thought you would."

The front door opened. Hannah smiled and fixed me with her beautiful eyes.

"Oh, look," she said. "My father's home."

"Hannah," he said.

I stood, and turned toward the voice.

Her father was wearing a dark-blue suit and shiny black shoes, the edges caked in drying mud. A small man, frail, who took small and careful steps, as if he were afraid of falling. He had a slight limp. But what stood out was his face, of course. It was a ghostly white, exactly as Henry had described it to me.

"Mr. Callahan," I said.

He smiled at me as he approached, hand outstretched. An open, guileless man, I thought. He looked like a very nice man. We shook hands. "James Callahan," he said. "And who do we have here?"

Hannah kissed him on the cheek. "This is Mr. Mulvaney," she said. "He's an insurance salesman."

"Really?" he said. He looked at his daughter approvingly. But he didn't believe her. No one would have. "So—you finally made that call."

"I felt like I had to," she said.

He laughed and looked at me. "Hannah thinks I'm in a flood plain. I keep telling her it's fine and not to worry. But she insists I get flood insurance. What do you think, Mr. Mulvaney? Are we in a flood plain?"

He gave me a hard look then, so that I'd know that he knew I was no insurance salesman. But I played along.

"I think it's a real possibility, Mr. Callahan," I said. "Were the sky to open, you never know what might happen here."

"I'm sure Mr. Mulvaney here knows what he's talking about," he said. "But I still think you should get another opinion."

"I intend to. I'd just told Mr. Mulvaney that, and he was about to leave."

"Wonderful," he said. "And how's Henry today?"

"Henry?" I spoke without thinking. It came out too fast, and too sharp. But I hadn't expected to hear him say that name.

Callahan looked at me curiously. "My grandson," he said.

"Of course."

And then, to Hannah: "Napping?"

She nodded.

"Good for him," he said. "I feel like one myself. First I'm going to get out of this suit, though, and then I'm going to go to my study and take a few notes."

"Notes?"

"James keeps a diary," Hannah said. "I call it his hobby. He writes down everything that happens to him."

"Because people forget," he said, pointing to his head. "And I don't want to forget. Not even the things I'd rather not remember."

"Sounds like a good hobby to have," I said.

"Maybe one day he'll let me read them," Hannah said, smiling.

"One day," he said. "I promise."

We watched him mount the stairs and didn't speak again until we heard the bedroom door close behind him. I looked at the baby. He was sleeping now, peacefully, on his back.

Hannah gave a smile a try, but it didn't quite work. "I imagine this comes as a surprise," she said.

"Something like that," I said. "But I think I'm catching up."

"Forgive me. I should explain."

"Oh, you don't have to," I said. "I think I've got it. Mr. Calla-han—we should call him by his real name now—he raised you to be a good girl. But you weren't."

"You're fresh," she said, blushing. "I wish you weren't."

"Forgive me," I said. "When I feel stupid I start to act tough."

She looked at the baby. "I made a mistake," she said. "A year out of college, I fell in love with someone who wasn't in love with me, and when things became complicated he left. I'm sure you've heard that story before."

I nodded. A little bead of perspiration rolled down my cheek. She noticed and opened a window. Then she turned to me and spoke softly, pausing when she heard even the slightest sound from upstairs.

"Luckily, Mr. Mulvaney, I had a home. And how fine a thing is that—*a home*. A place that's always here for me to come back to. That's all a person really needs, I think. As long as that's out there, this haven, you can afford to make a couple of mistakes. When you have a home, mistakes have time to turn into blessings."

"Like magic," I said.

She walked to the crib and lifted the child out of it and held him close, as though someone might take him away from her.

I looked at her and the baby, and I sighed. I'd figured this all wrong. It wasn't the first time I'd screwed up so perfectly, and it wouldn't be the last. But no one in this little drama was who I thought they were, and that made me feel like I should pack it up and go into business with my brother. He owned a dry cleaner's.

I picked up my hat and turned to go.

"So," I said. "Why didn't you tell me the baby's name?"

"Do I have to tell you everything?" she said.

I looked at her, this beautiful woman standing there holding her perfect baby in this Eden she called home. Birds sang outside in the trees, and the sky was blue, and if it ever got really hot you could order up a breeze the way you would a glass of iced tea. It just goes to show you, I thought. Sometimes, somewhere, and for reasons you would never guess or believe, someone is happy.

As I was leaving, she called out to me. "Mr. Mulvaney," she said. I turned. "Yes?"

"I wonder why Henry said he'd killed him."

I smiled, and thought about answering. But I didn't want to be the smart guy; I didn't need to be. I got in my car and drove away.

I drove back to my office. There were no phone calls or messages or any sign from the outside world that I was known to exist, and so I pretended not to, and it came as something of a relief.

I went for a walk. The night air was thick as peanut butter, and in a black wool suit—the only one I had—I was warm. Memphis is not so much a big city as it is a lot of small towns randomly stitched together. Walking in it at night, I always felt like I was trampling on someone's front lawn. Even a place like Joe's Clam Bar, the sick light of its red neon sign leaking into the dense night-shadows like blood. But Joe's would welcome me, and so would the next place, and the place after that. I took my time visiting my neighbors.

In any other case, I'd have told the truth to all parties involved. Not this one. I couldn't imagine what it would be like to tell Hannah all I'd learned about Henry, or to go back down to Mosgrove's Chinese Circus and find Henry Walker and tell him what I'd learned about Hannah. It was my job, and I was only a messenger. This is what I should have done.

But I didn't. Instead, every morning I woke up, fed my cats, drank a glass of orange juice, had a bowl of cereal, followed by a cup of coffee. Then I'd drive down to my office. When I said earlier that I ran a small private-detective agency, I should have said how small

it is: I am the only one in it. There is no one else. I wish I had a secretary I could buzz through a fancy intercom system and ask to do
something for me—bring me a Danish, or get Mrs. Blandersmith on
the line. But that would entail some very serious life changes I knew
I couldn't afford. I got a little desk calendar to mark the days as they
passed, and at the end of each one I could look back on it as another
day I didn't tell Hannah Callahan or Henry Walker the truth.

Hannah was calling me almost every day by then. I didn't know
what to tell her, so I didn't tell her anything. *I'm working on it* is
what I usually said, using my gruff, scary voice, which apparently
wasn't that gruff or scary, since she kept calling back. I even recognized her ring after a while—it had a sweet lilt at the end of it—and
I stopped answering. She let it ring for a while, too.

Why was this so hard for me, a man who had built his life on finding and telling truths? All I had to do here was tell it. But for the first
time in my life, I wasn't sure whether it was worth it or not. For any
of us. I didn't think Henry really believed he'd killed Mr. Sebastian:
he only wished he had. It was the wish of his life. He made up a story
to go along with the wish, a good story, something he could tell over
and over again to anyone who would sit still long enough to hear it,
and if they all believed it maybe he would come to believe it, too, a
little more each time, until, through its repetition, the reality of his
own life would be obscured, and in its place . . . in its place he would
see something else. Henry Walker's life was two stories, really: guilt
from having killed someone he never did kill, and mourning the
death of someone who was still alive.

The telephone never stopped ringing.

I spoke for about half an hour, and then let the story wash over
Rudy, JJ, Jenny, and Mosgrove. It was hard to tell what they were
feeling, but each of them—especially Jenny—was riveted. Jere-

miah and Rudy shook their heads, their eyes on the sawdust floor, and JJ put a wad of tobacco in his mouth and started chewing. I heard a horse clop by outside the tent. I heard someone say, "Next week, you're glue!"

After some very deep thinking, Rudy was the first to speak. "Well," he said, "Henry was a storyteller, that's for sure."

"That's a certain fact," Jeremiah said. "I, for one, never believed a word of anything he said."

"Who did?" JJ said. "This takes the cake, though. The cake and the icing, too."

"Took it with a grain of salt," Jeremiah said. "If that."

Rudy rubbed his big, scarred jaw, thinking. "There's a difference between a storyteller and a liar, though," he said. "I didn't think he was a liar."

"He never lied," Jenny said. "Never." She clearly believed that, with all her heart.

"I don't know, Jenny," JJ said. "He was here a full year before I figured he wasn't a Negro. Which I discovered by accident, walking into his trailer when he was still halfway through his makeup. Talk about a shock."

"But," Rudy said, still figuring, "if Henry *did* lie about this one thing—and let's just say, for the sake of argument, he did—that would mean he never killed the devil."

He looked at Jenny. The ashes from her cigarette had fallen all over her chin and chest, and he swept them off with a featherlike touch. "Which would mean . . ." Rudy said, trailing off into silence.

"You okay, Rudy?" Jenny said.

"I'm okay," he said. "I'm just thinking things through."

JJ laughed. "I for one never bought that," he said. "Never. *Nobody* can kill the devil. That's why he's the devil."

"JJ has a point," Jeremiah said. "That's been historically established. No one can kill the devil."

Jenny's eyes dashed back and forth between us. Since these were the only part of her body that seemed capable of any real movement, it was the equivalent of somebody else sprinting down three city blocks. Her exertion was real, and it appeared to exhaust her.

Then her eyes rested on me.

"Do *you* think he was the devil?" she asked me.

"James Callahan? He didn't look like the devil to me," I said. "He loved his daughter, he kept a diary. He was a natty dresser."

"Which is how the devil does," JJ said. "If he always *looked* like the devil, we'd know him for the devil. We wouldn't have problems with him then."

"*Exactly!*" Jeremiah said, and his voice took on the determined cadences of a professional orator. "Were we to see him coming at us, we could say, *Get thee behind me, Satan!* That sort of thing. His art is to appear to be another thing altogether, something good, or nearly so. Like this James Callahan, for instance." He paused to give the subject some of the deep thought it deserved. "Yes. I think he could, in fact, be the devil. But that's no more than an educated guess."

"Actually," I said, "I have a different view. I don't think the devil had much to do with this at all. And I don't think Henry ever met him. If the devil does exist, I think he's taken the last thousand or so years off. I think he figures we're taking care of things just fine."

No one looked at me. They let my dime-store wisdom hang in the air.

Jeremiah looked at me and laughed. "That's rich!" he said.

"Very rich," JJ said. "No devil. That's cheesecake."

Rudy still seemed puzzled. As Jeremiah and JJ laughed and laughed, Rudy was shaking his head, the thoughts battling within him like warriors. He just couldn't let it go. Finally, he sighed a giant sigh.

"So what you're saying," he said, "is that *everything* Henry told us was a lie?"

I didn't want to break his heart, so I didn't say anything. But Jenny, whose heart was already broken, did.

"He didn't lie," she said. "You have to know what's true to lie, and Henry didn't. He didn't know the difference."

And then, for reasons I've yet to fathom to this day, Rudy started crying. He tried not to, but the tears came, and once they did there was nothing he could do. "Henry didn't kill *anybody?*" he said. "Not even a man?"

"I didn't say that," I said. "He killed somebody, all right. It just wasn't the devil, and it wasn't Mr. Callahan."

"Who?" Rudy implored. *"Who?"*

I had every eye in the tent on me then. JJ, Jeremiah, Rudy. I could even hear the rusted hinge of Jenny's neck grate as she tried to turn her gaze toward me. I'd never had a more captive audience in my life, or a stranger one, all of them willing now, even eager, to hear my take on his story, after which they would tell me their own. Then we would subtract everything we didn't know from everything we did, and in that way, I hoped, come up with something that was something like the truth.

A Car Ride

May 20, 1954

The night had finally come. The Fleetline's headlamps only just cut through it as the car fishtailed with a death wish around every unseen curve. There was a moon and there were stars, but they seemed very far away now, glittering and glowing to no purpose.

Tarp drove. Corliss sat beside Tarp. Jake and Henry sat together in the backseat. On the radio the DJ needled the next platter: "Life Could Be a Dream," by the Crew Cuts. "I love that song," Tarp said. When it came on, he turned it up and made everybody be quiet while he listened, and sang. *"Life could be a dream . . . If I could take you up to paradise."* But even as he sang it out with his whole heart, he didn't take his foot off the accelerator. The car was like his own personal carnival ride. "I could do this in my sleep," he'd said early on to no one in particular. Later it was *Watch this*, and, grinning, he took his hands off the wheel going fifty miles an hour. In the rearview, Henry watched him close his eyes. The black of Tarp's suit melded with the black of the night, and the soft green light from the dashboard reflected up to his face and made him look ghostly, like a head, floating there, laughing.

Now they were going sixty, so fast that even the slightest turn was a hard one. Their bodies moved like trees swaying back and forth in the furious wind. Occasionally the car would hit a dip in the road, and for a moment they would actually take flight, the car and its occupants, and you could believe that it was the beginning of something spectacular, if that was something you wanted to believe. Something like lift-off. But then, almost as soon as they were up, they fell back hard, as if Earth had reached out with a possessive hand and grabbed them, unable to let them go.

Think *fly*! If this had happened a long time ago, Henry thought, that's all he'd have to do, all he'd have to do is to think the word *fly* and they would have flown. Henry could've made that happen. "Hold on to your hats, boys!" he'd say, and off they'd go. Tarp, Corliss, Jake, and Henry, all of them in the lime-green Fleetline, floating past the cold white moon. Thinking this, Henry couldn't help smiling.

It hurt to smile, though. It hurt to blink, to breathe, to be inside his own skin. He had given up making an inventory of everything that had been broken or cut or torn or cracked or severed or burned. He was what he was: barely alive. He had lost a bucketful of blood, he was certain of that; how big a bucket, though, he wasn't really sure. But he felt lighter now than he ever had before—in head and body—a level of pain that somehow had been transmuted into a woozy pleasure—and he realized this must be because of the missing blood. That was the only thing he didn't have now that he'd never lost before. A new loss for a man who had lost everything else.

When the song was over, Tarp turned the radio down and slammed his hand into the top of the dashboard. "*Damn*, that's good," he said. And he sang it some more, screaming into the wind, boom sh-booming. He had to catch his breath, he was singing so hard. "You like that song, don't you, Corliss?"

Corliss nodded and said that he loved that song and that he loved the Crew Cuts. "They're from Canada," he said.

For some reason, saying this made both of them glance back at Henry. Tarp laughed and punched the dashboard again: Henry figured he always needed to be punching something. *"Canada,"* he said. "Is that where you're from, Henry? Someplace crazy like that?" Tarp caught Henry's gaze in the mirror and smiled at him. They were like old friends now. "So—how's it feel to be white again?" Tarp asked him.

Henry didn't answer. He didn't know the answer, and even if he had known it, he didn't feel he could move his jaw to say it.

"Feels good, don't it? Don't it? When Jake said—you remember what he said, Corliss?—when he said, *Well he ain't a nigger either,* I thought he'd gone and lost his fucking mind for damn sure. Didn't you, Corliss?"

"For damn sure," Corliss said.

"But damn if he wasn't right," Tarp said. "How'd you figure that, Jake?"

But Jake didn't answer, either. His mind seemed to be elsewhere. Tarp one-handed them around an S-curve, and Henry fell into Jake, and that served to bring him back to the here and now. "I didn't figure it," Jake said. "I mean, there was just a lot of blood around his eyes and all, and I was trying to wipe it away, and—you know how it went."

"It's a good story," Tarp said. "No one's going to believe it, but it's a good story."

Henry wasn't sure whether he'd missed something. Tarp didn't make sense. Every few seconds he might have been falling asleep, but it was so sudden and so brief it was hard to tell what was really going on. It felt like the world had been torn apart and stitched back together in small bits and pieces, but not the same as they were before. Something had changed, was missing, and Henry couldn't figure out what it was.

There was a small pool of blood by his foot on the floor, darker than the darkness. For a few moments Henry was consumed with watching it roll back and forth across the rubber floor mat until Tarp braked for a branch that had fallen across the road, and with the stop the blood flowed beneath the seat and disappeared. Even when the car resumed its normal impossible speed, the blood never came back.

"He's not looking so good," Jake said, too softly to be heard. So he said it again. "Henry's not looking so good."

"*What?*" Tarp said, irritated. Tarp didn't know if he'd heard him, and if he did didn't know if he wanted to.

"Henry's a little pale," Jake said.

Corliss laughed. "Was that a joke?" he said. He turned to look at Jake. "That's a joke, ain't it? He's pale—pale because he's not a nigger, right?"

"No," Jake said. "Pale because I think he might be dying."

Henry's eyelids trembled like wings. They trembled like the wings of the bird Jake had saved, the one later killed by the cat. Henry remembered the story about the bird.

Tarp tried to get a bead on the situation in the mirror, studying Henry as his left hand clutched the wheel, seeming to guide them magically through the cloak of utter darkness surrrounding them. Tarp knew how to drive a car.

"Hey, Henry!" he said, like he was trying to wake him up. But Henry didn't say anything. Henry's eyes were open and he was looking right at him, but he didn't say anything. Tarp looked back and forth from the road to the mirror. "Henry, Henry, Henry! You hanging in there, big man? Tell me you're hanging in there, buddy! C'mon. Bring a smile to your new friend's face."

Tarp couldn't look at him for long. There was something about the way Henry was now that made it hard to look at him too long.

"I don't know that he figures we're his friends, Tarp," Jake said. "Us being the ones who made him like this."

"You little son-of-a-bitch," Tarp said. "Saying something like that now. I told him I was sorry. I told him that if we'd known he wasn't a goddamn nigger none of this would have ever happened. You think I don't feel like shit, Jake? I do. You think I don't feel like an idiot? It was a mistake. An honest mistake. But the thing I keep going back to is this: why did we *think* he was a nigger? Why? *Because he had a fucking sign that said he was.*"

"That's just exactly right," Corliss said. "He had a sign."

"He could've told us. He could have said something. He could have said something like . . . oh, I don't know, but maybe something along the lines of *I ain't a nigger!* Know what I'm saying, Jake?"

The two brothers looked at each other in the mirror. "I know what you're saying," Jake said. "It was almost like he wanted us to."

"He just has to hold on," Tarp said. "He just has to hold on a little longer, until we get him home."

"*Home?*" Jake said. "Why are we taking him home? We need to take him to the hospital, Tarp. Look at him."

"He does not look good," Tarp said, giving Henry another once-over in the mirror. "But I think if we get him home and out of the car and see what's really going on with him, then we'll have a better idea of what to do." Tarp coughed up a laugh. "I did beat the shit out of him. But the thing is, I held back there a little toward the end. I did. And I didn't shoot him, so . . ."

Jake stared out the window. "I reckon you'll get a medal for that."

"I'm so sick of you and your crap," Tarp said. Then he turned the radio up to drown out whatever Jake's response was going to be, to drown out all the other sound. It was Perry Como. "Don't Let the Stars Get in Your Eyes."

Henry opened his eyes. He realized his head had been leaning on Jake's shoulder, but he didn't know for how long. All he knew was that his head was there, and Jake hadn't done anything to make it not there, and that was a good thing. He had been gone for a while to a different place, Henry thought, he'd been in two places at once. For the first time in a long time, he thought of Marianne. It made him feel lonely, thinking of her, but, then, she'd always made him feel lonely, even when she was alive. Everyone he thought about made him feel lonely. He couldn't bear it. Going to a place alone when you used to go with someone together—this was hard.

Tarp caught a glimpse of Henry in the rearview then, and Henry him. "You awake, boy?" he said.

Henry opened his mouth to speak, but no words came out. He was trying to say, *I'm not your boy.* But he couldn't manage it. All he could do was smile.

Tarp smiled back. "See, Jake?" he said. "The man still has spirit. He can smile. I'm no doctor, but to me that means he's okay. Means he's gonna be fine."

Jake looked at his own shoulder: there was a blot of red on his T-shirt, blood that had seeped out from the edge of Henry's mouth. "What are we going to do with him, Tarp?" Jake said. "We ain't got no use for him anymore. Let's take him on to the hospital, where they might just be able to do something for him."

Corliss was humming along with the song, and he hummed until it was over. "That's a good song. That old Perry Como can sing, can't he?"

Tarp nodded. The cigarette was smoldering, hanging from his lips. "I want Mama to meet him," he said.

"Perry Como?" Corliss said.

"Henry," Tarp said. "I want Mama to meet Henry."

Both Corliss and Jake looked at Tarp. It was like they heard him but didn't understand what they were hearing.

"You want *Mama* to meet him?" Jake said.

Tarp nodded. "I want him to do a magic trick for her."

The road had straightened out, was as smooth as a carpet, and Henry realized it had suddenly become paved. He even saw some other cars going the opposite direction, blowing past like rockets.

He heard Tarp say *magic trick*.

"She'd like that, Jake," Tarp said. "You know she would."

"If that's what you wanted," Jake said, "maybe you shouldn't have broken his arms."

"I didn't break his arms," Tarp said.

"That was me," Corliss said. "I'm pretty sure that was me." Then Corliss turned around in his seat and looked at Henry, and his eyes were as big as a cow's eyes and just as sad. "I'm real sorry," he said. "I really am."

Jake said, "What kind of magic trick were you thinking, Tarp?"

"I don't know," Tarp said. He was looking at Henry in the rearview, thinking about it. "Maybe the one where you know which card someone has but don't let on that you do until you make them think you don't. You know that one?"

"The one like he did to me?" Corliss said.

Tarp nodded.

Okay, Henry tried to say. The word or something like it seemed to slip from his lips on the wings of a breath.

It was just a sound, but it was close enough. Tarp heard him say it, and so did Corliss—"You heard him, he said *okay!*"—so Jake gave up. He was tired of trying to keep living things alive. It was just too hard.

Henry closed his eyes, then opened them, but like a door in the wind they slammed shut. Now they felt locked. He felt like he couldn't open them, and never would again, hard as he tried. Think *open*. That's all he'd have to do and they would open. And they did.

Corliss had been thinking on something and finally decided to share with the others. It was complicated, so he spoke slowly. "If we had killed him before we found out he wasn't a nigger, we would have killed him thinking he *was* a nigger, and if we had, who knows if we'd ever known the difference."

"You lost me there, Corliss," Tarp said.

Corliss sighed. "I just mean, we would have always thought we'd done something we hadn't." He thought his thoughts again. "I wonder how many other things are like that."

"Almost everything," Henry said.

Tarp, Corliss, Jake—they were all astonished by this, completely and utterly astonished. The force and clarity of Henry's words, after only making sounds of pain for so long. The fact that he could talk at all. Henry's eyes were wide open: they were like the eyes of a baby, taking everything in. "Almost everything is like that," he said again, and all of a sudden, in what felt like one golden moment, it was like nothing had happened to him at all. The pain in his body disappeared. Henry felt fine now. He actually felt *good*. He'd survived. Was it possible that his jaw had never been fractured, his ribs broken? That the blood he saw running like a stream from the side of his body was actually little more than the leaf cuts he got in the bushes outside his mother's window when he and Hannah watched her die? Could he have made all this up, too? His window was halfway down, and the cool, damp wind surged across his face, and he felt it and breathed it in, and as he did he breathed in something else, too. *Life.* Henry felt it in his lungs. Life was seeping back into his body; it came from the air and the wind. Like dissipated spirits of everyone he had ever known coming together for him, *in* him, just to keep him alive. Before this moment of salvation came, he'd wished he'd been killed back there, in the field, just the way Corliss imagined it could have gone. Not because he wanted to die—he didn't—he just couldn't see the point in living. But now there seemed to be a reason. Or not a reason, really, nothing that definite and sure: a hunch. He had a hunch now that there was a reason to live.

"See, Jake?" Tarp said. "You stupid shit! I told you he'd be okay. I told you." Jake was pleased with himself. "The thing you have to remember is that I'm almost always right. Okay? That's something you need to get your fucking head around."

Henry thought he heard Jake grinding his teeth. Looking down, Henry could see he had that penny in his left hand, and he was rubbing it with his fingers.

Jake, Henry whispered. Henry was reaching out to touch him, the tips of his fingers moving toward his shoulder, when Jake grabbed Henry's fingers and held them, tight, in his right hand, still rubbing the penny like a rosary with the other.

Jake flipped the coin and caught it.

"Which is it, Henry?" Jake asked him. "Heads or tails?" Flipping and catching the coin without even looking at it. His voice rose to the pitch of the wind and the throb of the engine, a voice full of anger, and Henry couldn't understand why. "Which is it, Henry? Heads or tails? Black or white? Good or evil? Alive or dead?" He waited for Henry to answer, and when he didn't, Jake let go of his fingers and looked away from him and flipped the coin a few more times, higher and higher each time, until it hit the car roof and fell to the floor.

Jake looked at him. Henry could feel the anger in him seep out of his heart until all that was left was sadness. Everyone and everything was quiet then. Tarp had turned the radio off. In the front seat, Tarp and Corliss sat staring straight ahead, out the bug-covered windshield, and for what seemed a long time no one said a word.

Henry saw a light. It was a bright white light.

It was a streetlamp.

Tarp slowed down. "We're almost there," he said.

He was going so slow now, Henry could see what was all around them. He saw they were driving through a little town, probably where Tarp and Corliss and Jake lived. There were houses and people and dogs and the shadows of flowers on the lawn where the wild lilies leaned over the monkey grass. The normal beauty of life.

"So, Henry," Tarp said. "You think you can do some magic for Mama?" Henry nodded; Tarp smiled. "That'd be great if you could. I think she'll really like that. She used to have a little dog. I can't even remember that mutt's name now, but it could dance on its hind legs like a circus dog. Never seen her smile as much as she smiled when that dog danced."

"Polly," Jake said. "Dog's name was Polly."

"That's right," Tarp said. "Polly." Jake and Tarp shared this old memory. Henry thought Polly was a nice name for a dog, real nice. "Don't fuck up the magic, though, okay?" Tarp said to Henry. "Just this one time?"

"She's dying," Corliss said.

This time Tarp really did hit Corliss, hard, right in the neck, and Corliss had to bite his lip to keep from hitting him back. "Goddamn you, Tarp," he said.

"Don't say she's dying, Corliss," Tarp said. "It might be true, but saying it only makes it worse. You don't have the right. She's not yours."

Corliss shut up like maybe he didn't have the right.

They pulled up in front of a house, and Tarp cut the engine, and for the first time the car was still. Tarp turned around to look at Henry.

"We're counting on you, okay?" They were friends now. "This is all going to work out for the best. You just wait and see. You're going to make an old lady happy. Can't beat that, can you?"

Henry shook his head, but only just enough so Tarp could see he was listening, taking things in. Tarp looked at Jake. "I'll go in and set her up in her chair," he said to him. Then he opened up the glove compartment and found some rags and threw them at Jake's chest. "Clean him up some more. Get all that black shit off his face. The blood, too." Tarp's face went sour then. "Something *smells*," he said. He looked at Henry. "Smells like somebody wet themselves. Well, damn. I don't think there's anything we can do about that now." He winked at Henry, smiled. Then he touched him, placing the palm of his hand on Henry's cheek and letting his fingers run down it, like a lover would. "This is all going to work out," he said. "Just you wait and see."

"And here's this," Corliss said, "in case you need it," and he placed the three of hearts on Henry's lap.

Then Tarp got out of the car, and Corliss followed him, and Jake and Henry were alone in the backseat. They looked at each other, the same as they would had they known each other forever. Jake picked up one of the rags and gently took it around the corner of Henry's left eye, and then softly down that cheek. To Henry he looked like a ghost, or a saint, or an angel.

"It don't carry much weight to say this," Jake said, "but I'm saying it anyway." He took a deep breath. "I'm sorry. Sorry about all of this. I never thought things would go this far—never, not in a million years. Even if you hadn't of turned out to be—you know—who you are." Jake's eyes were full of a sweet sadness, but they had been from the moment Henry saw them. Jake was trying hard not to hurt him as he tried to clean him up, but sometimes he did, and Henry flinched, and when Henry flinched, Jake flinched with him. "It's just that some of this, it ain't coming off," he said.

Finally, he stopped trying and just looked at Henry, shaking his head. "It's not coming off," he said.

Henry's head fell backward against the seat cushion, and from there he had a great view of the world outside the window. It was so beautiful. There were great oak trees with leafy tops as big as clouds hovering above the houses. Streetlamps beaming on every corner, bats and bugs diving in and out of the light as if they were dancing. The houses around them were small, simple. But everything you needed for a house—porch, door, windows, and a warm light glowing within—was there. Life was everywhere. An old man wearing nothing but a pair of shorts wandered into his line of vision and then wandered out of it, shuffling around a corner. He was on a walk, Henry figured, a little stroll before bed. Something he did every night. You could set your watch by his walks. Henry thought, *A yellow cat on an old stone wall*, and there it was, a yellow cat on an old stone wall, all four legs folded in beneath its body. And there was a man and a woman. They were young, Henry's age or younger, walking hand in hand. He watched them. Then Henry heard a girl laughing, but he couldn't see her, couldn't tell where the laughter was coming from. Just the laughter of a girl somewhere close to him in the world.

Jake straightened Henry's shirt and wiped away some of the dirt on his shoulders, tried to blot up some of the blood. But it was a waste of time. Henry still looked like he had been beaten half to death, and there was no way to get around that.

Jake sighed.

"Well, I guess we should be getting on in there," he said. "Mom's probably waiting in her chair. And don't worry about messing the trick up. She can't see worth a damn." Jake opened the car door with one hand and took Henry's arm with the other, and gave him a gentle tug. But he didn't move. Henry was mesmerized by the world. He didn't want to stop looking at it, ever. A girl's laughter, the old man, the couple walking hand in hand: *people lived like this*. People lived in the world as if the world were a place for them to live. As if it were made for them. And the remarkable thing was—it came to Henry, just like that—it *was* made for them. For him, for us. That was why the world was here. Good Lord. Why had it taken him so long to figure this out? That this life, this world, was something he could be a part of, too?

Jake pulled harder, but Henry still didn't move. "I can't carry you in there all by myself, Henry," he said. "You're going to have to give me a hand, okay? Henry?"

Henry had a vision. He could live here. He could live in this town. He saw his life unfolding before him. He'd get a job, it didn't matter what it was, and find a place of his own. He'd plant a garden in the yard. He'd take long walks before bed at night. He'd join the parade of life that was out there now. Sure, he'd be a stranger at first, but that wouldn't matter; everybody is a stranger at first. Gradually, all that would change, though. He'd go on his walks, and when he met somebody there on the street he'd stop and talk, and they'd be friendly, welcoming, warm.

That young couple, for instance. He'd meet them.

You must be the new man, the husband would say, smiling, extending a hand. They'd shake, and take a deep breath of night into their lungs. *My name's Jim,* the husband would say, *and this here is my wife, Sally.* Henry would shake her hand and smile, and then someone would make a comment about the night, the weather, the starry sky.

And then they'd stand there. They'd stand there for a long moment, until Jim would have to say, *And you? Who did you say you were?*

And that's where the vision stopped, because Henry didn't have the answer. *I don't know* seemed like the wrong thing to say. But that's all he could come up with.

"*Henry.*" Jake took him by the shoulders and shook him hard, as though he were trying to wake him up. Henry wouldn't wake up. He wouldn't open his eyes at all. Jake put his arms around him and tried to lift his body up, but he had never felt anything so heavy in his life. "Henry," Jake said again, one last time.

But Henry didn't even recognize the name. Not now. He didn't know who Henry Walker was. There was a time he did, a time he must have known, but that was a long time ago. Years ago, before any of this happened, before his mother and his father and Hannah and the devil, before Tom Hailey and Bakari, from the darkest Congo, before the war and Marianne La Fleur and Kastenbaum and all the rest, all he'd have to do is think *Henry Walker.* Think *Henry Walker,* and Henry Walker would appear, whoever he was, radiant, on fire with life, and all the more beautiful because of it.

Think *Henry Walker.* Just think it. That's all he'd have to do and it would be done, and he would know.

acknowledgments

I kept this book to myself until I wrote the entire first draft, and then I showed it to three people: Laura Wallace, Ellen Lefcourt, and Joe Regal. They read it and told me where I went wrong and where I went right, and without them this book wouldn't be this book.

So thank you Laura, thank you Ellen, thank you Joe. Then Christine Pride—a real maestro—brought it home, cleaned it up and sent it out into the world. Thank you Christine. And did I mention Laura? My wife, Laura, my sweetest friend. XOXOXOXOXOXOXO-XOXOXOXOXOXOXOXOXOXOXOXOXOXOXOXOXOXOXOXO-XOXOXO I love you.